GHOST OF HONOR

HAUNTED EVERLY AFTER MYSTERIES
BOOK THIRTEEN

REGINA WELLING

ERIN LYNN

CONTENTS

GHOST OF HONOR

CHAPTER ONE

t first, I wasn't surprised to see Ernie Polk walk into the atrium. He'd been invited to the wedding, after all. It was his expression that gave me my first pang of worry. He didn't look like he'd come to offer us his best wishes. Instead, he had his cop face on.

What now? I thought as he spotted me standing beside Drew, saying goodnight to one of the guests.

Ernie wasted no time crossing the room. Dread built in me with every step he took.

"Drew Parker," he said without glancing in my direction. "I'm placing you under arrest for the murder of Jerry Kaminski."

Over Ernie's shoulder, the ghost of Dolly Tibbets winked out—presumably to find and welcome the town's newest ghost to the post-living community. I had no illusions whatsoever that Jerry would have gone into the light, and neither, it seemed, did she.

"Jerry's dead?" And for once, I hadn't found the body. Should I feel bad for feeling good about that? Probably. The relief lasted about a nanosecond before the enormity of the situation hit me again. "What happened?"

"I'm not at liberty to give details about an ongoing

investigation." Ernie began to read Drew his rights. "You have the right to remain silent."

"And that's just what you'll do." Patrea had appeared at my side. "Let him take you into custody." Not that Drew had put up a struggle. "And don't say a word until I get there."

"Until we get there," I insisted. "I'm coming with you."

I didn't care that I was still wearing my wedding dress. I didn't care if all of these people were my responsibility. I only cared that something was happening to someone I loved, and I needed to do whatever I could to make it better. That's who I am—who I have always been —the kind of person whose mind immediately goes into problem-solving mode whenever there is a crisis. It's not just a skill but a personality trait.

But Patrea touched my arm while Ernie finished his spiel and pulled me aside. "Not this time, Everly. This is what I do, and you need to trust me. I've got him, okay?" I wasn't the only problem solver in my immediate group of friends.

"Stay and deal with things here," Drew finally said. "I'll be fine. I haven't killed anyone."

"I know that." I glared at Ernie, who should have known better. He didn't even flinch, which didn't bode well. Thanks to him, my bright and shining, perfect day was now a tarnished mess.

By now, guests were filtering in from other areas of the house to see what the fuss was about.

"What's going on here?" Junior Pease's booming voice

cut through the murmurs like a chainsaw through balsa wood.

I didn't remember inviting him, but since they were both active in the VFW, Drew could have, or Junior could have been someone's plus one. Either way, he planted himself squarely in front of Ernie and Drew, his face reddening to match the color of the lobster puff appetizers we'd had earlier. His question was rhetorical since it didn't take a giant leap to see what was going on here.

"You can't be arresting a veteran on his wedding day in front of God and everyone. I won't have it. Do you hear me, Ernie Polk?" Junior's voice cracked with indignation, his hands clenching. "You oughta be ashamed, slapping cuffs on this good man like he's nothing but a common criminal! Explain yourself."

The room seemed to hold its breath, guests exchanging wide-eyed glances. Even the music went quiet. I could practically feel their collective disbelief morphing into a thick fog of speculation that would surely blanket the entire town with gossip by morning.

Ernie declined to elaborate. "I'm doing my job. That's all you need to know."

"Junior, please." Drew's words tried to cut through the older man's fog of anger, but they went ignored, lost in the sudden swell of conflict.

"Shame on you, Ernie!" Junior continued, jabbing a finger towards the officer whose jaw twitched beneath his stern facade. "This isn't how we do things here. We look after our own, and we certainly don't drag them away on what should be the happiest day of their lives. Your mother would be mortified."

"Enough, Junior," Ernie finally growled, his patience wearing thin as river ice in spring. "Step aside."

But Junior was a force unto himself, a gale that wouldn't be stilled. His outburst echoed off the walls, stirring up a storm within the once-serene reception. And just like that, my wedding had turned into a scene straight out of one of those thrilling crime novels – minus the thrills and double the drama.

Worse, now that more of the guests had been drawn to the source of the conflict, a commotion swelled like a cresting wave, crashing down to wash away all remnants of wedding cheer. Not that Ernie hadn't done that already.

My father stepped forward, his presence like a lighthouse amid the brewing storm. He placed a firm hand on Junior's shoulder, leaning in with the quiet authority he always carried.

"Junior," he said, voice steady and clear, "lets you and I have a word outside, hmm?"

There was something about the way Dad squared his shoulders, the imperceptible nod, that settled even the most obstinate folks down. Maybe his years of standing in front of high school students gave him the presence needed to deflate Junior's bluster. The older man's eyes flickered toward my father with a hint of respect.

"Fine," Junior huffed, allowing Dad to steer him away from the crowd, albeit with one last glowering look at Ernie, who paused as he took Drew's arm.

"I didn't kill Jerry Kaminski." Infused with certainty, Drew's voice echoed across the room.

A murmur of agreement spread throughout the guests, but I knew their support could be fickle. By morning, the roots of doubt would be set in the fertile soil around the local grapevine. Phone lines would burn with talk about attending a wedding where the groom had been arrested. Some would decide he'd done something to earn it.

Staring out at a sea of faces, I disconnected from the joy of the day. My mind churned with questions, each colliding into the next until my mind was filled with them. What evidence could possibly connect Drew to Jerry's murder? It was like making sense of a jigsaw puzzle with half the pieces missing.

I knew Drew—the rhythm of his heart and the absolute force of his convictions. There wasn't a shadow of a doubt he was innocent. But the truth would be the only thing to set him free. It didn't look like Ernie was overly concerned with finding it, but I certainly was.

A hush fell over the room as Ernie escorted Drew out. He held his head high, meeting people's gazes as he went. I watched him go, my heart thudding like a drumbeat against my ribs. Love as fierce as anything I'd ever felt settled over me, along with the absolute knowledge that I'd find a way to fix this.

"What the hell just happened?" Jacy's voice cut through the fog in my head as she reached out, her touch grounding me back to the moment. Her eyes were wide, mirroring the question marks flying around in my head.

"I don't know," I admitted, the words tasting sour. "But we're going to find out."

"I'll call you as soon as I know anything." Patrea's voice sliced through the silence, decisive and unwavering. She was already moving, her tall frame straight and her stride purposeful as she hurried after Drew and Ernie. "We'll fix this. Don't worry."

"Hey." Neena's Southern lilt was gentle but firm as she grasped my arm. "We're with you on this. We'll turn Mooselick River upside down if we have to."

"Bet your ass," Jacy chimed in, her gaze steady. "Right. First things first, we deal with all of this." She circled a hand to indicate the remnants of my wedding celebration.

Their words were a balm to the sting of fear and confusion. As Junior Pease's agitated voice rose once more in a crescendo of anger, a peculiar calm settled over me. His outburst might have rattled the guests, but I had seen enough of life—and death—to recognize the tremor of genuine emotion as he re-entered the room with my father trailing behind.

"Junior, that's enough," I said softly, not unkindly. My voice didn't carry far, but it wasn't meant to. It was, for him, a reminder that chaos wouldn't serve any of us well now.

Junior ran a hand over his white beard and scowled as he turned to me, his stoop-shouldered frame heaving with the effort to contain himself. I met his gaze squarely, letting him read the determination in mine. I could see past his bluster to his loyalty to those who served in the armed forces. It clung to him like cobwebs in an abandoned house.

"Sorry, Everly," he muttered almost inaudibly over the remaining whispers of the crowd. "I can't stand seeing a good man taken down like that. He's a veteran who stood for us when asked. I can't do less than stand for him now."

"That's fine, but the best way to stand for him is to stop making a scene." The disrespectful words were out before I could think better of them. Sometimes, that happened—my mouth running off without consulting my brain. But right now, there was truth in the recklessness.

"Sorry." Junior's head dipped in chagrin, and he finally quieted.

I looked at Jacy and Neena, their faces set with the same resolute expression that I felt etching across my own features. We would turn every stone, chase every ghost—literally and figuratively—of a clue until Drew was back where he belonged.

"Okay," I said, my voice steadier than I expected. "Looks like the party's over. Let's move these folks along."

I sucked in a deep breath, the kind that's meant to steel your nerves—or at least that's what I told myself. Only about a third of the die-hards remained.

"Everyone," I called out, my voice echoing slightly through the expanse of the atrium. "Please, let's not let tonight be remembered for...well, this little hiccup." I smiled, and it wasn't entirely forced.

"Ernie is just doing his job," I continued, weaving through the crowd to gently guide people towards the exit. "You know how he gets—a dog with a bone. But this is all a big misunderstanding. I'm sure of it."

A murmur of agreement rippled through the room, and I felt a tiny flicker of triumph. Calming an agitated crowd was no small feat, but this wasn't my first time.

"Let's give Drew and Patrea some space to sort this out," I suggested warmly, hoping my natural calm would be contagious. "We'll have this mess cleared up faster than Martha Tipton can organize a bake sale."

Laughter trickled out, relieving some of the tension as the guests filtered out, their murmurs and backward glances containing a mix of support and speculation. I stood at the threshold of what was supposed to be the happiest day of my life, now turned into a scene right out of a 'how-not-to' wedding planner's guidebook.

As the room cleared, I refused to let the mask of confidence slip enough so anyone could peer behind it and see the unease lurking just beneath.

What on earth could Ernie have found to pin on Drew? My mind raced through every conversation, every shared glance. With his easy smile and open heart, Drew was about as likely to commit murder as I was to start a polka band. Something didn't add up.

I rubbed my temples, feeling the ghost of a headache beginning to form. I wasn't Jerry's biggest fan by any means, but his unrequited crush on me wasn't anything I couldn't handle. And while Drew had found some of

Jerry's comments annoying, they weren't annoying enough for Drew to kill him over.

With the guests gone and only my closest friends and family remaining, I turned to find Patrea's husband, Chris, standing nearby.

"Well," I said, "for a wedding venue trial run, I guess that was one for the books. You don't think Patrea will consider this an omen, do you?"

Always the master of understatement, Chris cocked one eyebrow. "Have you met my wife?"

Of course, practical Patrea wouldn't let what had happened tonight stand in her way.

"She'll fix this." Chris held my gaze. "Don't worry. Drew will be home before morning if I know my wife."

I nodded, hoping he was right, then turned to join Drew's family for a moment where they'd clustered around his mother, who sat in one of the chairs.

"Who's this Kaminski fellow?" Drew's father asked, concern wrinkling his brow.

"Jerry Kaminski. Patrea hired him to do some plaster work during the renovation, and he developed...let's call it a crush for the lack of a better term. On me. It was nothing," I said when fire flickered in his eyes. Like father, like son. Protectiveness must run in Drew's family. "Harmless, really, which is one reason I'm certain Drew had nothing to do with his death."

"My son is no murderer," Drew's mother said, her voice watery with tears.

"No, he's not," I agreed. "And we'll prove it. Don't you

worry. Patrea's the best attorney I've ever met. She'll do everything she can for him, and so will I. Maybe you should go back to the inn and get some rest. I'll call you the minute I have more information."

"Come on, Mom." Drew's brother took her arm and helped her stand. "Everly's right. There's nothing more we can do tonight."

Nodding, she let Tom lead out without any further fuss.

"Everly, you're doing great," Jacy whispered, her hand gently squeezing my shoulder once they'd gone.

"Room check complete," Neena said as she and David re-entered the room. They'd slipped out when I wasn't watching to ensure no guests lingered. "It's just us now."

"Okay." I exhaled, allowing the brave face to slip just an inch—not too much, mind you, as I wasn't alone yet. I could fall apart at home, but I had no intention of doing that here.

"Do you want to come home with us?" Mom offered, slinging her arms around me and squeezing me. "You don't have to be alone tonight."

"I'll be fine, Mom. But I appreciate the offer." I needed the time to process and settle myself.

Except, I must have been closer to the edge than I realized because instead of the tears stinging behind my eyes, a hysterical giggle burst out. "Looks like we've got ourselves a real-life whodunit. Except, instead of Colonel Mustard in the library with the candlestick, we've got

Chief Ernie in the wedding venue with a pair of handcuffs."

That a sob followed the levity was the only thing that kept my mother from giving me the same disapproving look she'd worn when I'd married a man she didn't like. Instead, she handed me off to my dad for one of his patented hugs that soothed everything. He held me until my breath stopped hitching and then let me go. So much for waiting until I was alone to break down.

"Seriously though, we'll get to the bottom of this." I squared my shoulders, my gaze sweeping over the faces of those who knew me best—those who knew the depth of my abilities and the lengths I'd go to for the people I loved. "Drew is innocent, and I intend to prove it."

"Not by yourself." Jacy took my hand and squeezed. "We're all in this with you. Whatever it takes."

It helped to be with the people who knew me best and wouldn't expect me to do this alone.

"Now, let's get you out of that dress," Mom said, tugging on my arm to get me moving.

With the distant murmur of my friends' voices in the background, I followed Mom to the bridal suite, catching sight of my tear-ravaged face in the mirror that had reflected my joy just a few scant hours ago.

"Come here, sweetheart," Mom said, her voice a soothing balm as she reached for the hidden zipper at the back of my dress, her fingers deft and practiced.

"Feels like I just got into this thing," I muttered, trying to muster a smile. My dress rustled softly, like whispered secrets, as she helped lift it away from my body and hung it on its hanger.

"You looked beautiful, Everly," she reassured me, running her hand over the fabric with a tenderness that made my heart clench.

"Yeah, a beautiful bride with a husband who's been carted off to jail on our wedding day." The sarcasm was there, but it lacked its usual bite. Standing in just my undergarments and bare feet, I felt suddenly vulnerable and exposed.

"Your father and I are so proud of you, Everly. Not just for today but for who you are. You're strong. Resourceful. You have such a big heart and a questing mind." She draped an arm around my shoulders, and I leaned into her embrace.

"Thanks, Mom. I will need all that to get Drew out of this mess." I took a deep breath, the familiar stirrings of determination rising within me. "I don't know what's happened, but I know Drew's innocent. And I'm going to prove it."

"Of course, you will," she agreed, handing me the pair of comfortable jeans and loose top I'd arrived in. "You've got your friends and family behind you, and that special gift should come in handy." She gave a wry smile, acknowledging the psychic abilities she'd passed down to me even if she didn't generally use them herself.

"Special is one way to put it," I said, pulling on the top and inhaling the comforting scent of home woven into the threads. It felt weird to be putting on everyday things after hours spent feeling like a Gatsby princess.

"Any sign of Jerry yet?"

"None." He'd have known better than to crash my wedding. Or maybe I was giving him too much credit. "He probably hasn't figured out I could see him."

"I suppose that's for the best. You should go home and get some rest, honey. Tomorrow, you'll need all your strength." She kissed my forehead, her lips warm against my skin.

"Rest," I echoed, though I knew sleep would be elusive. Too many questions were swirling in my mind, too many ghosts—both literal and figurative—haunting the edges of my consciousness. Plus, I knew I wouldn't get a wink of sleep until Patrea called to tell me what she'd learned.

Efficient as always, Mom had my dress packed up and the bag slung over her arm before I finished gathering the rest of my things.

"You can leave that here, I think. Patrea won't mind. I'll have to come back tomorrow to deal with the gifts and whatnot, and I need to call the airlines and cancel our flight. If you don't mind keeping Molly tonight, I'll pick her up in the morning."

"Whatever you need, dear. Let's go back down and see what else needs doing." Mom slipped her hand in mine, and together, we walked back down the curving staircase to where my friends waited.

"Call me the minute you hear anything," Jacy ordered while her husband, Brian, enveloped me in a hug.

"No matter what time," he whispered in my ear.

"Will do."

"Same goes for me." Neena hugged me next. "Unless you want me to come stay the night. I'm happy to keep you company."

"I think I'll be fine." I turned to David, the other member of my close-knit group. "You'll take care of Drew's folks?"

David owned the inn in town where Drew's family had booked rooms. He'd given them the friends-and-family discount, but I planned to pick up the bill anyway. I just hadn't told any of them yet.

"Consider it done." Being the least physically demonstrative of the bunch, he patted my shoulder.

I let them bundle me into my car and spent the ride home trying to tame my errant thoughts.

CHAPTER TWO

A whip-poor-will's chant echoed from nearby as I fumbled for my keys. Its haunting melody couldn't drown out the echo of Drew's handcuffs clicking shut still bouncing around in my head. The night air brushed my bare shoulders as I finally found the right key and shoved it into the lock. All I wanted was to get inside and close the door—put a barrier between myself and the chaos that had overtaken what should have been our perfect day. And let the tears come again.

I should have known it wouldn't be that easy. I didn't even manage to make it inside before yet another obstacle jumped between me and the solace of being alone.

"Everly," a voice hissed from the shadows as the now-familiar chill raised goosebumps along my arms.

I spun around, banged my elbow on the doorframe, and cursed at the sight of Jerry Kaminski—or rather, his ghost—hovering at the foot of the steps. Great, just what I needed.

Dolly must have sent him here.

"Jerry!" I snapped, a little louder than I intended. "You can't just pop up like that! You'll give me a heart attack—

which, granted, would make our conversations a lot more convenient."

"Sorry, Everly," he mumbled, looking sheepish. "But we need to talk. Dolly said you might be able to help me."

Dolly Tibbets, the head of the ghostly welcome wagon, could have waited a day before sending the ghost I least wanted to see to my front door. She probably thought she was helping, but still.

I sighed, watching as my breath formed a misty cloud in the chilly air. Even the afterlife couldn't stop Jerry from being a nuisance. "Look, Jerry, I've got a lot on my plate right now. My husband—the guy I should be on my honeymoon with—is sitting in jail, accused of murdering you. We both know he didn't do anything of the sort, so unless you're here to give me a clue who actually did the deed, I'm really not in the mood."

"But I was murdered, and Dolly says you're the local ghost avenger. I thought you'd want a chance to prove it was not your man who killed me," Jerry said, moving closer. Because he was new, his outline shimmered with each movement, like a reflection in rippling water, but the rest of him looked solid enough.

"Let's get one thing straight," I said, holding up a finger. "I have every intention of clearing my husband's name, so you'd better get it into your head right now that it wasn't Drew who killed you. If getting him out of jail means helping you, that's fine. But don't think for one second this means we're pals."

Unlike some of my other ghosts, he wasn't threatening to hang around annoying me until I did what he wanted. He didn't have to because I had no choice.

"Of course, of course," Jerry agreed quickly, looking like a dog that'd just been scolded. "Whatever you say."

I didn't trust the submissive act, and half a second later, he proved my instincts correct when his gaze locked onto my cleavage. Ghosts already feel slimy when I come into contact with them, but this was a whole other level of disgusting. I wasn't impressed, but getting Drew out of jail was a moral imperative, so Jerry would get my help whether he deserved it or not.

"Good." I finished unlocking the door and headed inside. "You can come inside so the neighbors don't think I'm standing on the front porch talking to myself."

As I dropped my purse on the table by the door, I could feel Jerry's eyes on my butt. "Quit staring, Jerry," I tossed over my shoulder and headed toward the kitchen to make a cup of soothing tea. The day had drained everything out of me—the joy, the hope, even the anger. All that was left was a dull determination to set things right and the unsettling company of a sleazebag specter who couldn't take a hint.

"Great house. Moldings could use some touching up, but they're pretty solid," Jerry said, finally focusing on something other than me.

While I made a pot of tea, we played a game I remembered from childhood...the one where you turn your back, and the players move closer, then you turn around and try to catch them. Only this time, it was me trying to catch Jerry staring at parts of my body he shouldn't be. Even though I knew he was doing it, he won the round.

Finally, I set the teapot on the table and settled in my usual spot without inviting Jerry to sit. The best he could do was hover over any seat I pulled out for him, but I didn't want to give him any reason to think he was welcome.

"If you're going to stick around, you need to know the ground rules," I said, pouring a cup and stirring in a large dollop of honey. "Rule one: No chit-chat when I have company that can't see you. That means no whispering anything, including whodunit clues in my ear, when I'm surrounded by the living. Period."

Jerry nodded, his figure beginning to blur around the edges. "Understood. No talking during...social gatherings."

"Rule two: I'm not your messenger pigeon. Don't even think of asking me to pass along 'I love yous' or 'Find my baseball card collection' to your family."

"Fair enough," he conceded. "There's nothing I need to say to anyone anyhow."

"Finally, rule three," I continued, feeling a little surge of power at laying down the law, "you do not—I repeat, do NOT—invade my private spaces. That means no popping up in my bathroom, bedroom, or any other area where you could catch me indecent or vulnerable. You get me?"

"I do," Jerry agreed, raising his hands in surrender. "You have my word, Everly." He looked sincere enough, but I wasn't buying a word of it.

"Good." I let out a breath, not realizing I'd been holding it. Maybe because part of me knew that dealing with a ghost who had a crush on me was like playing with an Ouija board in a haunted house—nothing good would come of it.

"All right then," I said, shifting gears. "Tell me everything you remember about the fight with Drew." The bachelor party had started and ended at our place in Drew's man cave, but had taken a temporary detour to Cappy's when the guys got hungry enough to head over there before Adam closed the kitchen. Bad timing.

Jerry's face turned serious, and for a moment, I saw past the spectral exterior to the man who must've once had hopes and fears just like any of us. "I was at the bar, drowning my sorrows. As you do. The next thing I knew, Drew was coming at me. He was furious, shouting things about how you were his property, and I'd better keep my distance, or he'd hurt me. It got heated, and..." His voice trailed off as his attention slid away, lost to the memory. "Well. Here I am."

"Are you sure?" I pressed, knowing the Drew I loved—the guy who happily watched sappy movies with me and rescued spiders from the bathtub—reserved his violence for the gym. He'd never been a hothead, and even his time in the service hadn't changed that basic piece of his personality. "That doesn't sound like him. Don't get me wrong—he could have taken you apart without breaking a sweat, but you'd have had to come at him or someone he loved first. He wouldn't be the aggressor."

Jerry met my gaze, a flicker of annoyance passing over his face. "That's how it happened," he insisted, but a waver in his voice gave me pause. "He came after me for no good reason."

"Okay," I said slowly, not remotely convinced. "I'll see what I can dig up. But remember, I'm doing this for Drew. Are you sure no one else wanted a piece of you?"

The annoyed flicker came again.

"I'm a lover, not a fighter," he said. "Or I was, I guess."

"What about customers or co-workers? Anyone not happy with your services? Did you fire anyone from your business lately?"

This time, I couldn't blame him when he took offense. "You saw my work. I was damn good at what I did. Learned from my dad, and he was the best. Ask anyone I ever worked with. They'll tell you the same. All my customers were happy."

I held up a hand. "Okay, I didn't mean to cast aspersions on your work. What you did at Patrea's place was top-notch, and I know she had no complaints."

"Of course not," Jerry fumed before fading out of view, leaving me alone with the creaks and groans of the old house. The silence felt heavy, like a blanket too thick for a warm night.

"Great, I'm married for all of five minutes and already

spending my evenings with a dead guy," I muttered to myself, trying to inject some humor into the situation. It fell flat, echoing in the empty space.

With a weary sigh, I stood up, the remains of the day's joy clinging to me like cobwebs, and went to retrieve my phone from my purse. Patrea hadn't called or texted. I would have heard the alerts, but I checked anyway and found no new notifications.

The silence of the old house seemed to amplify each little noise, turning the soft ticking of the clock in the hall into a booming pronouncement of Drew's absence. My fingers twitched, longing for the warm, reassuring weight of Molly's furry head on my lap. I pictured her there, wide brown eyes reflecting concern—or maybe just a plea for treats. Either way, she'd been a comfort to me in the past.

"Could use your slobbery kisses right about now," I murmured to the shadows, but the thought of heading over to my parent's place, where Molly was enjoying what was supposed to be our honeymoon sleepover, made me wince. Mom's well-meaning questions and Dad's bear hugs were more than I could handle tonight.

"Besides," I said to the empty room, "it's not like you'd be any help with ghostly interrogations, Molls." My attempt at humor was as stale as the leftover wedding cake we'd left sitting on its table at the Wentworth house would be.

Note to self: find time to pick up leftover cake and wedding favors tomorrow.

I settled on the couch, curling up under the afghan that Grammie Dupree had crocheted for me—a riot of colors that managed to be both flashy and comforting all at once—and finally indulged in the misery I'd been trying to hold back. The best thing for me now would be sleep, but sleep, like peace, proved elusive. Every time I closed my eyes, I saw Drew's face going pale as Ernie read him his rights and felt the knot of worry tightening in my gut.

As the hours passed with no word from Patrea, I tried to cling to the hope that she was too busy working a miracle to let me know how things were going. That the opposite could be true was not lost on me, either.

The thought of climbing into bed alone held no appeal, so I stayed where I was and turned on the TV for comfort. I drifted into a troubled sleep once or twice through the long night.

With dawn came the golden slant of sunlight through the living room curtains and a resolve that felt like steel in my veins. With no word yet from Patrea, I burned off some of the worry by scrubbing the upstairs bathroom, but not enough to take the edge off. Finally, sometime after eight, I grabbed my phone with hands that didn't shake—much—and tapped out a message to Jacy and Neena:

I'm up. No word. Need you.

I knew they would come. They always did, no matter the circumstances. Jacy, with her ability to cut through any BS she might encounter, and Neena, with the gentle charm that could coax secrets out of a stone, were more than just friends. They were the sisters of my heart.

"Okay, Dupree," I said to my reflection in the hallway mirror, ignoring the faint redness that still rimmed my eyes. "You can get through this. It's just another mystery. You've done this before." But this time the stakes were higher than ever.

The moment Jacy's bubblegum-pink minivan pulled into my driveway, a flutter of hope lodged itself amidst the tangle of nerves in my stomach. She bustled in with enough coffee to caffeinate a small army and an expression that meant business.

"Neena's on her way. She said we needed the sustenance you can only get from baked goods, and since Patrea's otherwise occupied, took it on herself to provide us with some."

"I'm not sure I can eat, but bless her for the gesture," I said, taking the latte Jacy handed me.

"Mabel said she'd send you a care package later, and that you are not to even think about paying for it. She picked up four more catering clients at the wedding and two wedding cake orders besides."

Without knocking, Neena walked in carrying a bakery bag that, despite my queasy stomach, smelled of sugar and spice and everything nice. "I got the last three eclairs," she said, brandishing the bag. "And June talked me into one of her mini chocolate pies. It's covered in whipped cream. Looks and smells like sin on a stick. Just what we need for stress-relief."

"Any ghost sightings yet?" Jacy asked as she plopped down onto my plush couch, setting her to-go cup on a coaster with a precision that betrayed her inner turmoil.

"More like pesterings," I replied, sinking into the armchair opposite her. The fabric was warm under my fingers, a comforting contrast to the chill that signaled a ghostly presence. I recounted the scene from last night, outlining Jerry's version of events, his desperation—the whole spectral sob story.

"That's a hot load of BS." Jacy licked a bit of eclair filling from the corner of her mouth. "Drew isn't that kind of guy."

Neena held a tiny slice of chocolate pie up to her mouth, preparing to take a bite, her eyes sharp when they met mine. "So, he thinks Drew did him in? Honey, that's colder than a well-digger's ankle in January."

"Brian says otherwise." Jacy's voice cut through, pinning me with a look that meant she had news. "He said there was a spat, but it was all just bluster. And Jerry? Three sheets to the wind and then some. He came at Drew with some nonsense about how Drew could never appreciate you for the woman you were, and probably didn't have the equipment to satisfy a woman, anyway."

My eyebrows shot toward my hairline. "Yeah, I've got no complaints on that score. What did Drew say?"

"According to Brian, he laughed it off at first, but Jerry got in Drew's face, poked him in the chest a couple of times, and even then, Drew stayed calm. He let Jerry shove him a few times, then just grabbed him by the arm and signaled for Adam. Adam and the bouncer escorted Jerry out the door, and Brian figured that was the end of it until Ernie showed up last night."

"I figured he was full of it," I muttered, feeling a flicker of annoyance at Jerry's selective memory. "I guess we'll need to dig deeper then."

CHAPTER THREE

e were still mapping out our plan, scribbling notes on a pad with a pen that had 'Mooselick River's Best Realtor' emblazoned on it—compliments of Maryann Payne, the only Realtor in town these days—when the doorbell chimed. My heart stalled, thinking it might be Ernie. Then, it kick-started into double-time as I saw Drew's parents, Quinn and Cheryl, through the frosted glass. They had that wary, weathered look of folks who'd lost their bearings.

"Come in." I accepted hugs and offered something to drink.

"No, thank you, dear." Cheryl patted me on the arm. "Have you heard anything?"

"Not yet." And as the minutes flitted past, my worry continued to mount.

"We were supposed to head home later today," Quinn said after they'd taken seats in the living room, and Jacy and Neena had gone into the kitchen to give us some privacy.

"But." Cheryl looked at her husband for reassurance. "We've decided to stay on in Mooselick River for a while.

With everything going on, we'd feel better being near Drew."

Since they'd been at her place for an extended stay to welcome the new baby, his parents had flown in from the other side of the country. If they didn't ride back home with Drew's brother, Tom, today, they'd be stuck here without transportation unless I could scare them up a rental car. At least until Ernie and his crew finished going over Drew's truck, which they'd hauled off on a flatbed to examine for evidence.

"We're not comfortable staying at the inn while you're here worrying yourself to pieces," Quinn said. "We'd like to take you up on your offer to stay here. You shouldn't be alone right now."

We'd made the offer when we'd thought they would only be here a night or two at most, but these people were my family now. What kind of wife would I be if I didn't say yes?

"Of course," I replied, my mouth dry. "You're always welcome here."

Their relief was palpable, a pressure release in the room. I made a mental note to add 'ghost-proofing' to my to-do list. Because with Jerry around and Dolly popping in whenever she felt like it, my house could quickly go from my sanctuary to Grand Central Station for the dearly departed. Or the not-so-dearly in Jerry's case.

"Drew will be so relieved," I said, with a strained smile that felt tight around the edges. Drew's folks nodded, their expressions etched with the worry that comes from having your world turned upside down and shaken like a snow globe.

"Thank you, Dear," Drew's mom murmured, her eyes brimming with unshed tears. They gave me one last grateful look before heading back to the inn to retrieve their suitcases, leaving me standing in the foyer feeling as if I'd just agreed to harbor fugitives rather than my in-laws.

"Girl, are you okay?" Neena asked, her concern wrapping around me like a warm hug.

"Sure," I replied, knowing my voice was about as steady as a three-legged table. "So long as Jerry follows the house rules. And I'll have to tell Dolly she needs to tone it down, too. No spectral shenanigans while we have guests."

"Good luck with that," Jacy quipped, her honey-blond hair bouncing as she shook her head. "Jerry doesn't strike me as the obedient type."

"Maybe not," I conceded, "but he wants my help, so he'll have to play by the rules."

Once the coast was clear and the sounds of Drew's parents' car faded, we reconvened in the living room.

"Okay, the obvious first step is information gathering," I declared, picking up my notepad with the kind of resolve that would've made my Grammie Dupree proud. "We need intel on Jerry. Who he rubbed the wrong way, who besides Drew might have had it out for him. Friends. Family."

"Call Martha." Jacy deadpanned, taking the last bite of

her tiny slice of pie. "She can make you one of her famous dossiers on him."

"It would help to know how he died," Neena suggested, crossing her legs and leaning forward to set her plate back on the table. "Then, we'll have to track his movements on the night. The guy must've left a trail of breadcrumbs we can follow."

"Or a trail of empty whiskey bottles," I corrected. "Even he admitted he'd had a few."

"Patrea will let us know what happened as soon as she can," Jacy said, her face grim. "Hopefully sooner rather than later."

I nodded. "Once we have a list, we'll talk to the people closest to him," I continued, trying to sound less concerned than I felt. "And we'll get the guys to give us a list of people who were at the bar that night."

"And let's not forget he mentioned he had an ex-wife," Neena added, tapping a manicured nail against her chin thoughtfully. "Tangled marriages have a way of unraveling into motives for murder."

"Speaking of marriage," I said, downing the last of my coffee, "mine's certainly starting with a bang. I need to find time today to go back to the Wentworth to pick up my dress and Drew's things. Deal with the leftover cake and the gifts. I guess I'll wait until I get his folks settled. Maybe we'll have heard from Patrea by then. If not, I'm going to the station no matter what she said."

"Don't worry about anything at the Wentworth," Jacy assured me. "Brian and David took the morning off to help Chris with the cleanup. I'll text Brian and have him gather your stuff and drop it here on his way home."

"Thanks," I sighed, wishing I was on a beach somewhere, my toes curled into warm white sand instead of rattling around riddled with worry in my soon-to-be invaded house.

"We all know Drew's innocent. It's just a matter of proving it, and this isn't our first time," Jacy said. "It's just a question of getting it done before the town decides to nominate Jerry for sainthood."

"Or paints Drew as the Devil." Neena nodded, their faces set with determination, and my heart swelled with gratitude for these women who'd stood by me through thick and thin. If anyone could help me prove Drew's innocence and get to the bottom of Jerry's untimely demise, it was them.

Rather than calling Martha, I reached out to my mom. I needed to make arrangements to pick up Molly anyway and let her know the latest turn of events. I pressed the phone to my ear as I paced the length of my front hall. "Hey, Mom," I said when she answered. "No news yet. Or not about Drew."

I told her his parents would be staying with me and that I'd come and get Molly once I had them settled in.

"I'd tell you to give Ernie a chance to do his job, but I expect that advice would go unheeded," she said. "Instead, I'll just offer whatever help I can. Even if that means dealing with things I'd rather let lie in peace."

She meant ghosts.

"Thanks, Mom. Do you have any idea who Jerry's ex-wife might be?" I put her on speaker so Jacy and Neena could hear the answer.

"Of course." My mother's voice blended with clinking dishes in the background. "You know her, too. She did my hair yesterday. Cindy Johnson. From Mara's salon."

That was a name I hadn't expected to hear.

"Did she get married again," I asked, biting my lip, "or is Johnson her maiden name?"

"Married. She has a new husband. Or newish, anyway. They didn't wait long after her divorce was final." The lack of a gossipy tone was a hallmark of Kitty Dupree's disdain for spreading rumors, but still, she managed to convey there'd been plenty of them floating around.

"Thanks, Mom." I hung up and turned to face my partners in crime-solving.

"Looks like we'll need to chat with Cindy."

Jacy snorted. "You'd be better off talking to Dolly or Mara. Cindy's one of those listener types. Rarely talks about herself but gets you to spill your guts while she's got you in the chair. It will take a subtle touch to get her to talk."

"Plus," Neena said, "she'll have heard the news by now. You know how fast the grapevine is in this town. You say boo to someone at the post office, and they'll have heard about it at the grocery store before you can pick a shopping cart."

"True," I said as we all heard the sound of a car pulling into my driveway. Drew's parents must have already been packed when they came to ask if they could stay. Unless it was Patrea. Hope had butterflies doing the cha-cha in my stomach until I looked out the narrow window beside the door and saw I'd been right the first time.

I put the Parkers in the nicest bedroom upstairs. The one closest to the largest bathroom. "Make yourselves at home, and if I can do anything to make you more comfortable, please don't hesitate to ask."

Cheryl put her hand on my arm. "If you wouldn't mind, dear, I'd like to putter around in the kitchen. Cooking soothes my nerves."

"By all means." Then I remembered we'd emptied the fridge ahead of our honeymoon and explained the situation to her. "I have an errand to run that won't take long. Make me a list, and I'll swing by the grocery store on my way back. Maybe by then, we'll have some idea what we're up against."

We would because I'd have hit the end of my patience by then and shoved my way into the police station, but I didn't need to show my pushier side to my new in-laws.

Ten minutes later, list in hand, I followed Jacy and Neena out the front door.

"I'm driving," she said as I squinted against the morning sun's glare reflecting off her car. By the jut of her chin, I could tell she wouldn't be budged, so I relented and climbed into the back, taking the spot next to little Wade's car seat. The drive to the salon was short, and as the engine hummed, I rehearsed what I planned to say to Cindy in my head. Jacy pulled into a parking spot, and we tumbled out, our footsteps syncing as we approached the familiar building.

"Let's keep it casual," I whispered, smoothing down my hair.

"Got it," Neena said, pushing open the door with a jingle that announced our entry.

The scent of hairspray and shampoo enveloped us as we stepped inside. Cindy, her hair a pleasant shade of brown with gold highlights today, was chatting with the only customer in the place. Apparently, early Thursday mornings weren't their busiest time. When her hazel eyes met mine in the mirror, Cindy's jaw tightened, but that was the only outward sign of an inward struggle.

"She knows," I murmured, and we pretended to peruse the selection of nail polishes near the front. "And we don't have an appointment." I scanned the room for signs of the ghost of Dolly Tibbets and came up empty, which was a relief.

"And you're supposed to be on your honeymoon," Jacy whispered. "I think that might be the biggest clue that something's up."

This had been Dolly's salon until she'd dropped dead right in the middle of doing someone's hair. Now, she haunted the place in a benevolent manner to keep an eye on her legacy and her daughter, Mara. And let's not forget the salon was a hotbed of gossip, which, once she realized I could communicate with her, Dolly passed on to me—in great detail whether I wanted to hear it or not.

"Everly, I didn't expect to see you here today," Mara said when she came out of the back room with an armload of clean towels. Her gaze flickered toward Cindy, then back to me. "But I suppose I know why you've stopped by." She lowered her tone. "Ernie already dragged Max in for questioning this morning, so take it easy on her."

That was the first piece of new information I'd had since the night before and one I took as a good sign. If Ernie was still questioning people, he might not be entirely fixated on Drew as the murderer.

As the hairdryer's hum slowly died down, Cindy carefully finished arranging her customer's curls, her fingers dancing like an artist creating a masterpiece until she whipped off the plastic cape and let the newly coiffed woman out of the chair. Our moment had arrived.

"Hey, Cindy," I called out, my voice casual as I could make it. She glanced up and offered a smile that didn't reach her eyes.

"I know why you're here," she said, her tone as flat as I'd ever heard. "My Max didn't kill Jerry."

"Neither did my Drew," I matched her tone.

"I didn't say he did."

"Same goes."

"We were hoping to chat for a sec. But only if you have time between customers." Jacy stepped in to reassure Cindy we meant no harm. "No one's accusing anyone of anything, but it would help if you could tell us about Jerry. Fill in some of the gaps that might help us clear Drew's name."

Cindy relented. "I suppose. Let's step into the back room; we'll have more privacy there," She led us past a line of shampoo sinks.

Once safely tucked away among stacks of towels and shelves crammed with beauty products, Cindy's stern mask slipped just enough to reveal concern. "What do you want to know?"

"Anything you can tell us," I admitted, fiddling with the hem of my tee shirt. "We're trying to piece together a list of people who might have a reason to want Jerry dead. Besides Max and Drew, I mean."

"Jerry was a charmer," Cindy began. One woman's charmer is another woman's creeper, I supposed.

"But only when he was chasing something—someone," Cindy began, her gaze distant. "He pursued me relentlessly, made me feel like the center of his world. But after we married, it was like I became part of the furniture. And before long, there was another woman."

"Did they…" Jacy trailed off, leaving the question hanging.

"Have an affair? I don't know." Cindy bit her lip. "But Jerry, he loved the chase more than the catch. It was his pattern. And he drank—a lot—which didn't help matters."

"Sounds like a real Casanova," Neena quipped, though her furrowed brow betrayed her concern.

"More like a dog chasing cars," I muttered, thinking of Jerry's annoying fixation on me. "Sorry you went through that, Cindy."

"Thanks. Once I shook him off, I did my best to lose track of him. Not easy in a small town, but it helps that I stay away from Cappy's. Especially on the weekends. I'm sorry I can't be more help." Her voice trailed off, leaving us in a silence thick enough to cut with shears and I knew she'd said all she had to say on the matter.

After murmuring our thanks, we left Cindy to her sanctuary of hairspray and highlights, stepping back into the buzz of the salon where two more customers had arrived.

"Okay, so Jerry's a serial crusher with a drinking problem," Jacy summed up as we exited onto the sidewalk, the afternoon sun casting long shadows behind us. "This isn't exactly news, other than the serial part."

"Which means jealousy could be a motive," I mused, feeling the weight of Drew's situation pressing down on me like the summer humidity. "He didn't seem bothered by the fact that I was engaged. That tells me he probably chased other women who already had men in their lives."

"Could be revenge, too," Neena suggested. "Either way, we need to dig deeper."

"Maybe talk to some of the other women he's 'chased'? See if any of them hold a grudge?" I proposed, already dreading the thought of stirring up more drama.

"All we need is another list," Jacy agreed, wrinkling her pert nose with its dusting of freckles.

"Speaking of lists, why don't you give me your grocery one and let me do the shopping for you? It'll speed things up and save you having to answer a hundred questions."

Thanking her for being considerate, I handed over the list and my debit card and stayed in the car while she and Jacy went inside. Once they'd gone, my thoughts centered on Drew and what might happen if I failed to find Jerry's killer.

"Everly?" Neena's voice cut through my sleep-deprived haze. "You okay? You're quiet."

"Thinking," I replied, staring at my house with no memory of the drive back. The truth was, beneath the layers of worry and weariness, a steely resolve was hardening. Drew needed me, even if I trusted Patrea to handle whatever Ernie might throw at him.

"Those cogs are turning loud enough to hear," Jacy teased, her smile gentle.

"More like grinding," I confessed. "I need to pick Molly up from my parents and start gathering data on Jerry, but right now, I'm more concerned with seeing Drew and finding out what's going on with him."

"Which you will," Jacy stated firmly, reaching over to squeeze my hand. "One step at a time, Everly. We'll figure this out. We always do. It's like catching killers is our thing now."

Their friendship soothed my frazzled soul, and my heart swelled with gratitude for these two women who'd stood by me through more than their fair share of murder mysteries.

"If you need us," Neena said, helping me carry the grocery bags, "we'll be at the shop. Keep us posted on whatever you find out from Patrea, and try to find some time to relax."

"Relax," I echoed with a snort. That was as likely as me sprouting wings and flying to Paris to take in the view. But the sentiment was nice.

CHAPTER FOUR

he thick metal door to the Mooselick River Police Station creaked in protest as I pushed it open, a sound so familiar it barely registered. Unfortunately, I'd spent more than my fair share of time here since I'd moved back to town.

Today, my shoes tapped on the tile floor, the sound echoing off the walls like a metronome measuring out my rising anxiety with each step. The place was saturated with the smell of stale coffee and something vaguely metallic—like handcuffs that had seen better days. I was there for Drew, determined to yank out whatever thorny information I could from Patrea about his predicament.

One of the two deputies who worked under Ernie sat where Carole Ann Wilmette usually did. I thanked whatever patron saint watched over those of us who had to overcome the impulse to throttle the perpetually annoying. Today, I would not be tempted.

"I'm over here," Patrea called out, her voice cutting through the quiet hum of the air conditioning. Having pulled together several of the uncomfortable waiting room-style chairs to form a work area, she looked up from a stack of papers. Dark hair framed a face marred by lines of weariness. Chris must have brought her a change of clothes because she'd left the reception wearing her bridesmaid dress and now had on a power suit. I couldn't help thinking she looked like the star of a gritty courtroom drama.

But this wasn't TV—it was messier. Real life didn't come with commercial breaks or neatly resolved plotlines.

"Have you been here all night?"

"Naturally. Drew's getting my best effort, and that means being present for questioning."

"Okay." I picked up her coffee cup from the chair next to her and sat in its place. "You know I would never question your work ethic, but not knowing what's happening is killing me. It's Drew we're talking about. Ernie can't think he killed anyone. What would be the point when he had nothing to gain? It's not like Jerry had a shot with me," I said, fumbling over my words like someone learning to juggle chainsaws—badly. "I think I made it pretty clear I wasn't interested."

"I know all of that." Her tone dropped, serious enough to pin me to my seat. "But Ernie found evidence placing Drew at the scene. And not just the 'I was passing by' kind of evidence. This is serious."

"Define serious." My breath hitched, and I suddenly became aware of how flimsy my chair felt beneath me, as though it might crumble along with my composure. "Drew doesn't go after people. He's all about self-defense these days, not aggression. You know that. "

"I know, Everly. And I know he didn't do anything

wrong." Patrea's eyes met mine, steady and reassuring. "But believe me when I say the situation is grave. We're talking beyond a shadow of a doubt stuff. Ernie doesn't have much choice about holding him, and Drew doesn't have an explanation."

"Grave? Are we still talking about evidence, or are we foreshadowing my future conversations with Jerry's ghost?" I lowered my voice to a whisper and tried to smile, but it felt more like baring teeth—a defense mechanism against the weight of the situation pressing down on my chest. Drew, my rock, was being squeezed between the hard place of evidence and the hammer of justice, and here I was, making ghost puns.

"You've seen him?" Patrea glanced toward the deputy to make sure he wasn't listening too closely. "What did he say?"

"He said Drew got all pushy-shovey with him at the bar, but Brian said that wasn't how it went down."

"Plenty of witness statements corroborate Drew's accounting of events, and all the guys have come in to make their statements, which is why I've been here so long."

"I didn't know that. I thought the guys were on cleanup duty. You'd think Jacy would have said something."

"Brian only just left a few minutes ago. She probably didn't know yet. The only sticking point is that Drew left the bar for a short time, and no one can verify his whereabouts. He said he was on the phone with a friend, and his phone log bears out his statement, but since phones are entirely portable, using one as an alibi doesn't hold up. He says he never left Cappy's parking lot, but he could have. That, coupled with his fingerprints on the murder weapon, and Ernie could easily make a case against him."

"His fingerprints on the murder weapon?" I repeated in shock.

"I'm afraid so." Patrea lifted a hand to run it through her hair agitatedly. "I've been trying to get hold of the friend he was on the phone with, but there's no answer, which also hasn't helped things."

"Which friend?" I figured I had a right to know, and when Patrea gave me the name, my heart sank a bit lower. "That's concerning. Pete's been struggling with PTSD since he came back from Iraq. Drew's been talking to him a lot lately because Pete's reluctant to seek help. Drew's been worried he'll do something drastic."

"That's what he told me, too. But Pete's not answering his phone and Drew's adamant that we not send cops to check on him in case that makes the situation worse. Part of what I've been doing here all night is trying to get Drew to relent and let me call on other resources to help this Pete guy. We'll need his testimony, but his well-being is the top priority right now."

"Agreed." I straightened up, clinging to my determination like a lifeline. "Okay, so Ernie has evidence, but we can't fully establish Drew's alibi until we can talk to Pete. Now that I know where we are in the grand scheme, I can start looking for ways to figure this out. There has to be some Drew-is-innocent evidence floating around out there."

"Good luck," she said, but her smile was as thin as tracing paper. "I'm afraid you'll need it."

"Thanks for the vote of confidence." I stood up, trying to swallow the fight simmering inside me. "Any chance I can see him before I go?"

Patrea shook her head. "Ernie's not letting him have visitors until later today, so I told Drew to get some sleep. I'm working on getting a bail hearing set for this afternoon. I want him home with you by this evening. I would have called you once I had everything lined up, you know."

"Patience is not one of my virtues," I smiled at her.

"I'm aware. I absolutely will call you when I'm on my way back from talking to the judge. You'll see your sweetie today, I promise. And by the way, you look like you could use a nap, too. Maybe you should get some rest so Drew doesn't see his new bride looking haggard."

"Thanks for the flattery. Your honesty knows no bounds." I rolled my eyes.

"It's one of my virtues." Patrea grinned at me, her face relaxing for the first time since we'd started talking. "Hell of a wedding, though."

"The best. I'm beyond grateful for everything you did to make it that way."

Patrea waved away my gratitude. "Remember that when I start relentlessly hounding you for feedback on how to make it better."

"You're moving forward with the Wentworth as an event venue, then?"

"Martha cornered me last night and tried to book the grounds for no fewer than three events over the next year already. She wants to start doing tea parties and form something along the lines of the Red Hat Society. I had two other people tag me to discuss the cost of doing a wedding there. I don't think I'll have too much trouble getting bookings. You were the best guinea pig I could have hoped for."

"Thanks, I think."

"Now, go home, take that nap, and try not to worry."

"What about you?" It would be indelicate to mention it, but she looked about as tired as I felt. "You've been up all night, too. It's beginning to show."

Patrea picked up her phone when it buzzed. "I'll head over to my office and stretch out on the sofa for a couple of hours. Don't worry about me, but I've got to take this."

Nodding, I took the hint and left her alone with her phone.

The nap sounded like a good but unlikely idea with Drew's folks in the house. Especially, because my brain refused to settle. Instead, it sifted through everything I'd learned, trying to untangle the living nightmare unfolding before me. Somewhere, if I thought about it hard enough, would be a thread of truth that could help. I just had to find it and pull until the whole messy situation unraveled in Drew's favor.

My butt just about landed on the seat of my car before I got a text from Patrea.

Since I know you've already decided to ignore my advice about a nap, maybe spend some time scaring up a few character witnesses. We might need them at the bail hearing.

Consider it done—I typed back. It helped to have something specific to do.

The little dots waggled for a bit, letting me know she was typing a reply.

Drew's reputation in Mooselick River is solid. And then there's the timeline. If we can prove a discrepancy, that will also help.

"Discrepancies are good. Discrepancies are our friends," I murmured. Now, to find one.

I'm on it, I responded—*I'll reach out to the ghost network to see if they saw or heard anything. Dolly gets around.*

Just remember—came the fast reply—*ghost stories are not admissible in court.*

Heat rose from the pavement, threatening that the day would get warmer as it went on. I considered a quick stop at the bakery for another coffee but figured the caffeine might make me jittery, so I turned in the opposite direction. The drive to my parents' place was short, but it felt like crossing miles of uncertainty.

The familiar creak of the front steps soothed me as I walked across the porch. Before I got to the door, it swung open, and there she was—Molly, my four-legged bundle of joy, bounding toward me with all the grace of a gamboling lamb. Her wagging tail thumped against my legs as she danced around me, her tongue lolling out in a doggy grin that could thaw even the frostiest mood.

"Hey girl," I cooed, scratching behind her ears. Her soft fur felt safely familiar, and her eager affection seeped into the cracks of my worn spirit. I knelt to wrap my arms around her, burying my face in the warmth of her neck. As always, Molly leaned in to rest her chin on my shoulder.

"Thanks, Molls. I needed that." I laughed softly as she wiggled and slid her tongue up my cheek. Standing up, I kept one hand on her head as I raised mine to meet my mother's steady gaze.

"Are you okay?" she asked.

"As much as I can be." Molly and I trudged through the front door. As soon as we stepped inside, the weight of the situation settled back on my shoulders like a heavy shawl.

"Your father's in the kitchen making lunch," Mom said, her voice laced with worry as she ushered me through the living room.

"Lunch? Is it that late already?"

Mom quirked an eyebrow. "It's more like brunch, I suppose. You know your father when he's anxious. He barely slept and then zonked out on the sofa for a couple of hours and woke up hungry."

I had to admit the scent of whatever he was making had awakened the appetite I hadn't been sure I'd ever have again. I'd barely taken more than a few nibbles of the sweet treats Neena had brought that morning and was surprised to find that I could eat.

"Is there enough for one more?" I asked as he turned from the stove where he'd just flipped a Monte Cristo sandwich to cook on the second side.

"For you? Always." He deposited the sandwich he'd been making for himself on a plate and set it in front of me, then went back to making a new one. "How are you holding up, honey?"

I sank into a seat at the table, Molly curling up at my feet, her presence a silent show of support.

"Patrea's doing everything she can," I began, recounting the evidence against Drew and how she'd hoped to get a bail hearing by the end of the day. "We need to find a couple of character witnesses willing to testify in a hurry."

Mom perked up. "I can handle that for you. It'll be one thing I can take off your list, and you have my word I'll do it well."

Overcome, I put my hand on hers and squeezed. "I have no doubt. Thanks, Mom."

She nodded. "Okay. What else?"

"Patrea said to start looking for anything that helps shore up Drew's alibi. Or gives more detail about Jerry's movements. Mostly chasing down people who were at the bar and asking if they remember anything helpful. I assume if Adam had cameras outside, he'd have given the footage to Ernie already, but someone could have seen something. It's a long shot, but I have to try."

Dad, who had been quietly listening, leaned forward, his blue eyes sharp behind his reading glasses. "You know,

Max Johnson probably knows more about Jerry than Cindy realizes. He'd feel it was his business to know everything about the man his woman had been tangled up with. It might be worth talking to him."

"His woman?" Mom raised an eyebrow at Dad's choice of words.

"That's how he'd think of her, and you know it."

"I do," Mom conceded. "And I also know he tends to see conspiracies around every corner, and half of what he says needs to be—"

"I know," Dad grinned as he interrupted her, "taken with a grain of salt the size of a chihuahua. But discounting everything he says could be a mistake. Even the weirdest conspiracy theories can spring from a seed of truth. Max's biggest sin is being prone to flights of fancy, but under it all, he's a decent guy."

As compared to Jerry, I read from his overtones. I poured some extra syrup over the last corner of my sandwich and took a bite.

"Thanks, Dad. I'll keep all of that in mind." I stood up, steadied by the thought that there might be another lead to follow. "And thanks for the food. It really hit the spot."

His hug before I left shaved off a bit more of the edge my nerves were perched on. No matter what, I had friends and family willing to help me.

Back at my house, I found more of the same. While Cheryl bustled around my kitchen, Drew's brother sat waiting on the porch, his face drawn and anxious. I settled beside him, Molly placing her head on his knee as if understanding the gravity of our conversation.

"He didn't do it," he said, breaking the silence. "And I have to go back to work tomorrow."

"I know."

We sat silently until I said, "I need to hear about the bachelor party, everything leading up to Jerry getting kicked out. Anything you can remember about Drew stepping out for a few minutes."

Tom rubbed his face, exhaustion etched in the lines around his eyes. "It started out as a great night, you know? I got a chance to meet Drew's new friends. We played video games, had some laughs, and then decided to hit the local joint for the pool tables, food, and a couple of beers. No one got wasted or anything. Just a low-key party like he wanted."

"No strippers?" I asked, nudging my shoulder against his.

"He threatened to pants me during the reception if I did." The admission lightened his mood slightly.

"Sounds about right."

"Anyhow, this Jerry guy, I guess, was hanging out at the bar. I can't say I noticed him until he came over and started talking smack about how Drew wasn't man enough for a woman like you. He said you needed a real stud, and he'd win you over one day. Drew put him in his place and told him to back off. That's when things got heated."

As Tom recounted the events, his words painted a

picture wildly different from Jerry's accusations against Drew. This one, I knew, was the actual version of events—one I expected to hear repeated when Brian and David showed up.

Brian's work van turned down my street as if my thoughts had conjured them and pulled into the drive. Tom rose to help the other men unload boxes that looked like they'd been hastily packed at the wedding venue.

"Hey, Everly," Brian said, his dark hair tousled and his brown eyes weary. "We thought you'd want this stuff sooner rather than later."

"Thanks," I said, ushering them inside. I could feel the weight of their concern as they stored the gifts in my front room—the one my mother called a parlor. Tom joined his family in the kitchen, leaving us to speak privately.

"Jerry was way out of line," David began, his tall frame slumping into a chair as if the memory itself were heavy. His voice carried the soft cadence of someone who had spent too many nights contemplating life's what-ifs.

"He kept pushing, saying things about you." Brian scowled as he replayed the memory. "And worse things about Drew. If he'd come at me like that, I'd have popped him one."

"I thought you were going to when you stepped in," David said, nodding toward his companion. "Brian told Jerry to take a hike before things got ugly." He directed that part toward me.

"But Drew didn't start anything? Jerry told...uh, I heard a rumor Drew got in his face first." Being in the know about my ghostly proclivities, they'd know where the rumor came from.

"He did not," Brian added, his usually easygoing demeanor replaced by a stubborn tilt of his jaw. "Anyone who claimed Drew did the provoking is an idiot because it was Jerry stirring up trouble all night. After he got in Drew's face, Adam kicked him out, and none of us gave him another thought. I know I didn't, and it didn't look like Drew did, either."

The temperature dropped a few degrees as they spoke, and I felt the familiar tingle at the back of my neck. Jerry appeared near the window, glaring at me.

"Don't listen to them. They're spewing lies!" Jerry's voice echoed in the room, a spectral sneer in his words. "I was just having fun until Drew lost it."

"Tell me about the phone call when Drew left. Was it very soon after Jerry got booted?" Sometimes, the best way to handle an annoying ghost is to ignore them.

"It's hard to say." David slapped his fist into his palm. "If I had any idea what would happen, I'd have paid more attention. It wasn't right after, though, I don't think."

"Twenty minutes at least," Brian said. "Closer to half an hour. I remember ordering some fries right after Adam went back in the kitchen, and I had eaten about half of them when Drew pulled out his phone."

"Uh-huh," I muttered under my breath, trying to focus on Brian and David's account while Jerry floated around, making faces and gesturing wildly. My attempts to tune him out were about as effective as trying to ignore a mosquito buzzing in your ear.

"Everly?" Brian's voice pulled me back, and I realized both men were looking at me, brows furrowed in concern.

"Sorry, just—" I waved a hand dismissively, "thinking about next steps."

"Right..." Brian said, not entirely convinced. "Well, we'll help however we can."

"I appreciate it," I replied, giving them a grateful smile. "If you could make me a list of whoever you remember being at Cappy's the other night, that would be great."

As they left, promising to make and send their lists, my gaze drifted back to where Jerry hovered, still ranting about his version of the truth.

"Can it, Casper," I hissed, finally losing my patience. "I've got a real live person to save, and your boo-hoo act isn't cutting it."

Jerry crossed his arms, pouting like a child denied dessert. I sighed, turning my attention back to the boxes and the growing list of discrepancies in his story. There was much to do, and the last thing I needed was a dead guy with an ego problem muddying the waters.

I scooped Drew's clothes out of one, bits of the confetti we'd been showered with dropping to the floor like a mocking reminder of how quickly celebration could turn into calamity. My fingers brushed against the cool cotton of the shirt he'd worn that morning, the sensation grounding me as I tried to corral my thoughts. Sensing my distress, Molly nudged her wet nose against my hand, her soft snuffle pulling at my heartstrings. "It's okay, girl," I murmured, though we both knew it was anything but.

Jerry's ghost had vanished, probably off to haunt a liquor store or something, leaving me alone with my spiraling worries. Drew was counting on me, and here I was, sorting through wedding debris like a festive janitor while I waited for Patrea to let me know about the bail hearing. There were lists to make, people to talk to, and all I could do was dither around with things that didn't matter.

"Focus, Everly," I muttered to myself, dropping the confetti back into the box with more force than necessary. The gravity of the situation pressed down on me, a weight that made my next breath shallow. I needed more information—something, anything that could cast doubt on the evidence piling higher with every passing minute.

Pacing the length of our living room, my footsteps muffled by the antique rug, I chewed over every scrap of what Drew's brother, Brian, and David had said. I had no doubt they were telling the truth, but none could remember precisely how long Jerry had been gone before Drew went outside. This felt like crucial information, even if I couldn't say exactly why.

My mind raced ahead to picture one outcome after another. The town loved him—his fitness classes were about the only thing keeping half the population's donut consumption from turning us all spherical—but love didn't trump fingerprint evidence. Worse, the town's love for him wouldn't last. Once the talk started and the doubts set in, his business would suffer even if he was acquitted.

I needed to find the real killer and fast. I'm good under pressure. That's usually where I shine. Working out a plan for getting the job done and following through until it is. Except today, with this, I struggled to see my way clear.

Maybe I should take a page from Cheryl's book and find something to do to distract my thoughts. Cooking wasn't my way, though, from the smells coming from my kitchen, I was glad it was hers.

Still trying to get my thoughts in order, I sank onto the couch, Molly hopping up beside me to rest her head on my knee. I scratched behind her ears, drawing comfort from her steady presence.

Sitting here wasn't getting me any closer to anything other than the nap Patrea had suggested. I needed to clear my head so I could think.

"Want to go for a run, Molls?"

She launched off the sofa like a rocket, chocolate fur gleaming in the light through the window, and danced her way into the hall to wait beneath the hook holding her leash.

"I'm taking the dog out for a walk," I called back to let Drew's folks know where I was going, then grabbed Molly's favorite rubber flyer and pocketed my phone in case Patrea called with news.

Molly fell into step beside me as I jogged down the drive and turned right to loop through the side streets.

We'd just made a left onto Oak when a car pulled up beside me. I turned my head to see Ernie pacing us in his cruiser. Other than maybe Freddy Kreuger, Ernie was the last person in the world I wanted to see.

"Everly," he put down his window and called out. I ignored him and kept running. "I need to talk to you."

I picked up the pace.

"Everly!" He got louder. I considered offering him a rude hand gesture but figured even if it made me feel better for a second, it wouldn't help Drew's chances. Instead, I kept running.

The zoom of his engine as he took off conveyed his frustration, but at least he'd left me alone. Or so I thought. It shouldn't have surprised me to see him parked at the entrance to Mooselick River's unofficial dog park—a plot of land behind the end of an empty, dead-end street. Half of me wanted to be churlish enough to turn and run the other way, but I didn't.

"What?" I also didn't care if he could feel the anger in my tone. As far as I was concerned, he'd become the enemy.

"I need to talk to you."

"Molly needs her exercise." I stepped away and whipped the rubber flying disc into the air, watching a blur of muscles and fur as Molly chased after it. "It's a public place, so I can't stop you from talking."

"It's private land," he countered. "But since the owners don't mind people bringing their dogs here, I'm not hauling you in."

"Go ahead." I turned to him and got the first look at his miserable expression. I consider myself empathetic, but this time, I couldn't muster a shred of sympathy. "Put me in a cell next to Drew, why don't you? Molly, too. We might as well all be locked up for no good reason."

"I don't think Drew murdered Jerry Kaminski," he said. "I'm not the enemy here. But I have to do the job, and the evidence is irrefutable. His fingerprints are on the tire iron used to bash Jerry's head in. Maybe you can explain how they came to be there, but Drew couldn't."

I sighed. "Neither can I because it doesn't make sense. Nothing about this makes sense. Drew wouldn't kill Jerry for having a stupid crush on me. We both know that. And his ego isn't so fragile that being taunted could poke a hole in it, so there goes your motive."

Ernie ran a hand over hair he'd let grow out a little from his usual brush cut. "Means and opportunity carry weight here, Dupree. You have to know I can't just dismiss the fact that his prints were on the murder weapon."

Seeing his dilemma, I sighed again. "I guess not. I don't suppose you could show me the crime scene photos? Or better yet, send them to me."

"I could lose my job for that." He gave me a look that carried an unspoken something. "But I could play with your dog for a few minutes if you don't mind holding on to my phone so it doesn't get broken." Deliberately, he unlocked the screen.

"Ah, sure." I took the hint, and as soon as Ernie's back was turned, I sorted through his files to find the folder labeled with Jerry's name. I opened it and pulled up the images to take a photo of each with my phone. For good measure, I snagged a shot of his witness list and the statements each had made, then wiped the screen on my shirt to make sure I hadn't left any fingerprints. Just in case. Ernie played with Molly until I cleared my throat.

"I think Molly's tired out now. Thanks for playing with her." I exchanged his phone for Molly's toy.

He nodded, and I felt a surge of hope for the first time that day. Ernie wasn't working against Drew, so he'd be willing to listen to any theory I might turn up. But then, just as I'd found my center again, he tossed out a statement that pulled me back down into the depths.

"He's not getting bail today."

"But you just said—"

"I know what I said, but I also talked to the judge, and there won't be a hearing today, so he's not getting bail until at least tomorrow, and maybe not until Monday."

"Because of you?" All my good feelings for Ernie evaporated like summer rain on hot pavement.

"What I know and what I can prove are not the same. You need my help with the former, you let me know. Until then, I have to work with the latter." Those were his last words as he climbed into his car and drove off, leaving me staring after him.

CHAPTER FIVE

The phone rang just as I walked back into the house. Drew's mother was still in the kitchen—working out her stress on a ball of cookie dough—and his father was out back running the lawn mower. The grass hadn't needed cutting, but he probably wanted to keep busy. It was Patrea on the line—the sound of her blinker in the background a surefire indicator she was finally heading home.

"If this keeps up," she said, not bothering with any sort of greeting. "I may end up in the cell next to Drew. We're not getting a bail hearing today, and probably not tomorrow, either. The only good news is that Drew stays put for now—he won't be transferred to Thomaston unless we bomb out at the bail hearing."

"Thank you, Patrea," I sighed, relief mingling with frustration. I hadn't known a transfer was even a thing. I'd have worried even more if I had.

"Ernie says Drew can have visitors tonight," she added. "He's acting weird, though."

"Drew?"

"No. Ernie. Based on the evidence, bail would have been set pretty high if it was granted at all. I think Ernie had something to do with stalling the hearing. Probably to give you time to figure out what happened before he has to send Drew to the state prison."

"I know. I talked to Ernie earlier. Just between you and me, he knows Drew didn't kill Jerry but hasn't turned up anything that would exonerate him. He...uh...well, I sort of gained access to the crime scene photos, and Ernie knows I have them."

"Okay," she said, her tone lightening slightly. "That lets me off the hook. I was trying to figure out how to get them to you without compromising my ethics. There's one more thing. Drew specifically said he wants only you to come tonight for the visitation."

"His parents won't be happy to hear that. They're staying with me until...for a few days."

"He knows. They've called the station several times."

"I didn't know. Look, just go home and get some rest," I ordered. "You've done all you can do for now. Are you okay to drive?"

"I've got more caffeine in my veins than blood right now," she said. "I'll be fine."

"Well, text me when you get there so I won't worry," I ordered before hanging up.

Dinner with Drew's folks was like chewing on tin foil —tense and metallic. They hovered over their plates, casting sidelong glances at me, all while Drew's empty chair screamed louder than any ghost I'd ever met.

"Everly, dear, maybe you can convince Drew to let us see him?" his mom ventured, her voice carrying just a hint of rebuke—as if it were my fault he didn't want to see them yet.

But I knew how she must be feeling. Or at least how I'd feel if he didn't want to see me. "He knows you love him, but I suspect he doesn't want you to see him that way. I'll do what I can."

At the jail, Drew's eyes were rimmed with red, not from tears but fatigue. "Did Patrea get home okay? She wouldn't leave even though Ernie grilled me for hours," he rasped, his hands clinging to mine through the bars. "He thinks I did it."

"She did. But you're wrong. Ernie doesn't believe you did it," I assured him, squeezing his fingers. "He told me as much, and I've got the whole Scooby squad on the case. We've already spoken with Jerry's ex-wife, and the guys are gathering a list of possible witnesses from the bar that night."

Drew nodded, his thoughts seeming to drift elsewhere. He needed sleep. "I'm less concerned for myself than I am worried about Pete. I promised he could call me anytime, but now, I don't have my phone. He could be trying to get in touch. Can you get one of the guys to check on him and let him know what's going on? Jack would be the best one to call."

"Consider it done," I promised, tucking away his request in my mental to-do list.

"I'm sorry," he said. "This wasn't exactly how I'd planned for us to spend our first day as husband and wife."

Thankful the watchful deputy was allowing us a bit of latitude—a perk of being his former babysitter, I pressed my face between the bars. Drew did the same and rested his forehead against mine. "The beach will still be there once we've cleared your name, and so will I."

"Love you," he said, then kissed me gently.

"Same goes," I said. "You need to let your parents come and see you, okay?"

"Like this?" He shook his head. They'd taken away his tux and put him in an orange detention uniform. "It's bad enough that you're here."

"The reality can't be worse than their imagination. I think they can handle it."

Reluctantly, he agreed. "Tomorrow. I need to get some sleep first."

After leaving Drew, I went home, gave his folks the news that he'd see them the next day, updated Jacy and Neena with a brief text, and collapsed into bed. I had no dreams that night, only darkness and the soft ticking of the clock. And Molly's comforting presence as she sneaked into Drew's spot.

Morning brought a less tense breakfast scene with Drew's parents.

"I have to go out this morning. I might be gone for a while," I gave his dad my keys. "Use my car. Do something to take your mind off things. Maybe even visit with Leandra and Hank for a while. I think they're up at camp." If anyone could distract them, it would be Leandra. At least they looked more rested than they had the night before.

Jacy knocking on my door put an end to the discussion. She came in with Neena right behind her, both their faces set with determination, and declined Cheryl's offer of something to eat.

"Thank you, but we have a lot of...errands to run this morning." Jacy caught my nearly imperceptible head shake and stopped short of saying we had suspects to grill. "You know, tuxes to return. Things like that."

"Do you mind driving?" I asked the foolish question because Jacy always wanted to drive. I just didn't always want to ride with her. Don't get me wrong, Jacy's a safe driver. She just likes a bit more speed than I do.

Ignoring Cheryl's mild dismay, we trooped outside.

"They don't know I have the photos or that we're tracking Jerry's killer," I murmured on the way to the car. Drew's parents didn't need to see the brutality captured in those images, and they probably wouldn't think our investigation was a good idea.

We huddled around my phone in Jacy's fit-for-a-princess mini-van—a vehicle that defied stealth. The tire iron in the photo was both rusty and antiquated. It was at least two feet long, bent at the end with the socket built in and pointed at the other. It looked heavy enough to do plenty of damage but not so heavy that a woman couldn't swing it if she had to.

"Looks like the one from Catherine's old Buick," I mused aloud, feeling a twist in my gut. That car had been more than a mode of transportation; it had been just one more saving grace handed down from Catherine Willowby, the previous owner of my house. I'd bought the place and all its contents, which included the Buick I'd recently gifted to my father.

"It does, doesn't it?" Jacy flicked the photo on the screen to make it larger. "They don't make them like that anymore. Even newer pickups have those short-handled jobbies now."

"What's the plan?" Neena took the phone from Jacy and scrolled through the images a second time.

"Max Johnson sells cars in Hackinaw," I said—a fact I'd read in Ernie's reports. "Let's pay him a visit at the dealership."

"Undercover," Neena chimed in, a mischievous twinkle in her eye.

"Right. Because nothing says 'covert' like your bubblegum chariot here," I quipped, unable to resist.

"Yeah," Jacy agreed, "But he's a man and, like most of them, will take one look at my baby and try to sell me something else."

"Bet he doesn't offer much for the trade-in," Neena teased. "But I'll take the bullet on this one. We'll tell him my car died and I'm looking for a new one. The prospect of a sale should soften him up."

On the way, I looked up the dealership and found a photo of Max, then suggested a detour past the crime scene, a place that felt haunted even in broad daylight. It looked the same as the photos on my phone, with tufts of tall grass slightly flattened from vehicles that had parked there. Crime scene tape fluttered in the gentle breeze, and the blood stain looked black against the patch of sandy gravel. Nothing new revealed itself until we had pulled away, the van's air conditioner humming a low growl under our conversation.

"Stop the car," I ordered, spotting another area where the grass had been disturbed about fifty yards from where Jerry had died.

We piled out to walk back to the area I'd seen, and there it was—a puddle of dried vomit, a silent witness to someone's distress. A few feet away, a perfect tire print was etched in the silty soil of a dried-up mud puddle.

"Check this out," I said, snapping photos. "What if the killer felt sick over what they'd done and pulled over here? It speaks to this being a spur-of-the-moment crime and not premeditated." My fingers trembled slightly as I saved each image. This could be evidence. It could be a breadcrumb on the trail to vindicating Drew. And I intended to follow it wherever it led. But at the same time, I did the right thing and walked up and down the road until I found the only spot that had service, and forwarded the images to Ernie.

"It makes sense to me." Jacy wrinkled her nose up at the remnants of someone's stomach contents. "I know I'd feel sick if I'd just bashed someone's brains in. Unless they really, really deserved it, I guess. But even then—"

"The problem is finding out who thought Jerry deserved it." Neena shivered.

"We both know who thought that." Jerry popped out of thin air. "You should have picked me. I never was the violent type."

"Shut up, Jerry," I said.

"He's here?" Neena glanced around but didn't see anything. She shivered again.

"Not for long," I said. "If you don't have anything more useful than unfounded accusations against Drew, you might as well find someone else to haunt," I told the ghost, who had drifted close enough to stare down at my cleavage. "And quit leering at me. You didn't stand a chance when you were alive, and you certainly don't now."

With a mocking salute, Jerry poofed.

"He's gone," I announced. "The jerk."

My phone buzzed a text alert.

On my way. Don't touch anything—Ernie had written.

As if I would. This was not my first time.

Ernie must have been nearby because he rolled up within five minutes, took a look at what we'd found, and dismissed us as if we were in his way.

"Well, thank you, too," I muttered as I slammed the van door behind me.

"Cut him a break," Jacy warned. "He's doing the best he can in a difficult situation."

"I know," I sighed, then thought about our current mission. "When we get to the dealership, one of us needs to check the employee parking lot to see if that tread pattern matches Max's tires."

"I'll do it. But how am I supposed to know which one is his?" Jacy wondered.

"Check them all, I guess. Or maybe we can get him to tell us what he drives. If we do, Neena can keep him talking, and I'll text you."

The bell above the dealership's front door jingled a cheerful tune that clashed with the knot of tension in my stomach. I hung back while Neena turned her charm up to ten and sauntered over to Max Johnson, who was wiping fingerprints off the hood of a hatchback with more enthusiasm than it probably deserved.

"Hi there," she drawled, casting a practiced eye over the lot. "I'm in quite the pickle and hoping y'all can help me out."

Max straightened up, his face brightening at the prospect of a sale. "What can I do for you, ma'am?"

"Well, my old clunker has left me stranded twice this month, and just last week, I had to deal with a flat tire," Neena lamented, clasping her hands together. "My late husband used to handle all the car troubles, bless his soul. I'm just at my wit's end here."

"Sorry to hear about your husband," Max said, matching her tone with a sympathetic tilt of his head. "Let's see if we can find something reliable and easy to maintain for you."

As they wandered among the rows of cars, I trailed behind them like a shadow, my gaze flicking over the vehicles as if I had any idea what I was looking at. In truth, I was more interested in Max—a man who thrived on conspiracy theories should feel right at home embroiled in a murder mystery. I just needed to find the key to getting him talking.

"Speaking of husbands," I piped up, seizing an opening when Max began extolling the virtues of a particularly unattractive sedan. "You're Cindy Johnson's husband, right? From the salon where I get my hair done."

Max's chest puffed out like a rooster, ready to crow at the mention of Cindy. "Cindy's the best thing that ever happened to me," he declared, pride coloring his voice. "She's got a heart of gold."

"I hear Jerry Kaminski thought highly of her, too," I nudged gently, watching Max's face for any crack in the facade. "It's such a shame what happened to him."

"Jerry's death was…" Max paused, his expression clouding for a moment before catching himself. "Tragic. But life goes on, right?"

"Right," I agreed, my mind racing. There hadn't been a flicker of guilt, but there was something—a hesitation, perhaps? I couldn't put my finger on it, and it nagged at me like a splinter.

"Anyway," Max continued, shaking off the momentary lapse. "This one's a popular model and generally considered quite reliable. Gets decent gas mileage, too."

"Is that what you drive?" Neena smiled sweetly, steering the conversation back where we needed it. "I'd love a first-hand opinion from someone who owns one."

"Sorry." Max shook his head. "You can't get a month's worth of supplies in this little baby. I figure it's a good idea to be prepared for whatever might happen. You never know when you might have to go off-road for safety."

Look for something that will go off-road and carry a month's supply of gear—I texted Jacy.

Already found it—she texted back with an attached photo of a former military vehicle sporting a huge brush guard, cages over the headlights, and what appeared to be hand-made armored panels. The thing had lights mounted front and back and sat high enough on over-large tires that I'd need a stepladder to climb in. The vanity plate read Mad Max. A glance told me all I needed to know. These tires were not the ones that had left the prints we'd seen earlier.

But as I pretended to inspect the price sticker on a nearby sedan, I couldn't shake the feeling that Max was holding onto secrets tighter than the lug nuts on his over-sized wheels. And I intended to unscrew them, one by one.

I tuned in just in time to hear Neena bring the conversation back to Jerry.

"The greens don't usually kill after an abduction, so it had to be the grays that got him," Max said, leaning back against the hood of a gleaming SUV, arms crossed as if shielding himself from more than just the summer sun's heat. "They're much more likely to cap someone after an abduction. Especially if things didn't go well with the testing. Jerry had a lot of flaws. That coulda done it."

"Greens?" Neena frowned in confusion. "Grays?"

"Aliens," Max said like it was information she should have known already.

"Like from space?" I asked, my voice threaded with a curiosity that was equal parts genuine and performed. "The UFO kind?"

"Yep," he replied, his eyes darting away from mine, fixing on some distant point over my shoulder. "The greens are more catch and release types. Take us up, see what makes us tick, then wipe our memories and send us back. The grays are different. They find something weird, they're more likely to do something about it. That's why I reckon. Jerry got tangled up in something bigger than all of us and didn't pass the sniff test."

I frowned, exchanging a glance with Jacy, who'd just joined us. Out of Max's sight, she twirled a finger near her temple. Neena, bless her heart, maintained her composure, though her lips twitched at the corners.

"He wouldn't be the first one taken around these parts. You wouldn't believe the stories I could tell you about aliens and government cover-ups."

"Sounds…intense," I offered, trying to keep the humor from spilling into my tone. Inwardly, I couldn't help but wonder if Max's conspiracy theories were a convenient smoke screen or if they genuinely clouded every corner of his judgment. "Seems more likely that he got on the wrong side of someone local. Maybe someone who had a personal grudge against him."

"Or," Jacy said, "someone he had a grudge against.

Maybe Jerry and some guy fought over a woman, and things got out of hand. These things do happen."

"Not on that road," Max shook his head. "Anyone gets in trouble out that way, it's gonna be grays."

"You know where Jerry was killed?" I tilted my head and looked at Max. "Were you in the area at the time?"

"Course not," he said. "I only heard about it after. Tuesday night is my UFO group chat. We got into an argument about interstellar travel and FTL drives that lasted until way after midnight."

"FTL?" I had to know.

"Faster Than Light. We won't have that tech for another century, at least. Not unless the scientists figure out how to power the ship that crashed in Area 51."

"I suppose not."

But Max was only just getting warmed up on the subject. "Do you have any idea how many people have been abducted by aliens in this county alone?"

I shook my head.

"If you're smart, you'll stay inside at night. We've got a couple of major hotspots for UFO activity between Hackinaw and Mooselick River. That's why they changed the roads. To keep people being picked up so often. But do the damn fools listen and keep to the safer areas? No, they do not. My mother got taken up. Never was the same after that."

That might explain some things.

"Well, all of that is just fascinating, but we should probably let you get back to work," I said, tilting my head toward Neena, who nodded in agreement. We'd pried everything out of Max that we could get for the moment, and then some.

"You've been a big help," she said. "I'll be in touch about that car."

"Sure thing," Max replied, though his relief at our departure was palpable. He fished out a business card from his shirt pocket and handed it to Neena with a salesman's smile.

"Keep me posted," he added, but there was a tension in his jaw that suggested we'd asked too many questions, and he'd prefer if we lost his number altogether.

"Will do," Neena assured him, slipping the card into her purse with a practiced grace.

As we left the dealership, the bright morning sun did little to dispel the fog of confusion that had settled over me.

"Something's not right with that one," Jacy muttered once we were safely buckled up in her car, which stood out at the dealership like a flamingo among a flock of crows.

CHAPTER SIX

"**I** know it's early, but let's grab a bite at Cappy's," I suggested once we'd driven away from Max's oasis of used cars and probable lies and crossed back into town. "Maybe Adam will be there, and we can get his take on the bachelor party fiasco."

"Good idea," Neena agreed, scanning the parking lot of Curated Collections as we passed. With the unflappable Judy left in charge of the shop, Jacy and Neena's joint business—half art gallery, half second-hand store—was in capable hands for the day. "I could go for a cup of clam chowder. It's to die for."

"Let's hope that's not a literal assessment, considering our current murder mystery," I said, earning a snort from Jacy.

We had our pick of parking spots since the lot was empty and made our way into Cappy's, where the air smelled of fried seafood and nostalgia, a comforting combination.

"Hey!" Adam's voice cut through the pre-lunch quiet. Since it was early, we found him handling the counter and the kitchen before his wait staff clocked in. "Take pity on me and sit at the bar. What can I get you?"

"Two cups of clam chowder," I said, taking my cue from Neena.

"Make that three," Jacy chimed in.

"Sure thing." Cups rattled as he pulled three sturdy white ones from a nearby stack. "What brings you in this early, as if I didn't already know?"

"You figured us out. We're trying to piece together what happened at Drew's bachelor party," I began, my tone gentle but firm as he slid our order onto the shelf and then came through the swinging door to retrieve the tray. "We talked to Brian and David, and now we need your side of the story."

He set a cup in front of each of us, took our drink orders, and filled those before he began. "I doubt I can offer you anything you haven't already heard. Jerry got loud, as he does after a few too many. He poked at Drew some but didn't get too far. Drew has too much control to let himself be provoked that easily."

This was not new information. We all knew that about Drew.

"When it seemed like Jerry might get out of hand, I stepped in and did what I've done a dozen times over the past few years and booted him out."

"There's a story going around that the bachelor party got rowdy, and Drew started the argument."

Adam shook his head, grinning through his neatly trimmed beard—a new look for him. "Nope, but it doesn't surprise me. People will say any damned thing, no matter if it's the truth or a lie. I saw the whole thing, and just between us, that was the tamest bachelor party this place has seen since I've been working here."

Nodding, I blew on a spoonful of soup. "And after?"

"At some point, Drew stepped outside. Being a Tuesday, we weren't busy, but I wasn't watching the clock, so I couldn't say when or for how long."

"Anything about Jerry's behavior stand out to you that night?" Jacy prodded, her detective instincts kicking in over the rim of her iced tea.

"Only that he was being his usual charming self," Adam replied with a dryness that could rival the Sahara. "Made a fool of himself, but it wasn't the first time. My Tuesday night regulars were used to him by now. If I'd known how things would end up, I would've paid more attention."

"So you didn't see anyone else leave around the same time Jerry did?" I mused, thinking someone else could have seen their opportunity to get rid of Jerry and taken it.

"Not that I noticed, and I would have. Like I said, Tuesday is our quiet night. No Karaoke, no trivia, no happy hour. It's usually just me handling the bar and the kitchen. It wasn't a busy night, even with your guys taking up a table."

"Thanks, Adam. You've been a big help," I said, offering a smile that I hoped was more reassuring than it felt.

As I spooned up the last of my chowder, I caught a chill that had nothing to do with being too close to the air conditioning vents. Half a second later, a familiar scent wafted through the air—a mix of hairspray and perm solution that could only mean one thing: Dolly Tibbets, the former hairdresser who had never met a piece of gossip she couldn't tease out and perm into something substantial was about to make an appearance.

"There you are." Dolly materialized beside our table, her curls bouncing as if she were still alive and kicking rather than hovering and eavesdropping. "I've been looking for you. You want dirt on Jerry Kaminski? I've got it. Why didn't you come by the shop?"

"Because I wanted to enjoy my lunch without a side of haunting?" I muttered, but I wasn't unhappy to see her. "And besides, we were at the shop earlier. You weren't there."

"Dolly?" Jacy shielded her mouth with one hand so Adam wouldn't hear.

"In the not-flesh," I confirmed. "Thanks for the info, Adam." I pulled out enough cash to cover our lunch and a decent tip and left it on the counter. "But we've got to dash."

Dolly followed us outside and into the van, as I knew she would. I took the back seat with her to keep Neena from having to sit too close.

"What can you tell us, Dolly?" I asked once the doors closed and Dolly made herself visible. Warm brown eyes twinkled mischievously beneath arched brows as if she knew every secret anyone in this town ever whispered. She probably did.

"It's about Jerry Kaminski," she said, her tone shifting

to somber. "Now, I won't say the world is better without Jerry in it because he wasn't so much a bad guy as one who suffered from a strong case of hunteritis."

"Of what, now?" Jacy spun in her seat.

"You know, hunteritis. It's where the thrill of the hunt beats the thrill of the catch, and once they get the girl, they lose interest."

"That's what Cindy said, too," Neena said. She was so used to the weirdness by now that her voice didn't hitch with fear when speaking to a spirit.

"Trouble is," Dolly continued in her best gossipy voice, "Jerry was also a wimp. He didn't have the stones to tell her that he wanted out of the relationship, so he did what wimps do and treated her like something he scraped off his shoe."

"He wanted to be the dumpee and not the dumper," Jacy said as she started the car for the ride back to my place.

"Right. Makes a better sob story to unload on the next unsuspecting woman that caught his attention. And there was always another woman who did."

"He cheated?" Neena's tone held a dark condemnation.

"To a degree, I suppose. While Jerry didn't have women falling all over him, he couldn't keep his hands to himself. It was only a matter of time before his wandering eye landed him in real trouble."

"Trouble like being murdered?" I asked, the pieces

clicking together in a pattern that had started long before it landed my new husband in jail.

"Exactly like that," Dolly confirmed. "Between the drinking and philandering attempts, Cindy put up with more than anyone should have to. She says he never got physical, but I always wondered if that were true."

"Did Cindy ever fight back, or did anyone ever stand up for her?" My voice was tense, concern for Cindy knotting in my stomach.

"Max did. He saw right through the steaming pile of crap Jerry liked to throw around, and it never did sit right with him how Jerry treated Cindy," Dolly replied, her warm brown eyes serious for once. "He started out as Jerry's friend but became her shoulder to cry on, her knight in shining armor, or whatever cliché you prefer. And Cindy, bless her heart, used Max to get a rise out of Jerry."

"Jealousy as a weapon," Neena mused, twirling a dark curl around her finger. "Get him to become the hunter again."

"Except it backfired, and Max and Cindy eventually ended up married," I pointed out, trying to keep us on track.

"Anyway," Dolly continued, "Cindy would tell Jerry how Max was everything he wasn't. Strong, caring, sober...It got under his skin something awful. But don't go thinking Cindy's all sugar and no spice. She knew what she was doing, stirring that pot."

"Sounds like there were no saints in that love triangle," Jacy said, tucking a chunk of blond hair behind her ear.

"Exactly," Dolly confirmed, her form beginning to fade. "And now I've given you more to chew on than that chowder. You're welcome!"

"Thanks, Dolly," I whispered as her presence dissipated, leaving behind the faintest scent of salon chemicals.

"Jerry, Max, Cindy," Neena listed, ticking them off on her fingers. "Weaving a tangled web. And it's starting to look like everyone's a spider."

"And Drew's a fly caught in it," I added, my heart clenching at the thought of him behind bars. "We need to sort the predators from the prey, fast."

"Right," Jacy agreed, gripping the steering wheel with determination. "So where does this leave us? Are we buying Max's UFO alibi, or is he our prime suspect?"

"Both are possible," I replied, staring out the window as Jacy pulled back into my driveway. "What we need is hard evidence, and we're not going to find it by chasing ghosts—figuratively speaking."

"Or literally," Neena added with a knowing look in my direction.

"Nope," I concluded, forcing a smile. "The way I see it, we need to put together a timeline for the whole love triangle thing. I don't think Max and Cindy have been married all that long, and since Jerry had moved on to me, I think the Cindy angle might be a long shot. Still, Max could be a champion grudge-holder, so we need to see if we can verify his alibi. Just to rule him out if nothing else."

"Got it," Jacy nodded. Her tail of honeyed blond hair caught the light as she rummaged through her purse, likely for gum or her phone. "I'm heading into work for the afternoon, but I'll keep my ear out there, and when I pick up Wade, I'll see what my mother knows. As a prime node in the gossip network, she hears anything worth hearing."

Neena stood beside the car, a grin on her face that might be considered evil if it wasn't on my behalf. "And I'll infiltrate that UFO group. If Max was busy arguing about little green men all night, we should be able to confirm it."

"Great," I said, feeling a surge of gratitude for these women who would stand beside me no matter what ghostly chaos I dragged into their lives. "I need to reassure Drew's folks and see what I can get out of Jerry when he inevitably shows up later. And remember, Max is quick to jump to conclusions—don't let him catch wind of what you're doing."

"Got it," Neena said with a half-smile, "I'll be as subtle as a ghost at a séance."

"Which is to say, entirely unnoticed by most," I shot back, allowing myself a small chuckle. "Text me whatever you find out. I'll do the same."

We parted ways then, each to follow through on our missions.

Drew's folks had taken my advice and my car. I wasn't

sure whether they were at the lake with Jacy's parents or just out for a drive, but I didn't mind the extra hour of peace to collect my thoughts.

While they were gone, I put together my version of a murder board with crime scene photos and sticky notes plastered over a folding presentation board and hid it away from prying eyes in my room.

When I heard them return and head straight for the kitchen, I gave them a moment to settle, then greeted them. The smell of fresh coffee mingled with the familiar scent of my favorite pine cleaner. When cooking hadn't kept all the nervousness at bay, she must have resorted to cleaning.

"There you are, dear. We need to talk," Cheryl said, her voice taut like a high-wire, and I could practically feel the tremble of her words through the air.

"Sure, Cheryl. What's on your mind?" I leaned against the counter, already sensing the direction of this impromptu meeting.

"Leandra told us you have a habit of getting involved in dangerous situations." When she glanced at Quinn for support, lines of concern etched her face, the kind that only a mother who fears for her child can wear.

Drat that Leandra! As much as I loved Jacy's mother, she was trouble on two legs when it came to me.

"I don't know what Leandra told you, but you can see that I'm okay. You shouldn't worry," I assured her, forcing a smile.

"Of course I'm worried!" she burst out. "You're family

now. My son's happiness is tied up in you, so even if I didn't already love you, I'd worry for his sake."

Quinn still sat, his bulk a silent sentinel. His gray-blue eyes met mine in a quiet plea for calm.

Unfortunately, I was destined to disappoint him, so I looked away.

"Everly," Quinn interjected, his voice a gentle rumble, like distant thunder promising a storm that never arrives. "We just want you safe. You understand that, don't you?"

I pushed off from the counter and moved closer, taking Cheryl's quivering hands in mine. "I do, and I promise not to do anything reckless. But fixing things is what I do, and I can't sit back and watch Drew end up in prison. Not if there's something I can do to stop it. I have to help."

"Your 'help' seems to land you in trouble," Cheryl countered, a quiver in her voice betraying the fear beneath her words. "Leandra said you were attacked by a crazed murderer right here in this house."

I grimaced before I could catch myself. "Okay, well, that happened."

"And then again when the woman who killed your ex-husband's attorney attacked you."

I held out my hands. "That happened, too, but there were extenuating circumstances."

"And didn't a drug dealer break your arm?" Quinn repeated another of Leandra's claims.

"It was just my wrist." The qualification didn't help, so I did what I could to mitigate the circumstances. "I'll admit trouble has a way of finding me. But so does resolution. I helped solve every one of those crimes and can solve this one, too, because it's the most important one of all."

Quinn let out a half-chuckle, half-sigh, reaching over to pat Cheryl's shoulder. "She's got spunk, that's for sure. Like someone else I married thirty years ago."

"Thirty-two," Cheryl corrected automatically, a faint smile touching her lips despite herself.

"See? Spunk," he said with a wink.

Realizing I wouldn't be moved, Quinn said, "But you won't do anything dangerous?"

"That I can promise." I always think I'm being careful, even when I end up in trouble, so it wasn't a lie.

Seeming appeased, Cheryl let me order food from Bertino's.

"Now," I said, stepping toward the cabinet to get a mug, "Let's have some of that coffee before it gets cold."

Just as I tipped up the container of cream, a familiar chill crept up my spine—a telltale sign that meant nothing good.

"Everly," came the unwelcome voice, tinged with the stubborn edge of a man who refused to let the grave silence him. Jerry Kaminski's ghost sauntered into view, hands tucked into his pants pockets, his gaze fixed on me with unsettling intensity.

"Not now," I hissed, keeping my back turned away from the table, hoping Cheryl and Quinn wouldn't hear.

But Jerry, the most annoying man on the planet and

now the most annoying ghost, ignored my plea. "I know you've got feelings for me, Everly. You can deny it all you want, but you're helping me, not Drew. I know because I followed you when you went to see Max today."

I felt the color drain from my face. Rule number one: never let the living hear you talking to the dead. Especially not your in-laws, who were already worried sick.

"Excuse me," I muttered, edging past the table. My heart pounded like a drumline gone rogue.

"Is everything okay?" Cheryl's voice was sharp and concerned, her eyes searching my face for answers I couldn't give.

"Fine, just...the coffee got me overheated. I need some air," I said, flat out lying my way toward the front door.

Outside, I rounded on Jerry. "That's strike one. I told you to stay away when there are people around. You're not racking up the points with me." Then inspiration hit. "Hey, Jerry. Why don't you tell me how you died?"

Unable to help himself, he thought about it too hard and, as ghosts do when they concentrate on the moment of their death, he poofed. I didn't even feel bad about it.

Back inside, I made excuses that seemed to mollify the Parkers before they left to visit Drew. I'd go see him once they returned, which they did an hour later, looking both relieved and still strained.

When I got there, Drew looked more rested than he had the day before, but I could tell by the set of his chin that seeing his parents had upset him.

"Mom's worried. She said Leandra told them her

version of some of our recent escapades," he said. "They said you told them you'd stop investigating Jerry's murder."

"That's not exactly what I said. I told them I wouldn't do anything dangerous, but you know I can't let this go. Not for your sake, and especially not if it means Jerry won't leave."

"I just wish I could be there to help."

"Me, too, babe. Me, too."

I left him with both of us feeling unsettled and went home to stare at my murder board for an hour after his folks went to bed.

Finally slipping between the cool sheets, I stared at the ceiling, tracing patterns in the plaster with my eyes. The house was silent, but in my head, the voices of my friends and the echoes of the day's conversations played on a loop. My heart ached for Drew, for the confusion and hurt this whole ordeal was causing.

"Please don't let this be my new normal," I whispered into the dark, the words floating up and vanishing like breath in cold air.

But there was no response, just the soft embrace of sleep as it finally claimed me, carrying me away from the tangled web of murder in Mooselick River and into the respite of dreams.

CHAPTER SEVEN

Despite my assurances I'd be careful, Drew's parents sat on me like an egg in a nest until I escaped to meet my friends at the Blue Moon Diner. Between them, Jerry, and not having Drew there, my house felt like it wasn't mine anymore. One more reason to get to the bottom of this mystery. If only we could narrow the suspect list from anyone and everyone, that would help.

Several patrons looked up when I walked in. I caught both sympathy and speculation as I glanced around the room on my way to the corner booth where Jacy and Neena already waited. Word gets around this town faster than a bird can fly, so everyone was getting to gossip about my love life again. Great.

The low murmur of voices formed a familiar sound-track to our impromptu strategy meeting as I sat at our favorite booth, the one way at the back corner nearest the kitchen.

"Patrea's running late," I said, tucking a damp curl behind one ear. The relentless sun had given way to a dreary, misty day that perfectly fitted my mood but played havoc with my hair.

"Coffee?" Thea Lombardi loomed, her usual scowl replaced by a sympathetic smile.

She should be careful. Her face might freeze that way. People would get the wrong idea about her and think she's always nice and not at seriously random intervals.

"Thanks," I said as she poured without waiting for my answer. At least that hadn't changed.

"I just wanted you to know," she said, leaning down and practically whispering in my ear. "I've been keeping my ear to the ground in case someone lets something slip that might help your man."

"Thanks, Thea," I responded, keeping my voice low as well. "I had no idea you cared."

"I hate to see a good man wronged," she replied, her voice softer than I'd ever heard it. "So far, I've come up empty, but if I hear anything, I'll get in touch."

"Thanks," I said again as she and her coffeepot headed for the next table. "That was...unexpected."

I exchanged glances with Jacy, who raised an eyebrow and nodded her head. "Highly."

"If the world comes to an end, we'll know why," Neena said as Patrea walked through the door and headed our way.

"Uh oh," I said as I slid over to make room for her. "You've got your lawyer face on. How bad is it?"

Patrea grabbed my coffee and guzzled it like it was the last cup on the planet. "It's not good. The evidence is against us, so the only way forward is to dismantle the prosecution's timeline. If we can introduce reasonable doubt about when the crime took place, Drew might have a shot, but it's iffy. Ernie verified the tire iron didn't belong to Drew, which would have explained his finger-prints and given us a chance to point out that anyone could have grabbed it out of the back of his truck."

"One step forward and one step back." Neena sipped her coffee.

"At the moment," Patrea agreed, holding up a hand to attract Thea's attention. "But it's early days yet, and I know you're all on the case. I heard Ernie talking to someone on the phone about some possible evidence found near the crime scene. I wish I had more information on that, but he's not required to share until he's certain it's pertinent."

"You're in luck, then," Jacy smiled. "Because we're the ones who found it."

Before I could pull out my phone and show Patrea what we'd found, Thea popped back around to take our orders.

"Just a grilled cheese for me," I said, not bothering to look at the menu. My appetite had taken off to parts unknown again.

"Don't you want soup with that?" Thea urged. "Most people go with tomato. You need to keep up your strength."

Where was the warning that everything I ate would end up on my hips or, worse, my backside? This new, supportive Thea was freaking me out.

"That's fine," I shrugged and let her add the soup to

the order. Once she'd gone, I cued up the images from the day before and slid my phone across the table. "Take a look at what we found."

As Patrea flicked her way through the series of photos, she frowned. "I see what you're thinking here. This had to be Tuesday because it rained overnight on Monday, so the puddle would have taken most of the day to dry to the point where the tire marks would show so perfectly. By Wednesday, the mud would have been completely dry, and you wouldn't see this much definition."

"That's what we thought, too," Jacy said. "But there's no way to prove it had anything to do with the murder."

Patrea raised her brows. "From what I overheard, Ernie thinks it might. He mentioned sending two samples to the crime scene techs to see if they could nail down the timing. He also verified the tread prints did not match his current suspect's vehicle. If whatever was in the vomit doesn't match what Drew ate at Cappy's that night, it could be enough to get him released. So, yay for the vomit."

"Ew." Neena screwed up her nose. "I'm about to be eating here."

So was I. And oddly, despite the gross talk, my appetite had begun to return. If what we'd found could be tied to the murder, it would be the first hard evidence in Drew's favor since this whole thing started.

"Send these to me." Patrea handed my phone back and waited until Thea, who had just arrived with our order, put our plates in front of us to continue. "Now, tell me what you learned from Max yesterday. I only got the bare details, and I need the whole picture. New evidence is only half the story. We need a plausible suspect. Preferably one with tires to match that print."

"Well, it won't be Max. We already checked," Jacy said around a bite of the meatloaf I knew was her favorite comfort food. "Or I did, anyway. He's got off-road tires on his prepper-mobile. Great big ones with beefy treads. Nothing like the ones at the scene."

Half of a cherry tomato popped off Patrea's fork when she gestured with it. "Unless he used his wife's car. We'll need to check that before he goes off the list. Did he give you any idea who else might have wanted Jerry dead?"

"Counting little green men? Not so much." I popped the last piece of the first half of my sandwich into my mouth.

"Gray ones, actually," Neena corrected. "According to Max, they pop down from their UFOs to grab unsuspecting townspeople left and right."

"He thinks we're their prime source of lab rats. They pick us up, test us, and drop us back off none the wiser," Jacy added.

"I assume he's been tested," Patrea said with a dry smirk. "Or he should be. Did he have a theory on why they didn't just return Jerry alive and well when they were done with him?"

"None that made sense. He rambled on about the

difference between greens and grays and how grays were more likely to cap someone—his words, not mine—if they found an instability."

Neena leaned across the table, her brown eyes twinkling with humor. "Max did not see the inherent irony in him calling Jerry the unstable one."

"Max would not see the sweet baby Jesus if the manger appeared before him and an angel dropped down from heaven to prove it," Jacy said.

"Still," Patrea tapped the photo I'd sent to her phone and said, "This could help cement the alternative narrative I've been working on. We need to establish reasonable doubt and that the real culprit had the means and opportunity. Even without an alternate suspect, it could be enough, but it would be better if we had someone else to point toward."

"Which brings us back to square one," Neena sighed, pushing a stray curl from her forehead. "Finding out who really had it out for Jerry and ruling out anyone who didn't."

"Leave it to Jerry to complicate things, even from beyond the grave," I muttered, half expecting the dearly departed to pop up with a snarky retort. Thankfully, the diner remained ghost-free—for now.

"On paper, Max might make the first list," Neena started, twirling her fork absentmindedly in her salad, "but I've been trying to wiggle my way into that UFO group he's using as his alibi. Let me tell you, those folks are tighter than a clam with lockjaw. I can't post in the group for six months, and I don't have access to any of the private boards, but I did manage to get in far enough to scroll back through their online chat in the main one. Max was all over it the night of Jerry's...incident."

"Could have been chatting from his phone, though." Patrea raised an eyebrow, the lawyer in her poking holes immediately.

"Could be," Neena conceded with a frustrated pout, "which means he might have still been able to—"

"Be anywhere, including where Jerry met his untimely end," I finished for her, frustration bubbling up. It felt like we were chasing our tails, but Max hadn't struck me as a solid suspect, so I'd hoped to be able to rule him out entirely and move on. Unfortunately, that didn't look to be the case.

"How did we do on the gossip front?" I turned to Jacy.

"Argh!" Jacy exclaimed, throwing her hands up so suddenly she nearly knocked over her iced tea. "Not good. You'd think with all the loose tongues in this town, Momma Wade would have caught something useful. But no, it's all 'poor dumb Jerry.' Apparently, he was considered as annoying as a mosquito at a nudist colony but harmless as a kitten."

"A kitten with an impeccable ability to create historic plaster, though," Patrea added. Jerry had once bragged about restoring some fancy cornices at the governor's mansion. Based on what we'd seen of his work, I didn't doubt him.

"Exactly!" Jacy huffed, rolling her eyes. "The man had

a reputation for chasing women, but when it came to his work? Flawless. He could sweet-talk the peeling plaster off the walls and restore them to perfection."

"Anyway," Neena cut in, bringing us back to the matter at hand, "we've been trying to find someone else who could have been at the scene and are failing epically. What about someone who could prove Drew wasn't? We haven't been trying hard enough there, I don't think. What if someone drove past and saw him in the parking lot?"

"Someone who didn't realize it was him, or if they did, they should speak up," Patrea mused, tapping her fingertip on the table. "Or that they saw anything relevant. Good thinking."

"I'll have my mother put the word out. Might as well use the grapevine for something good for a change."

With a plan in place, we decided to order dessert.

The clinking of silverware and the hum of conversation had a soothing rhythm, a stark contrast to the mental gymnastics of figuring out Drew's defense. My fork was halfway to my mouth when the bell above the door jingled, heralding Junior Pease's entrance.

Even if there'd been any place to hide, I wouldn't have known I should until his gaze lasered in on me and he changed direction.

"Ernie Polk's as blind as a bat in broad daylight," Junior bellowed, striding towards our booth with a determined stomp that made his beard quiver like a flag caught in a storm. His round-shouldered frame loomed over us, his eyes blazing with outrage and sorrow. "Arresting an innocent man—bah!"

"Junior," I said, easing my fork back onto my plate. "What's got you all riled up this morning?"

"Injustice." He failed to elaborate, then pulled a crumpled piece of paper from his coat pocket and smoothed it on the table. "I need your signatures on this petition to open a pet cemetery here in Mooselick River. It's high time."

"Pet cemetery?" Jacy echoed, eyebrows arched in surprise while Neena leaned in, her curiosity piqued.

"Yep. My poor Mrs. Spiffles, may she rest in peace," Junior said, his voice softening as he touched his heart. "She was the best cat that ever lived and deserves a proper headstone, but the town ordinance won't allow me to put one on my own property. It's just not right."

"Mrs. Spiffles?" Patrea asked gently, always the first to comfort someone in distress.

"Run over last week," he replied, his gaze growing distant. "And the coward didn't even stop. Just left her there in the road like...like garbage." The last word came out strangled, and I watched as Junior's eyes glossed over with unshed tears.

"Junior, that's terrible," I said, my throat tightening in sympathy. "We're so sorry."

"Awful," Jacy added, her usual playful sarcasm subdued by the gravity of Junior's loss.

"Of course, we'll sign," Neena promised, reaching for the petition. "Won't we?"

"Absolutely," I agreed. As I scribbled my name on the dotted line, I couldn't help but think about the hidden layers in Junior's plea. A pet cemetery seemed like such a simple thing, yet beneath it lay the weight of grief and longing for justice, even if only in memory of a beloved cat.

"Thank you, girls," Junior said, his gratitude mingling with the shadows beneath his eyes. "Means a lot to me. More than you know."

Patrea passed the petition to Jacy, who signed with a flourish before sliding it across the worn Formica tabletop to me. "Can't say no to a final resting place for our furry friends," she quipped, trying to lighten the mood.

"Definitely not," I echoed and scribbled my signature below Jacy's, the pen squeaking against the paper.

Neena followed suit, her expression thoughtful. "I hope this helps, Junior,"

He carefully folded the petition, tucking it back into his coat as he nodded his thanks and approached the next table of diners, leaving us in the wake of his heavy-hearted departure.

"You want your usual, Junior?" Mabel's voice boomed from the kitchen entrance, wiping away the remnants of our collective melancholy. "Or can I add a little cinnamon to your oatmeal?"

"Just the brown sugar. You know that's the only way I like it."

"Every day. It's the same thing. You could try something new for once."

Junior waved her advice away but accepted the bowl once she'd dished it up from the pot she kept heating on the back of the stove all day and doctored it the way he liked it.

"As for the four of you," she flipped open the counter and approached us, her apron dusted with flour, a determined look in her eye that told me she'd been eavesdropping. Classic Mabel.

"You didn't ask for my opinion, but you're getting it anyway. Between Max and Cindy? If we're talking passion or spite, Cindy's the one with fire, even if she hides it under that sweet veneer. But killing Jerry? I'm not buying it. Even if Max worked up the guts to take action, neither would let it stew that long," Mabel declared, leaning in and using her inside voice so no one else would hear.

"Jerry was a piece of work," I muttered, "but he didn't deserve to die.

"Anyway," Mabel continued, undeterred, "I'd bet my graham cracker pie recipe it was someone else. Jerry was sniffing around plenty of other women before you caught his eye. If it was me, I'd stand around at the bar for the regulars he used to drink with. Might shake loose a few names."

"Thanks, Mabel," I said, feeling a surge of gratitude for the diner owner's gruff wisdom. "We'll check it out."

"Good," she replied, giving us a curt nod before retreating to her kingdom of stainless steel and sizzling burgers.

"You guys up for our regular Friday night at Cappy's?"

"Are you sure you want to be seen there?" Jacy asked, arching an eyebrow. "I mean, people will be talking."

"Let them," I replied, scooting out of the booth with purpose. "They've talked about me before. Why should now be any different?"

CHAPTER EIGHT

The rain picked up from a gentle mist to a steady fall, and my low fuel warning dinged as I pulled away from the diner. Annoyed at the inconvenience, I turned in the opposite direction from home and headed to the Gas-N-Go. At least they had one of those huge canopies to shelter under while I filled up.

"Hey there. Is your friend still thinking about that new car?" Max Johnson's voice sliced through the gentle patter like a buzzsaw through balsa wood. His eager face loomed from the other side of the pump before I could hook the nozzle back in its slot.

"Sorry, Max," I said, my words laced with fake apology, "I don't think she's decided."

"Okay." He seemed way too excited for the attempt at a gentle letdown, almost bouncing on the balls of his feet as he followed me inside. "I've been connecting the dots, and I'm telling you, there's something big going down in Mooselick River. Jerry found out about it, or else he was involved, and that's why he's dead."

"Something big?" I raised an eyebrow. Max's big and my big might be two different sizes. "Are we still talking alien abduction theories?"

"No. This is way bigger than that."

"And what would our local plasterer have to do with anything big other than his bar tab?"

"Everly, this is serious." Max leaned closer, lowering his voice to a conspiratorial whisper. "It's the Benevolent Brotherhood of the Black Bear. I think it's a front for a crime ring."

It was a good thing I hadn't just taken a sip of the cherry cola I'd grabbed from the cooler. I'd have choked on it.

"Max," I sighed, grabbing a candy bar to give my hands something to do besides throttling him for dragging my dad into his theories. "The lodge is about as criminal as Mrs. Leary's knitting circle. They raise money for the fire department and host bingo nights, not criminal proceedings."

"Ah, but that's what they want you to think!" His eyes were wide, earnest. "Think about it. Who would suspect? It's the perfect cover. And Jerry, well, he was up for membership. I think he stumbled onto a whole host of illegal activities. That's why he's gone! Someone died there just last month. That has to mean something."

"No!" I said, my tone flat as the pancakes at the church fundraiser breakfast. "Let me stop you right there. First of all, Bill Cavanaugh's death had nothing to do with the lodge. It was a personal thing. Second, you can't go around accusing one of the more civic-minded groups in town of nefarious activity."

"Pull the other leg," he pressed, "you know I'm right

about this. There's more going on in this town than meets the eye."

"Sure, and the bait shop secretly sells mermaid scales," I said, giving him a pat on the arm. "I'll leave the spy games to you, Max. I've got a husband to save, and you're not helping."

He looked a little deflated but unlikely to drop his pet conspiracy. "I know things. You have no idea."

"Okay, Max. Let's hear it then," I said, leaning against the coffee counter, arms crossed, a half-amused smile playing on my lips. "What are these things that you know? Is the lodge controlling the town's water supply?"

He leaned in closer as if the Slushie machine might be eavesdropping. "Probably, but that's beside the point," Max whispered, his eyes darting around like moths in a lampshade shop. "I think someone in the lodge is using their position for something nefarious. Like a crime ring."

I raised an eyebrow as the scent of conversational BS hung heavy in the air. "I don't think so. Those guys are likelier to throw out their backs playing checkers than mastermind some sort of crime ring."

"Ah, but that's where you're wrong!" he countered, fervor igniting behind his eyes. The dramatic flair would've been more at home on a stage than in front of the Slushie machine. "It's always the ones you least suspect. You're just overlooking the signs because one of 'em is closer to you than you think."

"Is that so?" I asked, the wrapper of my candy bar crinkling in my tightening grip. His words were starting to sound less like the ramblings of a conspiracy nut and more like the beginnings of a bad thriller novel.

"Everly, your father…" Max paused, gauging my reaction as if he was about to reveal the colonel's blend of herbs and spices.

"My father, what?" The warning in my tone was unmistakable, but Max didn't catch it.

"He's way deep in it. He might even be the boss."

The humor drained from me, and so did all color on my face. "My father?" My voice carried a sharpness that made Max take a step back. "You think my dad, the man who teaches high school kids how to use a table saw without cutting off their fingers, is some kind of crime boss?"

"Look, I know it's hard to swallow, but—"

"Hard to swallow?" I cut him off. "Try impossible. You're talking about a man who wears socks with sandals and gets his students to fix the town gazebo for next to nothing every time it gets hit with disaster. The most illegal thing my father has ever done is jaywalking because he forgot where he parked at the diner."

"Hey," Max implored, hands held up defensively, "all I'm saying is that people can surprise you. They wear masks, pretend to be something they're not."

"Maybe you do, but the only mask my father wears is a snorkel mask, and that's when he's pretending to be a submarine at the lake." A breeze wafted across my face as the door opened and closed behind the next customer. "If you're going to accuse my dad of something, you better have proof thicker than Mrs. Henderson's Scrabble dictionary."

"Everly, I—"

"Save it," my tone was final as I put the candy bar back on the shelf. I no longer had a taste for something sweet. "Next time you want to float a theory, make sure it has a flirting acquaintance with reality and doesn't involve insulting my family. If you'll excuse me, I've got someplace to be."

Even then, I didn't get far because he followed me back outside.

"If you'd just take a second to listen, you might see things my way."

"Fine. Say your piece, then," I said, leaning against the side of my car, "if you're so sure about all this cloak and dagger stuff, where's your evidence? And I mean hard evidence—the kind that doesn't sound like it came straight out of a B movie."

Max scratched at his stubble, eyes darting around as if expecting some secret agent to jump out from behind the pump. "Well, uh, it's just that there are things people talk about, whispers, y'know?"

"Whispers?" I arched an eyebrow. "What people are whispering? I need names."

He shuffled awkwardly, the conspiracy theory he'd woven unraveling with my every word. "I don't know. Just people. They're talking, and if they are, there has to be truth to some of it. I might not have pictures or documents, but—"

"Let me stop you right there," I held up a hand, cutting him off. "My Grammie Dupree used to say everything that comes after *but* is BS. So, if you can't come up with something rock solid and provable about the lodge or any of its members, you need to let this one go."

"Okay. Fine. Whatever you say." He didn't have any proof and wasn't convinced, but wasn't that the basic creed for people like him? "But—"

"What else is rolling around in that tin-foil-lined head of yours?" I asked, much less amused now by his doggedness.

"There's Mitch Castle. He and Jerry have had bad blood since they were kids. Mitch hated Jerry's guts."

"Mitch Castle?" I repeated, mulling over the name. I knew Mitch from helping Patrea with her first remodel. He worked at the lumber yard one town over and had delivered materials once or twice. From what I remembered, he was on the shorter side, but what he lacked in height, he made up for in attitude. There'd been a minor dispute about the number of trim boards she'd ordered, and he'd given her a hard time. The customer, in his opinion, was not always right. Not even when they had paperwork to prove it.

"Right. Old grudges die hard, and Mitch—well, he's got more muscles than common sense. Everyone knows he couldn't stand Jerry."

"Go on." My skepticism was taking a backseat to genuine curiosity. If *everyone* knew about this so-called grudge, wouldn't Ernie have at least brought Mitch in for questioning? He hadn't been on the list of suspects.

"It started as your classic boys ragging on their buddies thing. Jerry dubbed him Mitchy the Midget, and it eventually got shortened to Midge. People usually outgrow that type of thing, but Jerry wouldn't let it go. One night at Cappy's, Jerry kept poking at him, and Mitch went off. He said if Jerry didn't shut it, he'd make him eat his words. Literally." Max's hands formed into fists, mimicking a rather dramatic punch.

"Now, we're getting somewhere." I conceded. An image of Mitch's bulked-up frame and a scowl that could curdle milk popped into my mind. He certainly wasn't winning any Mr. Congeniality awards.

"See?" Max perked up, sensing he'd finally landed one of his theories. "Mitch had a motive."

"Maybe so," I murmured. "When did this happen?"

"Couple of years ago. Back when me and Jerry were still friends. I think they buried the hatchet after that, but you never know."

"What does that even mean?" I mused. "Burying a hatchet seems like a weird thing to do. And if they did bury it or whatever, why would Mitch wait this long to get revenge?"

"He could have faked the reconciliation. Maybe he'd been planning to kill Jerry for years," Max urged, getting deeper into the drama of it all. "I figure Mitch Castle has been nursing that grudge for at least a decade. All that anger bubbling away under the surface? It's enough to drive anyone to do something...drastic, but he bided his time. Once everyone thought they'd put the unpleasantness behind them, he pounced."

I tapped a finger against my chin, considering the possibility. If nothing else, it was a lead worth following up on. Jerry, the way-too-friendly ghost, was a constant reminder that I needed to solve his murder and get him to move on. Preferably before he drove me up the wall or got my husband locked up for life.

"Okay, Max," I finally said, pushing off from the side of my car with a newfound sense of purpose. "You've got my attention. But remember, this is just another theory until I find some real proof."

"Of course, of course!" he exclaimed, visibly buoyed by my interest.

"Thanks, I guess. But don't go spreading rumors about my dad." I started towards my car, the wheels turning in my head. One thing was for sure: I had some sleuthing to do. And maybe it was time to pay Mr. Mitch Castle a little visit.

I tossed a casual wave to Max as I pulled out of the parking lot and headed in the opposite direction than I'd planned. I needed to track down this lead in case it was a hot one. Drew's folks could walk to the police station to see him.

The thought of Drew, with his unwavering support and those arms that promised safety, steeled my resolve. I couldn't let rumors and small-town gossip drag his name through the mud. He deserved better. We both did.

Halfway through the nine-minute drive to the lumber yard, Jerry popped into the passenger seat, bringing the chill of the dead with him.

"Whatcha doin', cutie?" I could let the attempt at flirting go if he wasn't also trying to get a look down my shirt.

"You didn't stand a chance with me while you were living, and you certainly don't now, so back off."

"What? I'm not breaking any rules, am I? There's no one around, and this isn't your bedroom or bathroom. I'm not asking you to give anyone a message. What am I hurting?"

"My gag reflex, for one."

"Where are we going?" You had to give him credit for being able to ignore anything he didn't want to hear.

"Foss's Lumber. I need to talk to Mitch Castle."

"What for?"

"To see if he's a murderer. What else?"

"Old Midge didn't kill me. You're wasting your time, but I don't mind going along for the ride." Jerry reached over and put his hand on my leg. The sensation was all kinds of creepy, and for more reasons than that the touch of ghosts feels both shivery and gooey. This was all about the sleaze factor.

"Did I forget to mention the rule about respecting my personal space? No touching, so get your hand off me and keep it off!"

He complied, but he took his time about it.

"No worries, babe."

"And don't call me babe."

The air in the car chilled another degree or two. "Someone got up on the wrong side of the bed this morning."

"Can it, Jerry. If it weren't for you, I'd be sitting on the beach with my new husband right now. Instead, I'm forced to talk to one of the grumpiest men I've ever had the misfortune to meet so I can clear Drew's name and send your sorry ass into the light where you belong. Do not mistake my willingness to make that happen for anything other than a deep-seated desire to be rid of you."

"You don't have to be so mean. It's like you don't even care about me at all." He faded away.

Truer words, I thought, then realized they weren't. Not exactly. I was sorry he was dead, and I had sympathy for him the same as I would for anyone unwillingly caught on the wrong side of the veil. Otherwise, he pushed my buttons, and he needed to get gone. Maybe Mitch Castle could help me with that.

"Time to see what skeletons you've got hiding in your closet," I said as I pulled into Foss's parking lot, a wry smile tugging at my lips. And not just the metaphorical kind—I had plenty of experience with the literal ones.

With summer in full gear, even in the rain, the place was bustling. I pulled up in the only empty parking space between two work trucks, one being loaded with wooden boards, the other with several bundles of roofing shingles.

It didn't take long to find Mitch. He stood out among the other workers for two reasons. First, being short in stature, his physique was anything but. Bulging muscles strained against the fabric of his sleeveless tee shirt as he hoisted planks onto a truck bed, veins popping on his forearms like road maps to workoutville. Second, he wore a scowl like my mother wore earrings—as if it were an everyday occurrence and as necessary as breathing.

"Easy does it, Hercules," I muttered under my breath, observing him from a distance.

His dirty blond hair was cropped short, and those pale blue eyes flickered across the yard with an intensity that could start fires. His nose, sharp as the teeth on the saw blades that lined the walls of the lumber shed, seemed to sniff out any excuse to throw his weight around.

"This ought to be fun," I thought wryly as I watched him bark orders at a younger worker who had apparently stacked some lumber incorrectly.

Mitch's voice echoed across the yard, a blend of drill sergeant and angry bear. "Do it right, or don't do it at all!"

I might agree with the sentiment, but the delivery left something to be desired. Browbeating employees was never the best way to inspire them.

As I watched him interact with his two colleagues, it was clear that Mitch's temper was a regular part of their day. One seemed resigned, while the other kept glancing toward Mitch fearfully. It didn't take much to see that a single wrong move and the guy was primed to go off like a jack-in-the-box in the hands of a crank-happy kid. I had no trouble imagining him holding a grudge against Jerry, the bully from his past.

I sucked in a sharp breath and marched towards Mitch Castle, who had momentarily disengaged from the chaos of the lumber yard. He was standing under the roof of a lean-to shed out of the rain, examining a clipboard with an intensity that, I assumed, matched his workout regimen.

"Hey there, Mitch," I called out as casually as I could muster, though my palms were slick with sweat. "Got a minute?"

Mitch looked up, his pale blue eyes narrowing at the interruption. "Depends. You buying or selling?" he grunted, the corners of his mouth twitching downwards in clear annoyance.

Selling what?

"Neither, actually." I flashed a smile that I hoped didn't look too forced. "I'm Everly Dupree. We met when Patrea Evergreen rebuilt that house in Mooselick River."

He nodded as if he recognized me, but I didn't think he did.

"What can I do for you?"

I took a moment to frame my answer and then decided to go with the bald truth.

"Since my husband was arrested for it, I'm looking into Jerry Kaminski's...unfortunate end."

"Kaminski?" His reaction was instant, a mix of surprise and something else—disdain, maybe? "I heard someone bumped him off. What's that got to do with me?"

"Word is you two had history," I said, watching him

closely. His hands tightened on the clipboard until I thought it might snap. "I thought you might have some insights."

"Insights?" He snorted, tossing the clipboard onto a bundle of planks. "Like a character assessment?"

I nodded, thinking the less I said, the more I'd get out of him.

"I don't know what you want to hear, but the guy was a jerk when we were kids. He picked on me constantly, and I spent plenty of time plotting his death back then. But people change."

"You're saying Jerry changed?"

He barked out a laugh that held no mirth whatsoever.

"Not hardly. He was still a jerk but if it weren't for him, I wouldn't have had the incentive to get ripped."

A hint of a bitter smile crossed his lips, then faded so quickly I couldn't swear it had been real or a trick of the light. Maybe he just suffered from resting cranky face.

"I didn't look like this when I got out of school. It took me a long time to figure out strength doesn't come from height, and I needed to grow into mine. I found body-building in my late thirties, and it's become a way of life."

"And what part did Jerry play in that realization?"

"A big one." Unflinching, Mitch looked me in the eye. "If I hadn't been so hellbent on beating the tar out of him, I might never have picked up my first set of free weights. By the time I had the ability to smack him down, I'd lost the desire."

I found that hard to believe—mostly because I heard

some tension in his voice, and there was a tightness around his eyes every time I mentioned Jerry's name—something I noticed Mitch was careful not to do. It was like poking at a cavity with your tongue; painful but impossible to leave alone, so I prodded for more information.

"You mean you and Jerry became friends?"

"I wouldn't call us friends, but we mended our fences some time back."

That tallied somewhat with what Max had told me.

"Besides, I was at a bodybuilding competition the night he was offed. Got a trophy and a bunch of witnesses to prove it. You can check out their video feed. The whole thing was streamed live." This time he did smile, and it reached all the way up to his eyes. For a second, anyway.

"Congrats on the win," I said, pretending to admire the formidable biceps he flexed for my benefit. "You mind telling me the name of the competition?"

He did, and I made a mental note. "If that's all, I've got work to do."

"Of course," I replied, putting him on the probably not list. "Just doing my due diligence. You understand."

"Sure," he said, picking up his clipboard with a finality that suggested, whether I liked it or not, the conversation was over.

CHAPTER NINE

The air outside the police station was sticky and thick enough to cut with one of the fancy cheese knives I'd inherited when I bought my house. I stood on the sun-warmed pavement, watching Patrea approach with the measured gait of a lawyer who had too much on her mind and too few hours in the day to sort it all out. I already knew what she was about to say, but we had decided it would be best if Drew's folks heard it from her.

"Mr. and Mrs. Parker," Patrea began, her dark eyes somber beneath furrowed brows, "I've decided not to push for a bail hearing until after the weekend. The evidence weighs highly against Drew, and we might do more harm than good if we rush things at this stage of the defense."

Cheryl stared at Patrea as if she couldn't comprehend the words she'd just heard. Quinn put an arm around her, trying to be the rock in a storm that was washing all their hopes out to sea.

"Are you saying there's no hope?" Quinn's quiet question hung heavy between them like the humidity.

Patrea offered a look that held more determination

than despair. "No, no. Quite the opposite. I promise we're doing everything possible to bring information to light that will completely exonerate him." She glanced at me then, a silent cue that there was more to discuss away from prying ears. "Pushing for a hearing before we've had a chance to get our ducks in a row wouldn't help Drew."

"You're sure." Cheryl tilted her head to study Patrea intently. What she saw led her to make her words a statement rather than a question.

"I am. Why don't you go on ahead and take a few minutes alone with your son? I need to speak to Everly." Patrea motioned me aside, and I followed, feeling the weight of Drew's parents' anxious stares on my back before they did as Patrea suggested and went inside.

"Okay," she said once we were out of earshot, her tone dropping to a confidential level, "Ernie hasn't been able to contact Pete. He's beginning to think it's for the wrong reasons."

My stomach flipped. "You mean he thinks Drew wants Pete to lie for him, and Pete doesn't want to?" I asked, my voice barely above a murmur.

"Something like that," she replied. "We need to find Pete and get him to come in voluntarily. It will go better for Drew and, from what he's told me, for Pete as well."

"Okay. Jack was supposed to stop by and see how he was doing, but with everything else, I'd forgotten to check in. I'll do that today. How long do we have before Ernie does something official? Sending cops after him won't help Pete's state of mind, I don't think."

"Until Monday morning. Then it's out of my hands." She gave me a grim smile and patted my shoulder before heading off to do whatever magic attorneys do when the law gets sticky.

Moments later, I stood outside Drew's cell for my turn with him. His parents would come in after we'd had a few minutes together. He looked tired and needed a shave, but when his eyes found mine, they were clear and warm as always.

"Hey, babe," he said, wrapping his fingers around mine between the bars. It was all the contact we were allowed, even after Ernie gave me a pat down that embarrassed both of us before he let me back there and, mercifully, left us alone.

"Hey." I forced a smile. "How are you holding up?"

"Like a kayak in a hurricane," he joked, but his eyes told me it was more than rough waters he was navigating.

"We need to talk about Pete," I started, ignoring how he shook his head. "Listen. I know you think he's too fragile to make a statement, but I suspect you're underestimating him. From everything you've told me, Pete was a hero in Iraq. Don't you think he'd want a chance to be one again? Because that's what he'd be if he could help cement your alibi."

He sighed. "I see no flaw in your logic."

"And Jack's the right guy to help bring him in? Because if someone else doesn't, Ernie will have to send the local PD after him. I know you'd rather keep him out of this entirely, but I think it's too late for that. Better if he comes in on his own."

He nodded. "I would, but all I could see was the possible stress I'd put him under. It didn't occur to me that there might be an upside for him."

Warmth flooded over me when he squeezed my hand. "Patrea says if I give her the word, she can hold Ernie off until Monday. Jack was supposed to stop in and check on Pete after work yesterday and said he'd call me with a status report. He didn't, and I didn't think to call him back. I'll do that today."

Absently scratching his cheek, Drew said, "Thanks. I didn't think our marriage would start out with you having to be my rock. To be honest, I kind of signed up to be yours."

"You know what?" I said firmly. "This just proves we can be each other's rock. We just need to get you out of here so we can roll on with our lives."

"Your humor is terrible," he said with a tired chuckle. Fine with me. That was precisely what I'd been aiming for.

"Someone has to keep your spirits up," I replied, grateful when a genuine smile broke through and transformed his face.

We stood together, our hands touching between the cold bars separating us, while I shared what little progress we'd made on the investigation and our plans for going forward until his parents came in. I got him to describe the section of the parking lot where he'd stood while talking to Pete that night.

"Okay," I nodded, trying to picture the scene. "We'll have to see if you would have been visible through that one window at the front. Also, I'm sure Ernie has asked already, but did you notice anyone leaving the bar while you were outside? Or driving past? Someone may have seen you."

Before I finished speaking, he'd already begun to shake his head. "Not that I noticed, but I wasn't paying close attention, so there could have been. If I'd known I would need an alibi, I would have kept a better eye on things."

I squeezed his hand as his parents came in and said, "You couldn't have known. I'm heading straight over to Cappy's from here. We're all gathering to review the list of people the guys remember seeing that night. Plus, Jerry's drinking buddies are Friday night regulars. I need to talk to them."

"Haven't the police already done all of that?" Cheryl looked at me less than warmly.

"Even if they did, people don't always tell the police everything," Drew said, his posture straightening as he called on some hidden well of strength to comfort his mother, who visibly struggled. Mostly with her annoyance at me, but plenty of other emotions crossed her mobile features—fear being one of them.

I hadn't told the Parkers that Ernie had already fed me the preliminary witness statements because I didn't think it would help anything, but it looked like I'd have to rectify that oversight. Sooner rather than later if I wanted my welcome to the family to hold up.

"How will it look if your wife is hanging out alone in a bar two seconds after you were arrested? Not to mention that you've only just been married." Disapproval scored her features as she curled her nose.

Drew opened his mouth to defend me, but Quinn said, "Let the girl alone, Cheryl."

Holding up my hand to stop Drew from leaping to my defense, I said, "This is a small town. People know me. They know I won't let this rest. Anyone who thinks otherwise, I don't care about their opinion. Besides, I won't be alone. I'll be with six other people who all want to clear Drew's name as much as I do."

"If you think that's best, who am I to argue?" Cheryl gave in with very little grace. In the one-woman race to be her favorite daughter-in-law, I was coming in second.

As I walked out of the station, I wondered what would be left of my newfound family once this ordeal had ended.

Jack didn't answer his phone, so I texted him to call me and prepared for the ordeal ahead.

Leaving my car for Drew's folks, I caught a ride to the tavern with Neena. As we walked in, the familiar scents of our Friday night hangout failed to soothe me or spark my appetite. The place was bustling with the dinner crowd, the clatter of dishes, music from the jukebox, and the hum of conversation creating a lively backdrop that seemed almost jarring after the hushed tension at the police station.

We spotted the rest of our friends. An assortment of barely-touched appetizers spread before them as they gathered at the table closest to the barstools Jerry and his drinking buddies usually occupied. Tonight, only one of the three stools was occupied by a man everyone called Scooter. Two more empty glasses sat in front of the stools on either side of him. One upright, the other turned upside down as, I assumed, a tribute to his dead friend. Busy downing one glass after another, Scooter paid no attention to anything else happening in the bar.

"Any word on Pete?" Patrea said as I sat down, her dark hair gleaming under the warm glow of the overhead lights.

"Not yet." I sat between Jacy and Patrea, leaving the seat beside David for Neena, who shot me a narrow-eyed look. Because, for once, I hadn't been trying to get them together, I returned her look with my best innocent face.

"Hey, sweetie," Jacy offered a one-armed hug once I'd settled in. "You look like you could use one of these." She slid a glass of house white across the checkered tablecloth toward me.

"Thanks, I might need two," I replied, taking a long sip that felt like the first full breath I'd had all day.

Neena and David sat side by side, the cramped space making their chairs a tad closer than necessary. At one point, David reached for the pepper shaker, and their hands brushed, lingering for a fraction longer than if the contact had been accidental. His gaze met hers, a silent conversation passing between them before they both looked away, a faint blush coloring Neena's cheeks.

"Ooh, did you see that?" whispered Patrea, leaning across me to include Jacy in the conversation.

"See what?" Jacy responded, feigning ignorance, though her eyes twinkled with shared amusement.

"Nothing," Patrea smiled, "Nothing at all."

Neena would probably shred us later.

Clearing my throat, I steered the conversation back to safer waters. "So, about Drew's case—"

"Right," Jacy interjected, leaning forward with an earnest frown. "Mom said she heard from someone who heard from someone else that someone knows something about a guy who passed by the bar when Drew was outside. She's tracking all the someones and somethings down to see if they pan out. I probably won't hear anything until tomorrow."

"If she can follow that web of gossip back to the original spider," I murmured, rolling my eyes but appreciating the lead nonetheless.

"Speaking of leads," I continued, "I ran into Max today, and he mentioned Mitch Castle might have beef with Jerry, so I went to see him." My words prompted a sniff of annoyance from Patrea. After giving everyone a quick rundown of why Jerry and Mitch didn't get along, I said, "It went about as well as you might expect. He denied all knowledge and offered an alibi."

"Let me guess," Brian said, his fork pausing mid-air. "He was somewhere lifting something heavy."

"Got it in one," I admitted. "Apparently, he won a trophy for it, and the competition was streaming, so we can check the video for times. Given the logistics, I don't see how he can be the guy, so as fast as he got on the list, he's off."

"Ruling people out," Chris said, his voice a low growl, "narrows the field."

"Did he suggest anyone else who might have had a motive?" David asked, finally joining the conversation.

"No, and I didn't think to ask." I glanced down to see Jacy filling my plate with things I usually would have chosen from the sampler platters. To appease her insistence that I eat something, I speared a French fry and dipped it in the ketchup she'd also added. "I dropped the ball there."

The jukebox was belting out a twangy country tune, the scent of fried food and beer heavy in the air, when Jerry's other crony, a man called Gomp, made his entrance —or rather, his spectacle. He didn't so much walk as he swayed to the stool next to Scooter. He must have started his drinking at home. I hoped he wasn't driving.

"Raise a toast to Jerry, our fallen friend." Scooter pitched his voice above the jukebox, his words sloshing around like the beer he splashed into his glass from the pitcher sitting on the bar.

"To Jerry," Gomp hiccupped, nodding so vigorously I

thought he might tumble off his stool. "And to having his killer behind bars."

I watched from our table, wincing at their volume as Gomp extolled Jerry's virtues for the entire room to hear. Neither seemed to realize how loud they were getting or how their misplaced loyalty to Jerry might fuel the gossip firestorm.

"Anyone know Gomp's real name? Or how he came to be called Gomp?" I leaned across the table and kept my voice low—not that Gomp could hear me over his own voice.

"I do," Jacy offered. "His name is Billy Watson, but he goes by Gomp because his father always called him Gompy." A Maine term for someone who tends to be clumsy. "I guess he fell down a lot when he was a kid. He used to come into the diner when I worked there. He's… talkative."

I could see that for myself.

"Good." Neena transferred two chicken wings from her plate to David's as if they regularly shared food. "That should make it easy to pry information out of him. The question is, who should be the one to try?"

"We'll do it," Brian murmured, his brow furrowed as he glanced at Chris and David. "See if they remember anything useful."

"Or anything at all," Chris added, his grumpy tone not entirely masking a note of doubt.

"We shouldn't have any trouble eavesdropping," I

said, curious about what they might let slip under the influence of their grief and the booze.

Spacing it out so they didn't seem threatening, the three men strolled over to the bar, flashing friendly smiles that could disarm even the most belligerent drunk.

"Mind if I buy the next round?" David offered, his voice gentle yet firm.

"Wouldn't say no," Scooter replied, brightening at the thought of a free drink. "Did you know Jerry?"

"Some. Not as well as you." With a chin nod, David signaled Adam to bring another pitcher, which appeared with three more glasses. Once theirs had been topped off, Scooter and Gomp swiveled their stools to face the three men who flanked them.

"But we were here the night he died," Brian said, sliding into the conversation like a smooth pebble across a still pond.

"You was?" Gomp frowned, confusion momentarily clearing the fog of alcohol.

Scooter leaned forward to get a closer look at Brian. "I remember you. You were with the guy that killed Jerry. Why'd he want to go and do a thing like that? Jerry never meant him no harm."

"But he did come at Drew, didn't he?" Having taken the spot on Gomp's other side, Chris leaned against the bar. "That's how it went down."

"That's not how I remember it," Scooter defended his dead friend.

"Maybe your memory's a bit hazy?" David prodded from his spot next to Scooter.

"Could be," Scooter conceded after a pause, the doubt seeping into his voice. "We was all pretty tanked, to be honest. Jerry was making noises about his new woman and said some asshole named Drew wouldn't stop chasing her."

I didn't know what was worse, being called Jerry's woman or Drew being called an asshole. Patrea put her hand on my arm when I might have risen to rush to both our defenses.

"Thass right," Gomp waved his glass for emphasis, slopping beer all over his pants. "I remember he said the guy was—what's the word? Diluted." He pronounced it die-luted, then shook his head. "Deluded. That's it. And he was going to straighten him out."

"Was that before or after he and Drew had words?" Chris wanted to know.

"Before," Scooter said.

"After," Gomp said with equal emphasis.

"No." Scooter shook his head so hard he nearly fell off his stool. "It was before. I remember because he said there wasn't anything else to do but set the guy straight."

"Anyone would do the same. Can you remember what happened after he set Drew straight?" Brian asked, his question casual but his eyes sharp and assessing.

"He got kicked out, didn't he?" Gomp looked to Scooter for confirmation. "We was going to go with him because he was still sober enough to drive, but we had to finish our beers, and I had to hit the john."

Scooter nodded. "When I looked out the window, Jerry's car was gone, so while Gomp went for a whiz, I called my old lady to give us a ride."

"Only the dang bathroom was full up," Gomp grumbled, then his face lit up as if he'd just solved a crossword puzzle. "I had to go outside to take a leak, but the lights was too bright in the parking lot, so I went across the road where it's dark and nearly got mowed down by some jackwad driving a gray pickup with a black cap."

"A gray pickup?" Chris echoed, perking up at this new tidbit. "You sure about that?"

"Yup," Gomp nodded, looking proud of himself. "It come out of nowhere. Nearly peed my pants twice, once from need, and once from near about getting run over."

"Sounds like you had quite a night," David said, trying to keep the mood light.

"Could've been a worse one if that darn truck hadda hit me," Gomp added, seemingly oblivious to the weight of his own words.

"Any idea how long it was from when Jerry left the bar until you had your near-death incident?"

"Long as it takes to finish off a pitcher," Scooter interjected. "No sense letting good beer go to waste. 'Specially when it was paid for by some poor schmuck who was getting married the next day."

He meant Drew. Did he not even realize Drew and the

schmuck were the same man? For that matter, did he realize his fly was open? Probably not.

With that, the guys returned to our table. "I think we've exhausted those particular sources," Brian said with disgust as he glanced toward Scooter and Gomp. They had already returned their stools to their original positions and were squabbling about whose turn it was to pay for the next round.

"Okay, so a gray truck." I used my elbow to nudge Jacy, who was staring into her wine glass like it might tell her the secret meaning of life. "Gomp nearly gets run over by one the night Jerry was killed. The driver could be a potential witness."

"Or the killer." Patrea voiced what we all were thinking. If Jerry had left as soon as he was kicked out of the bar, the driver could have nearly killed Gomp on his way to or from the murder site. Depending, of course, on how long Scooter and Gomp lingered over that final pitcher of beer.

Either way, this was the first new piece of the puzzle we'd uncovered. Now, it was time to see if we could figure out where it fit. To that end, we vacated our front-and-center table for one nearer the back of the bar, where we wouldn't be as easily overheard.

"I need to get the general order of things straight. Do any of you remember seeing Gomp leave the bar?" I wished I could ask Drew, but Ernie wouldn't let me back in to see him at this time of night.

Squinting while he considered the question, David

finally shook his head. "I didn't."

"Me, either," Chris said. "My back was to the bar, though."

"Did you see them leave?" I asked.

"It was a little while after Drew came back in, I think." Brian ran a hand through his hair as if that would help clear up his memory. "I heard Scooter tell Gomp to hurry up before his wife got any more pissed off than she already was, and Tom was telling us about the time Drew fell out of a tree trying to save what he thought was a cat, and it turned out to be an opossum."

"We need to know how long it took Scooter's wife to get here once he'd called her," Patrea pointed out.

"I can help you there," Brian said. "I know where he lives from my meter-reading days. It's not far. Wouldn't take his wife more than five minutes. Give her an extra five to get ready. Or maybe ten if she's like Jacy, so we're talking fifteen—give or take."

After a moment to catalog the information and align it with what I'd already heard, I said, "Jerry and Drew argued, and Jerry got kicked out. David ordered fries. Ten or fifteen minutes later, David's fries came, and he ate a little more than half of them before Drew's phone rang and he went outside. At the speed David eats, Jerry must have been gone almost half an hour before Pete called."

"Sounds about right," David said.

"We know the phone call with Pete lasted about twenty minutes because Ernie noted the time stamp from Drew's phone. We also know Drew had come back inside before Gomp went out to pee and nearly got hit by a car while Scooter called his wife. Gomp and Scooter left ten to fifteen minutes after that. Does that sound right?"

All three guys nodded.

"Which means," Neena picked up where I'd left off, "the driver of the gray truck couldn't have seen Drew outside but could be the killer because Gomp said he went across the road."

"Exactly." Jacy nodded, her eyes bright with excitement. "Anyone driving on that side of the road would have been coming from the direction of the murder, not going toward it, and the timing makes sense for it to be them. Now, all we have to do is find the truck and match the tire prints to the ones we found at the secondary scene."

Shaking her head, Patrea said, "I hate to put a damper on your theories, but we have no proof that the tire prints were connected to the murder."

"You're right," I said, defending Patrea when everyone else groaned. "But it's the best lead we've got."

"Still." Brian leaned forward, his brows knitting together. "A gray truck...there's got to be at least a ten of those owned by people who live in or around Mooselick River. It's a popular color. We need to narrow it down."

"And it might not even be local," Neena said, wrapping her hands around the glass of cola she'd switched to drinking since she was driving. Her eyes flickered to David, and he gave a small nod of agreement.

"She's right. It could have been someone passing

through?" David added. "Someone not used to the roads around here. It's a good theory, but there's not much to back it up."

"Let's just assume it was the killer," Chris mused, his voice steady. "They've just bashed someone over the head, and they're so freaked out they don't even notice Gomp when they go by. It makes sense to me and speaks to the level of forethought. This was a crime of convenience, not premeditated."

"Exactly." I tapped my fingers on the table, the gears in my head grinding into action. "We've got to think about this from every angle. Who benefits from Jerry being out of the picture?"

"Every woman who now never has to deal with him?" Jacy quipped. "Or just someone who owns or had access to a gray truck that night and didn't like his face."

Nodding along in time to my tapping, Neena said, "Jacy's right. This doesn't feel like murder for financial gain. It's more likely to be someone who just had it in for him. The motive was probably revenge."

"Right, we're looking for someone who doesn't just dislike Jerry but who developed a deep-seated hatred for the man," Patrea said, her lawyerly logic shining through.

"Again," Jacy said, setting her drink down. "Every woman who ever had to deal with him. But so far, we haven't found anyone who hated him enough to resort to this level of violence. Either we're talking to the wrong people, or someone's lying."

"Someone who felt wronged in some way," Patrea

speculated, her tone grave. "Are we sure it wasn't one of the women he chased and discarded?"

"That list could be endless. Let's focus on what we know for sure," I insisted. "And keep an eye out for gray trucks."

The band was just stepping up to the stage when Adam wiped his hands on his apron and ambled over.

"Mind if I join in for a sec?" he asked, pulling up a chair without waiting for an answer. The smells of fried onions and grilled burgers lingered around him like an aura.

"Of course," I said, scooting aside to make room. "What's up?"

Adam leaned in and rested his elbows on the table, his expression serious in a way that spelled trouble. "I've seen you all in action before, so I know you're working on finding out who killed Jerry Kaminski," he began, glancing at each of us. "And there's something I think you ought to know."

"Do tell," Patrea prompted, her eyes sharp behind her glasses.

"There's this guy who lives just out of town. Don Giacomo. Goes by Donnie." Adam scratched his chin, leaving a streak of cooking oil. "He and Jerry worked together when that young couple who opened the coffee shop had some work done on their place. Well, Donnie came in here one night and proceeded to get drunk off his rocker, cursing Jerry's name to high heaven."

Don Giacomo hadn't rung any bells with me, but the

name Donnie did. "Donnie," I repeated, racking my brain to pull up a face to go with the name. "Dark hair, sunglasses perpetually stuck on the back of his head? Plays bass in the little combo Bess's nephew put together?"

"That's the one," Adam confirmed with a nod. "He does the music thing on the side and works carpentry jobs wherever anyone will hire him. From what he said, Jerry had found out Donnie had lied to his boss about taking time off to help his grandmother. But instead, the guy was living it up with some woman he met in Hackinaw. Jerry blabbed, and Donnie not only got the sack, but after that, the two biggest outfits in the area refused to hire him again."

"Ouch." I winced, picturing the scene. "That does sound like a motive for holding a grudge."

"More than just a grudge," Adam added, lowering his voice. "The night he got fired, Donnie was here drowning his sorrows. He kept saying he'd make Jerry pay."

"Did anyone take him seriously?" I asked, leaning forward. My pulse quickened at the thought of a new lead —a solid one.

"Most folks just figured it was the booze talking," Adam admitted with a shrug. "But now, with everything going on—"

"Thanks, Adam," I said, my mind already racing with the possibilities. "This is huge. We'll look into it. I don't suppose you know what kind of vehicle Donnie drives."

"An old truck," he replied, standing up and heading back to the bustle of the kitchen.

"Looks like we've got a new name on our suspect list," Jacy murmured, scribbling in her notebook.

"Seems like Jerry's habit of sticking his nose where it didn't belong might have caught up with him," I said, feeling a mix of vindication and trepidation. "At least we have a couple of new leads. For now, I suppose I should get home before Drew's mother finishes sewing a big red M for Meddler to all of my clothes. She's concerned about the optics of me being here as it is."

"I'll drive you." Neena glanced back toward David, and I sensed a certain amount of reluctance on her part to leave before he did.

"Miranda dropped me off on her way home." David tilted his head and looked at Neena. "You mind if I ride with you?"

"Not at all," she said. "The more the merrier."

Or the fewer, I thought, beginning to feel like a third wheel.

CHAPTER TEN

The summer sun hadn't even had the decency to peek through the curtains before Jerry decided to break another ghost rule. There he was, standing at the foot of my bed like some annoying specter of bad decisions, grinning that half-cocked grin I'd come to loathe.

"Jerry, what part of 'stay out of my bedroom' don't you understand?" I hissed, clutching the sheets to my chest. Not that I cared, but my hair was a mess—a testament to a night spent tossing and turning over clues that just wouldn't click into place—and I needed coffee before I had to deal with him.

"Come on, honey, I just—" he started, but I cut him off with a wave of my hand.

"Out! Do you have any idea how thin these walls are? And if Cheryl and Quinn are in the kitchen, they'll hear me talking." I groaned, envisioning the mountain of awkwardness awaiting me beyond my bedroom door if they did.

"They're not." His eyes strayed to the spot where the edge of the sheet met my skin. What a sleazeweasel. Molly growled at him. Smart dog.

"Get out anyway," I pointed toward the door because

that's what you do with a solid person, not remembering he wasn't one.

"Fine, I'm going," Jerry said in a tone that suggested anything but compliance. He didn't move an inch, but his form flickered like a poorly tuned TV station.

"I can still see you," I said, my tone dry as day-old toast. "Get out."

With one last look toward the bed, he turned and walked through the wall. If he hadn't already been dead, I might have wanted to kill him myself as I struggled out of bed and into something resembling daywear.

As fate would have it, the moment I opened my bedroom door, Cheryl descended the stairs and headed for the kitchen. Jerry, who had been waiting just on the other side, followed me, commentary track unchecked.

"Morning, honey." Cheryl looked up, her eyes clouded with concern that had become all too familiar since Drew's arrest. "Did you sleep okay? You look a bit... frazzled."

"Fine, fine." I echoed Jerry's earlier lie, offering a smile that felt more like a grimace. "Just the weather making my hair...express itself." I gestured toward my unruly mop, hoping it might distract her from the bags under my eyes. "And Molly hogged the bed."

Hoping that would distract her, I went to the back door and let Molly out to water her favorite patch of lawn while I filled her food bowl.

"Or else it's your taste in men keeping you up at night," Jerry muttered, hovering close enough for me to feel the chill that clung to him. "You should have saved yourself for someone who wasn't a murderer."

If looks could poof ghosts, mine would have sent Jerry wherever spirits go when they've exhausted their energy and need to recharge. A break from him certainly wouldn't hurt my feelings.

"I really am fine," I reassured Cheryl, pouring myself a cup of coffee with a hand steadier than I felt. "I've got a few new leads to follow up with today. Maybe something will break our way."

"You can't seriously be thinking about poking around again." Cheryl dumped yeast into a mixing bowl and added warm water to help it bloom.

"Oh yes, she is." Jerry's insistence hummed annoyingly at the edge of my consciousness, like a mosquito determined to ruin a perfect night's sleep with its buzzing.

"New leads. Viable ones," I repeated firmly, both for Cheryl's benefit and to convince myself. "Nothing dangerous and nothing that'll interfere with what the police are doing, I promise."

Cheryl nodded, accepting my vague assurance while flicking on the mixer with a gesture that bordered on aggressive. Meanwhile, Jerry hovered near the refrigerator, his expression one of mock innocence as he continued to slander my husband with inane comments.

"Maybe you could spend some time at home today," Cheryl suggested, pulling a dozen eggs from the fridge. "We've hardly seen you since the wedding."

"I will not," I responded to Jerry's outrageous suggestion that I file for an annulment just as Quinn walked into the kitchen. When he caught sight of his wife's devastated expression, he gave me a look that made me squirm and think back to what she'd just said. Oh crap. I'd totally offended my new mother-in-law. Way to go, Dupree.

"I'm sorry. I didn't mean that the way it sounded, and of course, I want to spend time with you both. I just need to follow up on these new leads first. You understand, don't you? I can't concentrate on anything else until Drew's home where he belongs."

"We understand," Quinn said. "This is a hard situation, and I know we're all doing our best to get through it."

"This is what you get when you marry a criminal," Jerry said, sending my blood pressure skyrocketing.

Looking at my reddening face, Quinn said, "Tell me about these new leads."

"I've talked to a man named Mitch Castle, and today, I'm looking into another man who didn't get along well with Jerry. His name is Don Giacomo."

Jerry snorted. Yes, ghosts can do that. "Donnie and Midge had nothing to do with my untimely demise. Midge might have the muscle, but he doesn't have the stones, and Donnie's too stupid to cover up a murder. If he'd killed me, he'd have told someone by now. His jaw's hinged at both ends and wags in the middle."

I spent half a moment trying to picture what that would look like and couldn't.

Seeming genuinely curious, Quinn asked for more information, which I offered while Jerry scoffed. "You're out of your mind. I'm telling you, those guys are innocent. You're barking up the wrong tree."

"Trees," I blurted out, desperately needing Jerry to shut up. Instead, I ended up on the receiving end of more concerned looks from Drew's parents. "Sorry. I was just thinking some time by the trees at the lake would be nice."

"Everly," Cheryl said gently, her voice laced with worry. "I hate to say so, but you seem quite overwrought. Maybe you should leave this investigation to Ernie. It's what he's trained for."

Jerry scoffed, a sound like a pig rooting through mud. "Let Ernie handle it? He couldn't find his hat if it were on his head!"

I'd hit my limit of dividing my attention between keeping up appearances and not letting Jerry see how much he was getting under my skin. "I'm sorry. I need to give Molly some exercise. I'll be back in a few minutes."

Making my escape through the back door, I gave Jerry a look that said he'd better follow me or else. I had no or else to threaten him with, but he didn't know that. Besides, he lived to annoy. Figuratively speaking.

"Now that I've got you alone, let's talk about us," Jerry said as he followed me down the back steps. Molly growled at him again.

"Good dog," I said, ruffling her fur. "I totally agree." Then, I tossed her favorite rubber ball for cover while telling Jerry, "There is no us. Why don't you take me over the events leading up to your death? I've heard everything up to you getting kicked out of the bar. What happened next?"

"You're finally trying to help me?" He moved close enough to send a chill across my skin, and I stepped back.

"Personal distance, Jerry."

"Fine," he said, moving back half a step. "Ask me anything."

Molly dropped the slobber-covered ball at my feet, then raced away in anticipation of the next throw. "Tell me what happened when you left the bar."

Pacing, he did. "There's not much to tell. I'd had a few, but I was okay to drive, so I headed home. I didn't get too far when I realized I had to take a wicked whiz, so I pulled over and whipped it out."

"Gah," I said. "Too much detail. Just get on with it."

"No, that's all of it. I don't really remember anything after that."

"Try harder," I ordered.

Obliging, he closed his eyes to concentrate. As he did, his edges began to blur. "I heard a vehicle pull up and was afraid it was the po po, so I cut things off midstream and zipped up."

"Then what?" I prodded as his entire body began to vibrate.

"Then I—"

He'd poofed, which was half the point of my prodding

him for answers. If I was lucky, he'd stay gone for the rest of the day. I sure could use the break.

Back inside, Molly zoomed to her food dish and practically inhaled the contents while Cheryl herded me toward the table and plied me with scrambled eggs and thin slices of the ham she'd cooked the day before.

"Do you always talk to yourself? Or do you have an imaginary friend?" Quinn wanted to know.

I choked on my orange juice, coughing discreetly into a napkin while Cheryl's brows furrowed in concern from across the table.

"Are you all right, dear?" she asked, reaching out to pat my hand.

"Fine, just...swallowed wrong." I cleared my throat, trying to regain composure while shooting my new father-in-law a reassuring look.

"No one has ever asked me that before, but I guess the answer is yes. Sometimes, I talk to myself. It helps me get my thoughts in order," I said, not convincing anyone. How was I supposed to break the news to Drew that his parents thought I was a nutjob?

The rest of breakfast passed in subdued silence. Finally, I slid the last of the dishes into the dishwasher and mumbled an excuse about errands that didn't fool anyone but at least got me out of the house. Blissfully alone, I searched a few social sites for Don Giacomo's name but turned up nothing to help me figure out where I could conveniently run into him.

Out of ideas, I headed for the salon to see if I could

ease a few more details from Cindy. I wasn't sure how much Jerry-free time I'd bought myself—every ghost's recharge time was different—and I wanted to make the most of it.

The salon was in full Saturday morning swing by the time I arrived, with blow dryers roaring and scissors snipping a rhythmic counterpoint. The tangy smell of hair dye and nail polish perfumed air that hummed with the chatter of women who liked nothing more than to pass on the latest gossip.

"You're back," Cindy's voice sliced through the cacophony, her surprise registering above the din. Her hair, darker than before, framed her face in a way that made her hazel eyes pop. I liked the new color better than the last, but I wouldn't say I enjoyed the suspicion on her face because I knew I was about to earn it.

"Hey, Cindy," I said, offering what I hoped was a casual wave. "Since Mara's not here, any chance you could work your magic on this?" I tugged at the hair I hadn't bothered to comb before I left the house. At least I had a good excuse for stopping by.

"I suppose I can squeeze you in between the Tupperware twins' dye jobs," she replied with a wink, gesturing to two elderly ladies whose heads were wrapped in foil like leftovers. "But I won't have time to talk."

Obviously, I hadn't fooled her with my humidity-driven hair woes.

"You don't have to." I lowered my voice, leaning closer. "But I do have news."

Cindy's expression sobered, the stylist's facade slipping just enough to reveal concern. "Say what you need to say at the wash station. It's quieter over there."

As we navigated the obstacle course of hair stations, I felt the weight of every eye upon us. In a town like Mooselick River, a whisper could be as loud as a shout, and since I was already on people's minds, I knew our tête-à-tête would be the day's hot ticket item by noon. But if it got me one step closer to finding Jerry's killer, I'd give them a show worth watching.

Cindy rinsed my hair with practiced ease, the warm water sluicing over my scalp a soothing distraction from my troubles. Too bad it only lasted a moment.

"What's up?" Cindy's voice was soft above the swish of water and the bustle of the salon.

"I talked to Mitch Castle, but he has an alibi." I squinted up at her, drops of water clinging to my lashes. "And then I heard about Jerry's squabble with Don Giacomo. Do you know anything about it?"

She hesitated, her hands stilling. "Donnie? He's a playboy. At least in his own mind, you know the type?" Her reluctance was as palpable as the damp air around us.

"I do. Sounds like he and Jerry had that in common."

"Not really. Donnie doesn't make women think he wants more from them than he does. He's honest that way, at least."

Had she been charmed by another of Jerry's friends?

"Look." She glanced around nervously, then lowered her voice. "I know about what happened with Donnie, but only because his mother is one of my best customers..." She trailed off, leaving implication hanging between us like the steam fogging the mirrors.

"So that means you know how Jerry got Donnie fired," I pressed, feeling the pieces shift and slide into place.

"Yeah, because he stirred the pot." A resigned sigh escaped her. "The guys had just finished up at the new bakery, and Jerry was working at Patrea's place. Donnie wanted in on the job, so Jerry got him in with the drywall crew. Except, on the second day out, Donnie called in sick. Said he needed to take care of his ailing grandmother for a few days. Donnie's grandmother died three years ago. He was holed up with a lounge singer in a cheap motel room in Hackinaw."

"I see. And Jerry blew him in for it."

"Pretty much. Donnie got fired—as he should have. But you know how many crews worked that job. Everyone who does construction in this town was out there, and they all saw what happened. Donnie hasn't had much luck picking up work around here the past few weeks."

The shampoo done, she sat me up. "Seems like a good way to stir up bad blood."

"Maybe," Cindy shrugged. "Maybe not. Donnie's like a cat. You know how they always land on their feet? His mother said he's got a line on something down in Bangor."

I allowed that I did and asked if she knew where I might be able to find Donnie.

"Sure. It's Saturday, so he'll be at the Starlight Lanes tonight. Donnie never misses the start of the summer bowling league."

Eyes wide, I said, "Spending his Saturday nights at the bowling alley isn't what I'd expect from someone known as a playboy."

"I suppose it is when their average is a 296, and the bars stay open long after the alley closes."

"Thanks, Cindy." My heart hammered at the thought of being one step closer to a viable suspect. "And Mitch Castle? He said they'd patched things up between them. Any chance he's still holding a grudge against Jerry?"

"Those two?" She laughed, a genuine note of amusement threading through her voice. "They called a truce years ago. I even think Jerry apologized, which shocked everyone who knew him. Speaking of Mitch, I haven't seen him in months. Is he still as handsome as ever?"

The question caught me off guard, and I noticed the wistfulness in her eyes. "He's...Mitch," I said noncommittally, but my mind whirled. Was there more to Cindy's past interactions with Mitch than met the eye? Wasn't she already married to another of Jerry's friends? How many of them had she burned through?

"Uh-huh." She smiled, and it was clear there were stories she hadn't told. "Just curious."

With her sturdy build and quiet manner, Cindy didn't strike me as the type to play around, but looks can be deceiving. Plus, if she was at the heart of the death, it would flip the script, giving Jerry a motive to harm Mitch or Donnie, not the other way around. I wasn't sure what to think.

"Thanks for the tip, Cindy." I sat up, the emerging puzzle both a challenge and a warning. "Looks like I need to make a date with some tenpins—and maybe a side of truth."

Nodding, she went to work with the blow dryer, taming my hair and applying some sweet-smelling product to counteract the humidity.

Stepping out of the salon, I squinted against the summer sun, my mind a tumult of leads and suspicions. A bee buzzed around me as I made my way down the side-walk, passing the bakery where the scent of fresh bread tested my resolve.

"Everly!" Neena's voice hailed me from across the street. I turned to see her waving at me from the doorway of Mabel's diner, her dark curls nearly as wild as mine had been. The humidity was no one's friend this summer. "Want coffee?"

Nodding, I darted across the street, dodging a bicycle that whizzed past, its bell dinging in reprimand. "Coffee sounds good," I said, stepping into the cool shade of the diner's awning. "And I've got news. You alone?"

"It's my turn to do the coffee run while Jacy hits the bakery. Your hair looks fabulous." She leaned in and sniffed, her eyes twinkling with curiosity. "What did you use on it?"

"Cindy did it. Used some new product at the salon. I'm sure Mara would be happy to sell you some."

I followed her inside, where we ordered iced coffees to go. "She tell you anything useful?" Neena asked, her voice low enough that no one heard.

"If you mean why Donnie got fired, then yes," I admitted, rubbing the back of my neck. "Even better, she told me where he hangs out on Saturday nights. Looks like I'll be checking out the bowling alley later. Donnie's in a league there, so it's a good place to talk to him—find out what he knows about Jerry's situation."

Her eyebrows arched, and she folded her arms. "You're going to talk to a potential killer alone?"

"Who says I'll be alone?" I retorted with a grin. "Care to join me for some suspect stalking—and maybe a game or two? I can call the others and see if they want to make a night of it."

"Darlin', I thought you'd never ask." Neena's grin was all mischief and excitement. "Count me in, but Jacy and Brian have a thing tonight with Brian's family."

"Okay. I'll check with Patrea and Chris and text you the time." I gave her a mock salute before turning toward home, feeling a surge of relief having her on board. Just her, though, because Patrea promptly texted back to say she and Chris had plans.

Back at the house, I clipped Molly's leash onto her collar, and we set off for another walk. As usual, she headed for the dog park, where she found a couple of canine companions to romp with. There, leaning against the fence with a coffee cup in hand, was Ernie Polk, watching the canine chaos with a bemused expression.

"Polk," I greeted him, tossing Molly's ball when she brought it back to me, then watching her race the other dogs to grab it.

"Dupree." He nodded, eyes scanning the horizon as if expecting trouble to parachute in. "You're not here to tell me you've solved the case already, are you?"

"Hardly," I said, leaning against the fence beside him. "But I've got a hunch. Don Giacomo—what do you know about him?"

"Generally harmless to anything that doesn't wear scanty panties," Ernie grunted. "Why?"

The term scanty panties nearly floored me, but I let it pass.

"Long story short, I think he's involved. And there's something else—gray trucks. How many do we have in this town? Any chance you could find out for me?" I asked, trying to sound casual. "Ones with black caps."

"Gray trucks?" He raised an eyebrow skeptically. "You planning on starting a new car dealership?"

"Someone saw one at around the time of the murder," I said, giving him my best 'trust-me-I'm-on-to-something' look. "Seems like someone with the means to do so should check it out. That's you."

Ernie sighed, the sound carrying the weight of a man who knew he would regret this. "You mean you haven't already hacked the DMV's database? You've got your nose in everything else."

"Wouldn't dream of it," I said with a feral smile, watching Molly chase her tail in dizzying circles. "Even if I had the first clue how."

"Right." Ernie didn't seem convinced, but he pushed off from the fence. "Leave it with me. Speaking of, the tire tread you found was off a Goodyear Wrangler. Truck tire."

"And do we know where people buy those around here?" Hope danced through my belly, leaving a trail of butterflies behind it.

"Only every single Walmart in the state. It's their most popular seller statewide."

The butterflies died. "Thanks, Ernie. You're a peach."

He snorted at that, shaking his head as he walked away.

The noonday sun beamed down from straight overhead as Molly and I made our way back from the dog park. The river gurgled in the background, a comforting soundtrack to my jumbled thoughts. I scratched at a mosquito bite on my arm—a souvenir from an overzealous bloodsucker with an apparent taste for ghost whisperers.

"Come on, girl," I urged Molly, who seemed more interested in sniffing every blade of grass than getting home.

My phone rang, its cheerful jingle stark against the peaceful sound of our footsteps. Martha Tipton's name flashed on the screen. Sighing, I answered, "Hey Martha, what's up?"

"Everly, darling, I just heard about Drew! I'm so sorry," she cooed, her voice thick with sympathy.

Just? Where had she been the past couple of days? In isolation? It wasn't like Martha to be uninformed. I'd have thought that even if she'd left the reception early, she would have heard about the arrest before Ernie settled Drew in the back of his cruiser.

"Thanks, Martha. It's a mess. But I'm going to clear his name," I said with more confidence than I felt.

"Of course you will. Listen, this is a dreadful time to ask, but Junior Pease is here asking if we could organize a pet cemetery fundraiser. Any chance you could whip up one of your brilliant ideas?" she asked, her voice blending hope and hesitation.

"You know I'd love to help, but my plate's so full stuff is falling off the sides right now. You're going to have to be the creative genius this time," I replied, half-apologizing, half-standing my ground, and not giving her one iota of information to feed back through the chain of gossip.

"I was afraid of that. We'll muddle through somehow. Keep your chin up!" she chirped before hanging up.

"Chin's up. Spirits are somewhere around my ankles," I muttered to Molly, who gave me a look that clearly said she adored me no matter how low my spirits had sunk.

Lunch with Drew's folks was slightly less awkward than breakfast, but it at least had the benefit of being ghost-free. Plus, I managed to talk them into spending the afternoon and evening at camp with Jacy's parents by telling them how much Molly loved a good swim.

And they wouldn't be there to disapprove when I left to go bowling later. Win, win, win.

With a few free hours on my hands, I did some online research that didn't provide any new information and walked over to spend an hour with Drew. I shouldn't have been surprised to find my parents already talking to him, but it gave me a chance to fill them all in on my progress and tell them of my plans for later.

The walk home cleared my head a little but nearly made me late. Turning onto my street, I saw Neena jumping into David's truck, still running, in my drive.

"Ready to bowl a strike or two?" She grinned, leaning out the window.

"Sure, but I thought it was just us girls tonight," I said, tilting my head to smile at the man who had become family to me over the past year.

"Change of plans! David offered to come along. Is that okay?" Neena asked, opening the door and beginning to get out so I could sit in the middle.

"Just move over." I waggled my eyebrows at her, and she blushed, which I found delightful.

"Hey," David greeted me, a shy smile creeping across his face. "Thought it might be a good idea to have some muscle along for the ride."

"Appreciate it," I said, trying to mask my surprise. "How's your bowling game?"

"I hold my own, Dupree," he replied, his eyes holding a hint of steel I hadn't seen before.

"So do I," I shot back, slamming the door and patting the dashboard. "Let's roll out."

On the way, I gave David the rundown on what I already knew, and we put a tentative plan in place to find out if Don Giacomo had any skeletons rattling in his closet. Or, better yet, clues about who had put Jerry in his grave.

CHAPTER ELEVEN

The neon Starlight Lanes sign buzzed like a swarm of electric bees, throwing its garish glow over the parking lot where David struggled to find a space. The summer evening clung to our skin, damp and warm, as we stepped out of the car and headed toward the sound of crashing pins and 80s rock seeping through the building.

"It's been at least five years, but nothing has changed," I told Neena, then got a look at her face. "Hudson used to bring you here, didn't he?"

Because of course, he did. Bowling had been her dead husband's ideal date. That hadn't changed since he'd been my high school sweetheart, and we'd rolled balls to the same music they were playing now.

The last time I'd seen him bowl hadn't been here, though. He'd already been dead when he rolled a mannequin head down my stairs to knock out his killer, the man who, at the time, had his hands around my throat. He'd scored that day, too, so I'd lived to tell the tale.

"Don't you worry about that now, honey," she drawled with the innate charm that could convince you to buy snow from an Eskimo, "I have nothing but good memories here and no reason in the world not to make a few more. Besides, it'll be worth it to see David wearing rented shoes."

David grunted, his tall, dark, and handsomely awkward frame unfolding from behind the wheel. "For the record, I look good in anything," he declared, though I caught a flicker of hesitation in his smile. Poor guy was still finding his footing after life threw him a gutter ball.

The moment we entered, the scent of waxed lanes and greasy pizza assaulted my nostrils, a nostalgic cocktail that somehow spelled 'community' in small-town Maine. As we approached the counter, a familiar figure caught my eye. There, lacing up a pair of fluorescent orange bowling shoes, was none other than my mother, Kitty Dupree. I looked around for my dad.

"Mom?" I exclaimed, the syllable bouncing off the walls louder than I intended. "What are you doing here?"

She looked up, her face brighter than the overhead score monitors. "Your father and I joined the summer bowling league. I never expected to see you here—not that I'm complaining about spending time with my favorite daughter." She winked, well aware of my status as the only contender for that title.

"Did you join because of the bowling or the chance to grill suspects between frames?" I joked, trying to mask my surprise. It wasn't like my folks to crash my Saturday night plans, but then again, murder investigations did make us do odd things.

"Can't a woman enjoy a harmless game of bowling?" she countered, her tone innocent, but I knew better. Kitty Dupree didn't do 'harmless' when her daughter might be in danger. Not that I thought I was.

"Of course," I said, accepting her hug and inhaling the familiar scents of lavender and determination. "Not that there's anything harmless about your game. Or Dad's, either."

They'd been league bowlers in the past but, over the years, had let the sport go in favor of other pursuits. She might be rusty, but I bet she'd get her mojo back quickly enough.

Neena chuckled beside me, elbowing my ribs gently. "Looks like she's in it for the win," she whispered, taking in my mom's perfect form as she threw a practice ball.

"So am I," I replied, slipping on a pair of clown-colored shoes and mentally preparing for a night of strikes, spares, and, most importantly, crime-solving.

Not being part of the league, David, Neena, and I ended up on fifteen, one of the end lanes set aside for regular bowlers to use. Donnie's team was on lane nine, and in a stroke of luck, my folks were on lane ten. My mother's interference might come in handy after all.

We'd barely laced up our bowling shoes when Ernie Polk walked in and joined the team on lane five. Mom caught sight of him as he settled his ball on the return rack, scowled, and zeroed in on her target like a heat-seeking missile while my father watched, his face resigned.

"Ernie Polk!" She said his name like it was a euphemism for something filthy, cutting across the alley with an intensity that made bystanders pause mid-swing. "I need a word with you."

"Kitty, this isn't the place," Ernie grumbled and looked annoyed that his attempt at a night that didn't involve law or order wasn't going well.

"Then find a place because I have something to say, and I mean to be heard," she retorted, hands firmly planted on her hips. Her voice carried over the clatter of pins, drawing more attention than a turkey on Thanksgiving. "I've been trying to catch up with you for two days, but you've been 'away from your desk' every time I stop by."

Dad moved out at the same time I did. Since he was closer, he got to them first, but I wasn't that far behind.

"Kitty," he said, his tone low and calming as he gently rubbed her upper arm. The look she gave him made him pull his hand back.

I bit my lip, glancing around at the curious onlookers. My mother's fierce loyalty to family and friends was both admirable and terrifying. But as much as I might enjoy watching her take a strip off Ernie's hide, this might not be the best time. "Mom, remember why we're here."

"I know exactly why we're here," she shot back, her gaze never leaving Ernie's face. The man squirmed uncomfortably, regretting his choice to spend a casual evening in the lion's den. "What I don't know is why Ernie thinks it's a good idea to go bowling when there's an innocent man behind bars. He should be out there beating the bushes until he finds the person who killed Jerry Kaminski."

She did have a point, but she didn't know he'd been feeding me information that might help rectify the situation. Here and now were not the time and place to tell her. Too many people were listening in.

"I can only follow the evidence, Kitty. You know that," Ernie said, defending himself.

"Mom, let's just—" My attempt to mediate was lost to the tension crackling between them.

"Look, I understand you're upset, but causing a scene here won't change anything," Ernie said, his eyes pleading for some semblance of peace.

"Upset? Upset doesn't even begin to cover it!" Mom's hands flew to her hips, her stance wide and unyielding. "And I will cause as many scenes as it takes until justice is served!"

"Justice will be served through proper channels, not through intimidation or harassment," Polk said, his voice firm but his eyes betraying a hint of empathy.

"Are you telling me you think Drew is capable of murder?" Before Dad or I could stop her, she got in Ernie's face again and wagged a finger under his nose. "Your so-called 'investigation' reeks more than these rental shoes!"

"What I think and what I can prove aren't always the same thing."

"Mom. Stop!" She wasn't helping anything. Secretly,

though, part of me cheered her on. Drew didn't deserve to be behind bars, and her outrage on his behalf felt good.

"Fine," she huffed, the fire in her eyes simmering to a low burn. I exhaled a silent sigh of relief. Crisis averted— for now, at least.

"Sorry," I mouthed to Chief Polk, who nodded stiffly before retreating to the snack bar, likely to drown his sorrows in a plate of nachos.

"Let's focus on the game, shall we?" I steered Mom toward her lane and stayed there for a minute to make sure she wouldn't go back to Ernie for round two. Not knowing what else to do, Neena and David kept up appearances by picking out their balls and putting our names into the electronic scoring system.

"Is it my turn?" Mom smiled at her teammates to gloss over the unpleasantness and picked up her ball. Meeting my father's gaze over her head, I figured we both knew better than to think the issue had been dropped. It was merely shelved, awaiting the perfect moment to resurface. And knowing my mother, that moment wouldn't stay shelved for long.

The clatter of pins and the murmur of Saturday night chatter filled the air as I rejoined my companions and waited for the right time to talk to Donnie Giacomo. Better to let him settle into his game first.

"All right, let's see if you've got any secret talents hiding up those sleeves," Neena teased, glancing over at David, who was cradling a glossy bowling ball as if it might hatch into something wild.

"Trust me, my talents are strictly inn-related," he replied with a crooked smile that didn't quite mask the interest in his eyes. "I haven't bowled since I was a kid, and then we only had candlepin. But I'll give it a shot."

"Go on, then. Impress me," she urged, giving him a playful nudge towards the lane.

David took a deep breath and approached the line, his tall frame bending into an awkward but strangely endearing form. The ball rolled down the alley with the tentative hesitation of a fawn on ice, but to our collective surprise, it knocked down a respectable seven pins.

"Look at you, not half bad!" Neena hooted.

"Beginner's luck," David shrugged as his second ball took down two more pins, though his grin betrayed a hint of pride. "Your turn."

As we continued the game with Neena and David exchanging tips and laughter, I couldn't help but feel a warmth at the sight. They were good for each other—Neena with the vivacious charm she'd begun to embrace again and David emerging from his shell, finding solace in her light.

We'd bowled a few frames with Neena firmly in the lead before I noticed Donnie and his team were taking a snack break. I decided we should do the same. I caught up with him and got into the ordering line behind him.

"Oh," I mumbled, plastering on my most casual face. "Hey, Donnie! Fancy seeing you here tonight. I didn't know you were in the summer league." Not surprising since the only thing I did know about him outside of the context of Jerry's murder was that he'd been on the framing crew when David had some work done on the Marlow Inn. Since I'd been helping David with his plans for the property, I'd met the subcontractors and most workers with Donnie being one of the latter.

"Hey! It's Everly, right?" He flashed a grin, turned to check his place in the line, then turned back and nodded toward where my parents were bowling. "That's your mother over there?"

"It is." I didn't elaborate. Now that I had him here, it seemed entirely ridiculous to be at a bowling alley while my husband was in jail, and worse, I wasn't sure how to bring up the subject of Jerry's murder.

When the line moved, he turned away and took a step forward, leaving me to contemplate the sunglasses perched ridiculously on the back of his head despite the dim lighting indoors. With the line dwindling ahead of us, I needed to say something before I lost my chance.

"Do you bowl here often?" I tapped him on the shoulder.

"I've been a league bowler every summer since I got into the junior league when I was twelve. Gives me something to do, and it's always a good time."

"Sure, sure," I said. "Speaking of good times, weren't you up in Hackinaw a few weeks back? Hanging with that cute blond singer?"

Donnie's smile tightened just a fraction, but he recovered quickly. "That was one hell of a night. Plenty of booze, a hot woman, and lots of laughs. Can't complain."

"More than one night, from what I heard." My voice was light, but I watched him closely, trying to read any flicker of guilt or unease.

"Ah, well…" He shifted his weight, scratching at his neck, and grinned. "I've got no ties, so I go where the fun is. Cost me a job or two, but Lita was worth it, if you know what I mean."

Based on his leering smile, I was sure I did. "Is she here? I'd love to meet her."

"Naw. She wasn't local or anything. She caught a gig at the resort, and when it was over, she moved on. Just one of those fun and done things."

If he was pissed about it, he hadn't told his face because the cheerful grin never slipped once.

"Shame about Jerry Kaminski, though. Didn't you work with him?" I carefully searched Donnie's face for signs of guilt.

"Damn shame." Instead of guilt, I saw only sorrow. "He was a decent guy. No matter what anyone says. Hey, wasn't it your man who got arrested for killing him? You don't look too broken up about it."

"Looks can be deceiving." My face flamed. I should never have come here. "Since I had no interest in Jerry or his intentions, Drew had no reason to kill him, but maybe you did."

"Over a lost job or two that I didn't even care about?" Donnie barked out a laugh. "Hardly. For what it's worth, Jerry could be a jerk, and he couldn't keep his eyes—or his hands—off of anything with boobs."

Being relegated to a thing with boobs didn't earn Donnie any points with me. "I suppose some women are flattered by that type of attention. Did he put his eyes or his hands on someone you wanted?"

Strong emotion flickered in his eyes but was gone so quickly I wasn't sure if it had happened or was a trick of the light.

"We didn't have the same taste in women. I figure his ex had something to do with his death. Or else that guy she married. You gotta be pretty pissed to bash someone's head in, ya know? A woman gets dumped, she's likely to hold a grudge."

"Did Jerry leave his wife?" That wasn't the way Cindy told the story. Talking to Donnie had brought up more questions than answers.

He shrugged. "Dunno. Just the way I figured it went down because he bragged about ditching the old ball and chain for a better model."

"You're up," I nodded toward the counter, wondering if Donnie had just broken this case wide open.

"Sweet," Oblivious to the undercurrents swirling around him, Donnie ordered a beer. "Anyway, I should get back to it. Got a reputation to maintain!"

"See you around," I said, unsure if I'd need to talk to him again. Unless he had a better motive than lost wages, I couldn't picture Good Time Donnie whacking someone with a tire iron. Not bothering to order, I headed back to my friends.

"Strike!" Neena's triumphant shout snapped me back

to the present, and I cheered alongside her, clapping my hands as David sent her a mock bow in admiration. Their laughter was like a peek of the sun through the clouds amidst the storm brewing just beneath the surface of this cheery Saturday night, and I noticed she put her hand on his shoulder as she passed him to sit next to me.

"Everly," a voice sing-songed from behind me, dragging out my name like a broken record. I spun around, feigning surprise at the sight of Jerry's unwelcome form strolling across the lanes, bowling balls zipping right through him until he got to mine. Ah, Jerry. Always showing up at the most inconvenient times.

"Ugh," I murmured under my breath, keeping my eyes fixed on the pins at the end of the lane as if I could will them to topple over with my gaze alone. He'd been gone most of the day, but I could have used more time. "What are you doing here?"

Jerry waggled his eyebrows, giving me a lopsided grin. "Just came for the scenery. You can't yell privacy at me here. This is a public place."

I'd leaned down to release my ball, which gave him a good view of my cleavage. Standing, I buttoned the top buttons of my shirt.

"Charming," I replied dryly, eyes flicking toward Mom, who was now scrutinizing the score monitor with the intensity of a hawk. She could see Jerry just as well as I could but preferred to pretend ghosts didn't exist and refused to speak to them unless it was essential.

"You got a spare. How about a little victory dance?" He

waggled his hips, and I was glad I hadn't ordered food earlier, or I might have lost it right there.

"Everything okay over here?" Mom asked, having noticed Jerry and, for once, decided not to ignore the situation.

"Yep, just picturing Jerry's face on the pins," I took a page from her book and pretended he didn't exist. "Makes the whole game more satisfying when the ball takes them down. Worth it to keep those strikes coming."

"Right." She eyed me for a beat longer before leaning close and telling me she'd spoken to Donnie and repeated the same basic story he'd told me. If he was lying, his lies were consistent.

Still there when it was my turn again, Jerry kept up a running commentary as I released the ball with a flick of my wrist, watching it hurtle down the lane toward ten versions of Jerry's imagined face with what I hoped was enough force to knock the pins into next week—or at least off of their smug little marks. The ball connected, and the pins scattered with satisfying force.

"Strike!" Neena cheered from behind me.

"Nice shot, Everly," David added, clapping me on the back as I turned around, trying to hide that I'd been holding my breath.

"Thanks," I replied, offering them a slightly smug smile. "Visualization is the key."

I sat, the worn faux leather clinging to the back of my jeans, and watched Neena take her turn. She rolled a decent spare, and David followed with a respectable seven-pin split but washed up on his second throw. They were flirting between frames, their laughter easy and light —a sharp contrast to the heavy aura clinging to my spirit like socks to my favorite sweater when I forgot the dryer sheets.

"Everly, your turn again," David called out, oblivious to my most recent ghostly encounter.

"Right, coming!" I stood, feeling the tingle of anticipation mingled with frustration. I grabbed the ball I'd chosen, a deep blue that matched the color of the evening sky outside the alley's large windows.

"What happened just before that tire iron came down on your head?" I whispered fiercely, picturing Jerry's face again while lining up my shot.

The question gave Jerry pause as he foolishly tried to remember.

"Wait." Jerry's eyes widened. "There was a scent— something distinct. I remember smelling it right before everything went dark."

"What kind of scent?" I prodded, my senses on high alert.

"Something sweet...like cherries. Yes, cherries!" Jerry exclaimed.

"Cherries?" I echoed, my mind racing. That was a new clue, at least. Not much of one, but something.

"Everly, your second throw?" Neena prompted.

I looked to see that I'd only knocked down half the pins.

"Your mother's quite the bowler." Jerry's voice slithered into my head, and I nearly jumped out of my skin. "And she fills out those jeans she's wearing, too. Hot mothers have hot daughters. It's a thing."

Furious, I countered, "Focus, Jerry. You smelled cherries, and then what?"

"I died." As I'd hoped, he focused hard enough to send his body into a case of pre-poof shivers, and then he was gone. I probably should have felt bad for making him go away again, but I couldn't muster a single shred of regret.

I quickly picked up the spare without his constant nattering in my ear. And still, I came in a close second to Neena at the end of the game, with David taking third.

Jack still hadn't texted by the time I got home, and when my call went straight to voicemail, I gave up and spent another night tossing and turning when I should have been sleeping.

CHAPTER TWELVE

"Well, hello there," Dolly walked through the door, and I mean that literally, without bothering to knock the next morning. Despite what you may have heard, most ghosts don't get off on knocking on walls, and while Dolly was no exception to that rule, she also wasn't like most ghosts. Dolly Tibbets wasn't just a presence. She had presence.

"Who's that, dear?" Cheryl called down from upstairs, where she'd gone to make up the bed she and her husband shared in my guest room. "I didn't hear the doorbell. Is everything okay?"

"Sure. It's just my friend Dolly. She just stopped by for a quick visit."

"Helloo," Dolly called up the stairs. I felt the blood drain from my face.

"Oh. That's nice, then. Does she want something to eat?"

"No. I can safely say that she doesn't."

"Okay," Cheryl sounded doubtful but didn't come down to see for herself if my hostessing skills were lacking. "When Quinn returns, please send him up here?"

My father-in-law had gone off with my dog for a walk around the neighborhood.

"Jeez, Dolly. What's with all the yelling? Cheryl heard you."

"I know." Dolly winked at me. "But she doesn't know me from a hole in the ground, so I thought it would be fun to pretend I'm still among the living. I get bored being invisible. Sometimes, I zip off to Bangor and walk around where people can see me just for fun."

In that getup? I thought but managed not to say. Dolly had died in the eighties, and so had her fashion sense. Well, except for her hairstyle, which was at least a decade behind. Unlike any other ghost I'd met, she changed her outfit occasionally, but her go-to look consisted of leggings—today's a pink and black leopard print—under one of the smocks that made up her hairdressing uniform. She wore her hair piled high, her cascading curls tamed with enough hairspray that you could smell it on her whether she appeared or not. Let's just say she'd stand out in a crowd.

"Even so, it would be better if you could be a little less corporeal when my in-laws are around," I whispered fiercely, hoping Drew's mother couldn't hear any of the conversation from upstairs. Seeing Dolly might be fine, but there would be questions if Mrs. Parker caught wind of any ghostly business. The kind I couldn't answer without either lying or freaking her out. I'd rather not do either of those things.

"Darling," Dolly ushered herself further into the house, "I would never dream of intruding on family time. But I simply had to tell you—I've found myself a pet!"

"A pet?" Like a pet project? Not Jerry. It couldn't be. No one in their right mind would make a pet project out of him. "What kind of pet?"

"The cutest little kitty cat you ever did see."

I blinked at the sheer absurdity. "So, you're what? Stealing food from the grocery store? Or from Mara to feed a stray cat?" There were worse things she could do, I supposed.

"No, silly." Dolly waved that away while stifling a giggle. "A ghost cat. One of the dearly departed. No feeding involved."

"But that's—" I sputtered, then rethought the situation. "Actually, kind of sweet. I didn't know pets could linger on this side of the veil."

"It's the first one I've ever seen. Must have some kind of unfinished business."

My brows shot up. "I can't even imagine what that might be. A half-dead mouse that needs eating? Or maybe a butthole that didn't get licked thoroughly enough?"

Dolly's laugh tinkled through the room.

"You've got me, but it's the most darling thing. She's white with wispy whiskers and a bushy tail that follows behind when she goes through walls," she cooed, clapping her hands together but making no sound.

"Shh," I hushed her. "Keep the ghost talk down. Or,

better yet, keep it non-existent. We'll talk about your phantom feline later."

"Fair enough. Now, tell me where you're at with Jerry because that boy needs to get crossed over. I caught him coming out of the bathroom at the salon the other day when Cindy had been in there. No decorum whatsoever with that one."

"I'm doing the best I can." I brought her up to date on the investigation and wasn't surprised when she pooh-poohed the idea that Jerry had broken up with his wife and not the other way around. "You know men, they're always trying to save face. Trust me, Cindy was the dumper and Jerry the dumpee."

Thinking she knew better than I would, I listened to the latest gossip, mainly to make Dolly happy, not because I was interested in hearing the story of Mr. Sanderson's toupee malfunction at the grocery store. "My friends will be here any minute to figure out our next moves."

"I'm going," Dolly held up a hand at what I'd considered a subtle hint. "Just keep me in the loop and let me know if you want me to haunt anyone in particular. I think I'd make a pretty good spy."

"Ooh, that's interesting. I might take you up on that. Pop back in later. But keep it quiet this time. You know, like spies do."

"Gotcha." Dolly waggled her fingers at me and winked out just as the doorbell rang.

"It's open," I yelled out, and then had to listen to a short lecture from Cheryl on personal safety. She came halfway down the stairs to deliver it and didn't seem to care if Patrea and Chris heard the gentle dressing down. And when she pointed out there'd just been a murder in town, I realized I'd lost the argument, anyway.

"I won't do it again. I promise." That seemed to satisfy her, so she went back upstairs.

Holding out the plastic container of baked goods I didn't know when she'd had time to make, Patrea grinned at me. "If I promise not to murder anyone, can I come in?"

"What's in the box?" I grinned back. "You know I'm a cheap date when it comes to baked goods."

"This and that," she waved her hand. "The almond croissants are my new obsession."

I was sold if they were anywhere near as good as her chocolate ones.

"One of them, anyway," Chris said without censure. In a whirlwind holiday romance, Patrea had won the heart of the man long considered Mooselick River's most curmudgeonly but sought-after bachelor. She'd softened some of his rough edges while he'd helped her slow down and appreciate a more balanced life.

"Once we get Drew out of jail, I promise I'll go back to being a tree farmer's wife with a couple of part-time gigs."

Having recently hired a paralegal to help in the town's only legal practice, Patrea renovated houses on the side. She was just as happy with a wallpaper steamer in her hand as she was arguing a case in front of a judge. House projects didn't come along every day, and the town's legal needs tended to be routine, so she had plenty of time to indulge her husband and her love of baking. Now, with the Wentworth project becoming a thing, I thought she might be overestimating her upcoming free time.

When the doorbell rang again, I opened it to let in Neena just as Jacy's pink minivan pull into the space beside my car while David parked his truck behind. The gang was all here, including Jacy's adorable son, Wade.

"Patrea brought baked goods and there's coffee and other beverages in the kitchen," I said once everyone was inside.

"Sweet tea?" Neena said hopefully.

"In the fridge."

Jacy handed Wade over to me so I could bury my face in his little belly and make him giggle. It was the best sound on earth, even if he tangled his fingers in my hair and Brian had to help me get loose. Finally, we all settled in the living room—the adults around the coffee table and little Wade in the portable playpen I kept in the closet for when he came to visit.

As my friends settled into the blue velvet sectional and mismatched chairs of the living room, the mood shifted from casual to focused. The warm summer breeze fluttered through the open windows, carrying the scent of freshly cut grass. On any other day, my heart would have been full. Today, it was on the edge of being broken.

"You first," Patrea said, offering a supportive smile.

"What did you learn at the bowling alley last night?" Her voice was calm but determined, like the steady hand guiding a ship through choppy waters.

"Not much," I responded. "My mother took a verbal swing at Ernie, which was fun to watch."

"Oh, I know all about that." Jacy held out her phone to show the newly minted Mooselick River Community Facebook group. "Someone posted a video."

There she was, in all her rage and glory, my mother giving Ernie a piece of her mind. If someone showed her this, she'd either be mortified or proud. I wasn't sure which.

"She didn't hold back," David said, his smile one of pride. "You've got to love Kitty when she's got her dander up."

He and my parents had become close when he'd moved to town and stayed with them for a few months. My dad and his had been childhood friends and kept in touch, so when David needed rescuing from his own demons, my father stepped in and helped out. Compassion was one of my dad's best traits.

"Even so," Neena said. "I noticed Ernie talking to your dad when we left, and neither looked upset. I wonder if she had a reason for making a scene."

"There is nothing I wouldn't put past Kitty Dupree when she's in mother-bear mode. I'll talk to her and see. Anyway, I got the chance to talk to Donnie. It was an awkward and fairly unenlightening conversation. He admitted he hooked up with the lounge singer in Hackinaw, and he definitely lost his job over it. He didn't seem upset. But more importantly, he said Jerry dumped Cindy, not the other way around."

Her left eyebrow quirked, Jacy said, "That doesn't sound right at all."

Quinn opened the door, and Molly bounded into the room, momentarily stopping the conversation. I sent him upstairs as Cheryl had asked and let things settle again before continuing.

"Dolly popped in this morning, and when I asked, she said Cindy definitely did the dumping. Either way, Donnie didn't seem too concerned about losing a job because of Jerry. Or for missing work in the first place. But still, there was a moment when I felt he wasn't being entirely honest. I'm just not sure about what."

I broke off a piece of flaky croissant and chewed it while I got my thoughts in order. "It almost seemed like he was annoyed that some women enjoyed the kind of attention Jerry offered. Or maybe he felt sorry for them. I don't know. It was just a vibe."

Jacy leaned forward, her elbows on her knees, her voice lifting to be heard over Wade's vrooming sounds as he played with his favorite truck. "Okay, so Brian and I took half the list of the people at Cappy's that night and tracked them down for a quick chat."

"I thought you had a date with Brian's folks." I should have known they'd still find a way to help out.

"That was between. Anyhow, other than confirming what we already knew, no one we talked to saw anything helpful. Everyone corroborated Drew's story about the argument, though. Jerry started it, but Drew did not engage. Every person I spoke to had already talked to Ernie and told him the same, so even if we didn't learn anything new, that has to help."

Chris chimed in next, glancing around the room. "While Patrea worked on her defense strategy, I took the other half of the list." His voice was steady and reliable, just like the man himself. "Everyone thought Jerry deserved to get booted, and most were happy to see him go. No one saw him after he left."

"And what about Drew?" Neena asked, her voice laced with concern. "Did anyone see him outside?"

"Well," Chris cleared his throat, drawing all eyes to him. "Actually, there might be something there," he began, hesitant yet earnest. "I ran into Jim Tarkington at the hardware store. He mentioned being at the bar that night, but he wasn't on the list."

"Now that you mention it, I do remember seeing him," Brian said, snapping his fingers. "Totally slipped my mind."

"Jim has a way of fading into the background," Jacy said.

"Anyway," Chris continued, "Jim remembered seeing Drew on his phone in the parking lot. Couldn't nail down a time, though."

"Jim Tarkington?" I quirked an eyebrow, committing the name to memory and trying to dredge up the memory of a face to match the name. "Is that the guy who played Joseph in the Christmas pageant?"

"That would be him," Brian agreed, nodding.

"He was sitting at the table near the window but only noticed anything when he got up to play a round of darts," Chris said. "He said Drew was pacing back and forth, and the conversation seemed intense, but he couldn't say what time it was. He didn't remember seeing Drew leave or return, so I don't know how helpful this is."

"Could be something, or it could be nothing," I mused aloud, tapping my finger against my chin. "Every little detail helps us nail down the timeline, but I don't think we're any farther ahead than we were before. Not without Pete's testimony, if he can even offer one."

"I'm still waiting to hear from Jack. I should know something soon. Otherwise, we're stuck where we've been since Drew was arrested."

"We're not," Patrea leaned across Jacy to pat me on the arm. "We've established possible motives, begun a list of suspects, and loosely established a timeline I can use to cast doubts when we go before the judge. There are still tire prints and gray truck angles that need work. Besides, you know how these things go. It always takes a minute, and if we can get anything useful from Pete, that should help me with the bail hearing. With Drew out on bail, we'll have more time to devote to the investigation."

I sighed. "It doesn't feel like nearly enough."

"You should know people have been calling my office offering to give character witness statements."

"She's right," Brian nodded, his warm eyes meeting mine. I'd known him as long as Jacy had, and as her other half, he had always been there for me. "Every single person I've spoken to has offered to stand up in court and testify that Drew shrugged Jerry off like he meant nothing. That should weigh in his favor."

Maybe it would be enough to counteract the evidence. My gut was not convinced. Still, as I guided the last of my friends to the door, my heart had been lightened by their unwavering commitment. "You guys are the best, you know that?" I said, mustering a grin.

"Right back atcha, sweetie," Patrea flashed me a smile.

"You're family," Jacy chimed in, her voice steady as a drumbeat, "and now, so is Drew. He's not going down for something he didn't do. No way, no how."

David clapped a solid hand on my shoulder, his gaze solemn but unyielding even though he didn't say anything.

Neena followed Jacy out after they'd hugged me, leaving Brian and the baby for last. "Give Auntie Everly a kiss." He leaned over so I could plant one on each chubby cheek.

Closing the door, I turned back to the living room, now strangely quiet. The absence of lively discussion left a hollowness that echoed off the walls.

"Everly!" Cheryl's voice, tinged with uncertainty, cut through my thoughts as she called down to me from upstairs. "Something odd happened. I think you need to see."

What now?

I found her in the room where they'd been staying, holding a decades-old pantyhose egg while her husband sat on the chair near the window, an odd look on his face. Having found several of Catherine's secret stashes, I know what I'd see when she pulled the egg apart and dumped the contents on the bed. From experience, I figured there'd be around a hundred and fifty dollars. That seemed to be her go-to amount.

"One of my socks fell behind, and when I pulled out the drawer to get it, I found this," she said, her brows knitting together as she offered the now-empty egg to me.

The question she asked was, "Were you hiding money in here?"

'Were you hiding money from Drew?' was the question I sensed she wanted answered.

"Me? Hide money in a pantyhose egg?" I laughed, taking the oddly literal nest egg from her hands and turning it over. "No. This is just one of the constant surprises lurking in every corner of this house."

Cheryl's eyes widened slightly, the corners of her mouth twitching upward. "So, you didn't put it there?"

"Absolutely not." I shook my head, still amused by the find.

Drew had known of Catherine's eccentricities before we'd reconnected. He'd come here to help his uncle deliver some items stashed away in the back rooms. He'd been asked to keep her secret, and he had, even from his parents. That sense of honor was just one more reason why I knew he hadn't killed Jerry Kaminski.

"This is the work of Catherine Willowby. She had more hiding spots than a squirrel preparing for winter. And trust me, you are not the first person to stumble on one of her hidden treasures."

"Really?" Cheryl leaned against the old mahogany dresser, her curiosity piqued. "Drew mentioned your house had some items left in it by the woman who'd lived here. I thought he meant a sofa too large to move or some stray pieces of furniture."

"Oh, it was a lot more than that." I explained that Mrs. Willowby had been a childless widow with no other family, and after she'd passed, the town had taken ownership of the house when the taxes lapsed. "It's my theory that whoever they sent to assess the place took a look around and decided it would be less of a hassle just to resell it with the contents intact."

Motioning for them to follow me, I led them to one of the smaller bedrooms I hadn't yet cleaned out. With a flourish, I dragged open the top dresser drawer to show the sheer detritus shoved inside.

Cheryl's eyes widened. "Are those unopened boxes of silk stockings?"

Grinning, I nodded. "How many pairs would you say are in there?"

"Good grief," she shook her head. "There must be two dozen at least."

"Probably." And even when I opened the closet door to

display carefully bagged garments crammed from one end to the other, I could safely say she hadn't seen anything yet. "Catherine liked to collect things, and what she collected, she kept."

"This is—" Cheryl had been rendered speechless.

"I consider her to be my benefactor. When my marriage ended, I'd had almost nothing and very little money. I'd walked into the town office to look for rentals or job listings on the notice board, and Martha Tipton had saved my life. She talked me into buying this place and everything in it for the back taxes. I went from being potentially homeless to owning a fully furnished home in less time than it takes for a background check to rent an apartment. There was even a car in the garage."

Shaking his head as if it were all too much to take in, Quinn said, "That is quite a story. Maybe you should write a book about your experiences."

"I'd have to make it a work of fiction because no one would believe the truth. And this is barely a scratch on the surface of it."

"Really?" Cheryl seemed delighted. "What else have you found?"

"Love letters in the attic, a collection of rare stamps inside a hollowed-out book, and a vintage bottle of wine tucked behind a loose brick in the cellar." I shrugged, feeling a kinship with the eccentric former owner. "Seems like Catherine believed in spreading her wealth around. Literally."

"Fascinating," Quinn said. "Was the wine any good?"

I barked out a laugh. "Your son wanted to know the same thing, and no, it had turned to vinegar. Being the practical man that he is, Drew looked up the maker and year in case it was valuable before we cracked it open."

Speaking of him, in the context of good times seemed to comfort his parents.

"If you're up for it, I can show you more. But you have to take a solemn oath to keep Catherine's hoarding proclivities a secret. She took great pains to keep parts of herself hidden from people in this town, and I wouldn't want her secrets to get out now."

Miming putting a key to her lips and turning the lock, Cheryl looked at me with twinkling eyes. "Mum's the word. I promise, and so does Quinn."

"Course I do."

"Okay, follow me." I led them downstairs.

"Jacy sold a fair bit of the extra furniture on consignment. In fact, she and Neena credit Catherine with being the reason they were able to open their shop," I began with a wry smile, watching as Cheryl's eyebrows rose in anticipation.

"Every drawer in this house was a surprise party waiting to happen." I chuckled, remembering the time I found a set of dentures grinning up at me from a velvet-lined jewelry box. "One time, I pulled open a drawer expecting linens and instead discovered a family of taxidermied mice wearing tiny top hats."

Cheryl snorted with laughter, her earlier anxiety melting away into curiosity. It was the first time I'd seen a light in her eyes since Drew's arrest. "I'd have screamed the house down."

"I nearly did," I said, leading them through the hallway toward the door to the addition.

"Behind this door lies Catherine's true legacy," I proclaimed, throwing my arms wide as we stepped into the cavernous space. Despite the sheer number of items I'd sent to Jacy to sell and the space we'd cleared for Drew's camping equipment, the volume of stuff crammed into the space was staggering. If a second-hand shop and a recycling center had a mad affair and somehow managed to spawn a love child, this was where it would go to live.

To give my in-laws the full effect, I hit the switches on the bank of light near the door and waited for their reaction.

"What the hell?" Quinn said as he took in the series of painted and collaged mannequin torsos with can lights set into the arm and leg holes that marched down the length of the ceiling.

"Catherine was an artist."

"Is that what we're calling it?" Cheryl murmured, her eyes wide as saucers.

Pride swelled in me for the woman I'd come to know through her journals and the multitude of items hidden away in her house. "Her work has a following, but no one in Mooselick River knew." That wasn't entirely true. Neena's husband—my ex-high school sweetheart—had taken his knowledge of Catherine's hoarding to the grave.

"She lived here in obscurity and turned the things she collected into works other people did."

"I've never seen anything like this."

"Exactly!" I laughed, taking in the organized chaos. "Catherine spent the years between her husband's death and hers tucking away herself and anything she thought she could use back here. She experimented with painting and pottery-making and, as you can see, collaged some of her finds to turn them into other things. I've been slowly going through it all, but it will take years to find all her secrets."

"It's exciting, isn't it? Knowing you could find another set of stuffed mice," Cheryl said, running a hand over a silk shawl that shimmered with embroidered peacocks. "Or the lost crown jewels of some obscure monarchy."

"Wouldn't that be something?" I smiled, amused by the thought. "I tell you, if these walls could talk, they'd have stories for days."

"She'd be glad you were the one to find and respect her things," Quinn observed from the doorway, his voice deep and steady. Despite his few words, I felt the warmth of his silent support filling the room like sunlight.

"I hope so. I barely knew her when she was alive, but everything I've found so far tells me she was an amazing woman," I said. "How can I not feel a kinship with someone who understands the value of a good hidey-hole?"

"Or a pantyhose egg stuffed with cash," Cheryl added,

her tone lighter now, playful even. "What will you do with your windfall?"

"Same thing I've done with all the others. I donate her egg money to children's arts programs in her name. I hope that's what she'd want."

"What a lovely thing to do. I'm sure she'd be pleased."

I hoped she'd be even more pleased that showing off her collection had created a moment of lightness between Cheryl and me. One we'd desperately needed.

CHAPTER THIRTEEN

My phone rang just as we came out of Catherine's back rooms. Jack's number flashed on the screen, and my gut warned me before answering that this wouldn't be a good call.

"Everly, it's Jack. Pete's missing," he said without any pleasantries.

"Missing?"

"He's not at his place, and the last time anyone saw him was on Wednesday," Jack replied, his voice tinged with urgency. "He could be anywhere by now, and I'm not as familiar with his habits as Drew."

"Okay, I'm on it," I cut in, feeling a gnawing in my stomach. Whether Pete could offer any help with his defense wouldn't matter to Drew nearly as much as the man's safety. "You hang tight. I'll go talk to Drew right now and get back to you. Can you give me fifteen minutes?"

"I'm not going anywhere. Tell Drew I'm sorry I didn't rush over here. I didn't think he'd bolt."

I didn't know Jack all that well, but I didn't need to know him to hear the concern in his voice. "It's okay."

The station wasn't far, but the drive felt eternal. Once

I'd parked, my flip-flops slapped rhythmically against the parking lot pavement as if marking time.

I pushed open the door to the station and scowled when Carole Ann Wilmette stared at me over the high counter where she handled incoming calls. Thankfully, Ernie was at his desk and assumed I'd come to see Drew.

"Come on," he said. "I'll take you back."

"Thanks."

When the metal door clanged shut behind me, I wondered if the sound of it bothered Drew as much as it did me.

"You're here early." Drew's voice broke through the silence, and my heart clenched at the sound. He was seated on the thin mattress that served as his bed, his broad shoulders hunched forward.

"I am," I said softly, coming to stand in front of his cell. His eyes lifted to meet mine, and there it was—that look. Pain and longing etched across his features so clearly I might as well have been reading the headlines in the Bangor Daily.

"Pete's missing," I blurted out. It felt cruel to drop the bomb without any cushioning, but dancing around the truth wasn't my style or what Drew needed. Time was of the essence.

"Damn it," he muttered, running a hand through his hair.

"I know." I leaned closer, gripping the cold bars. "Jack called. He wanted me to get a list of places to look. Do you have any idea where Pete might have gone?"

Drew leaned back on his bunk, his gaze drifting to the ceiling before he answered. "There's a hidden beach just south of Port Harbor," he said with a sigh. "You won't find the access road on any map or GPS." As he reeled off a very detailed set of directions, I started an email and made notes on my phone.

"Beach near Port Harbor," I echoed, typing rapidly. "Anywhere else?"

"Augusta, maybe," he continued, scratching his stubbled chin. "The Veteran's Memorial Cemetery. He goes there to visit the grave of a buddy from his platoon." His eyes were distant now, shadowed by memories I couldn't fathom.

"Got it. Cemetery in Augusta." My fingers were a blur as I added notes. "And didn't you say something about an old church in Belfast once?"

"Right, St. Francis, the one he went to as a boy. He might seek refuge there if things got too heavy." Drew's voice was laced with concern, only for Pete and none for the precarious thread his own future hung upon.

"Okay. Jack's going to start searching," I said after sending the list. The quick buzz of my phone confirmed Jack's reply: 'On it.'

"Tell him thanks," Drew muttered, his gratitude mingled with frustration for not being the one to conduct the search.

Before I could offer any more reassurances, a chill snaked along the back of my neck—the telltale sign of a spectral presence. Turning slightly, I saw the unwanted form of Jerry Kaminski standing far too close for my comfort. At least Ernie wasn't within hearing distance.

"Jerry's here," I explained to Drew, not even trying to mask my annoyance. Jerry's fixation on me had been problematic enough when he was alive; dead, it was downright exasperating.

"Consorting with the enemy, I see," he said, his voice tinged with the bitterness only the wrongfully departed possessed. "I thought you had more sense than to tie yourself up with the likes of him. If only the jerk could hear me. Got a few choice words for the man who killed me."

"Pretty sure he's got a few for you, too," I muttered. "You know you can show yourself to the living if you really want to. You just have to want it bad enough and focus." It was one of those psychic tidbits that felt less like wisdom and more like a parlor trick.

"Really?" His brow furrowed skeptically.

"Really," I assured him. "Give it a go."

With a determined squint that would've been comical under different circumstances, Jerry concentrated. Slowly, the edges of his figure became more solid until, not nearly as imposing as he might wish, he stood before Drew.

"Hello, Jerry," Drew greeted the apparition of Jerry Kaminski with as much warmth as he deserved, which is to say none at all.

"This moment brought to you," I quipped, though my heart wasn't quite in it, "by Mooselick River's very own ghost whisperer. And the letter C for contemptible creepy chowderhead."

"That was uncalled for," Jerry insisted.

"I know a lot more letters, Jerry. Do you want me to use them?"

The smarmy smile fell off his face as he turned to Drew and began to reel off the list of things he'd miss out on now that he was no longer among the living.

"Summer barbecues, man," Jerry lamented, his voice grating with annoyance. "I'll never flip another burger, never taste that charred, smoky goodness." He threw his arms wide, nearly passing through the bars before he caught himself. "And weddings! I won't get to see my sister say 'I do' or tie one on at the reception."

As Jerry continued to list the things he'd miss—Christmas mornings, first dates, even the simple pleasure of feeling rain on his skin—I saw Drew's hard stare melt into something soft, empathetic. His eyes, usually so full of determination and warmth when he looked at me, now held a deep sorrow as they locked onto Jerry's.

"Even the hangovers," Jerry said, almost wistfully. "I'd give anything for just one more blinding headache."

"Dude," Drew said, the sympathy in his voice somehow reaching across the barrier separating life from death. "I'm sorry you won't get to do any of those things again. I didn't kill you, but missing out on all that life isn't something I'd wish on my worst enemy."

"Didn't you, though?"

"Look at me, Jerry," Drew ordered, his voice intense.

"You weren't my enemy. At all. You were an annoyance to me and nothing more. To be honest, I felt sorry for you more than anything because you never had a shot with my wife."

"God's honest truth," I said, holding my hand up.

It was then I saw it—the moment Jerry's ranting ceased, and his eyes narrowed, scrutinizing Drew's gaze with a newfound intensity. There was a flicker of realization there, a silent communication that passed between them.

"Hey," I stepped forward, breaking the stillness. "What was that look all about?"

Jerry turned to me slowly, the edges of his form beginning to waver like the heat haze on asphalt. "He didn't kill me." Jerry looked flummoxed, his earlier fervor gone.

"About time you got a taste of the truth," I said, throwing my hands up in disgust. "I've been telling you that since the beginning."

"Sorry about that. No hard feelings, eh?"

Before I could tell him there were, Jerry dissipated into nothingness, leaving behind a silence that hummed with unspoken words.

"That was fun," Drew said softly, bringing my attention back to him.

"Your eyes always do speak volumes, my love," I replied, giving him a smile. "At least I won't have to hear him rant about my poor choices in men anymore."

"There's that silver lining you always seem to find. Now, if the clouds can clear enough to shine some light on the truth before I go mad in here, that would be good."

"It's that bad?"

Drew's eyes flickered with a hint of mischief, the kind that led to spontaneous midnight picnics by the river or an expedition into my dusty attic. He leaned in, his voice barely above a whisper. "Carole Ann puts the emergency line on speakerphone sometimes."

"And?" I arched an eyebrow, pressing closer to the cold metal bars, intrigued despite myself.

"And I can hear the calls from here," he chuckled lightly, shaking his head. "You know Mrs. Casellas? She's in Riley's Silver Sneakers class."

"Cute little old lady who wears those bedazzled jogging suits?"

"That's the one." He nodded. "It seems her husband had a fall last night and needed some help getting back on his feet."

I didn't see what was so funny about that. "Was he hurt?"

"Not badly, or else I wouldn't be laughing about it, but he'd taken a little something to help things out in the bedroom." When I frowned because I didn't get it, he elaborated. "A little blue pill."

"Oh." It dawned on me what he meant, and my brain treated me to a mental image I could have lived without, but I still didn't see the humor in the situation, so I said so.

"Carole Ann put the call on speaker, and I heard Mrs.

Casellas yelling, 'Wally fell and broke his willy. I need someone to come and get him up.'"

"No!" I gasped, both hands covering my mouth as a giggle escaped me.

"Yup, the next call was from someone I didn't know." Drew's eyes sparkled with unrestrained glee. "This guy said he'd had a theft and needed the police to come. When Carole Ann asked for the particulars, he said he'd cut himself a piece of pie before he went to the bathroom, and when he came back, it was gone."

"We have a pie thief in town?"

"When Carole Ann asked if he knew who might have taken it, this guy went on to describe the suspect. Said it was a 'suspicious-looking raccoon' with shifty eyes and a bushy tail that had come in through the pet door."

"Stop it!" I clamped a hand over my stomach as laughter bubbled up. The image of Ernie slapping the cuffs on a trash panda was too much. "That can't be real."

"Cross my heart," he replied, grinning now. "Carole Ann told him to call animal control and hung up on him."

"Only in Mooselick River," I managed to say between chuckles, shaking my head in disbelief.

"Sometimes I think we're living in a sitcom no one told us about," Drew mused, the humor in his voice tinged with warmth.

The heavy pall that hung over us lifted for a moment, replaced by the ridiculousness of small-town life. The kind of place where everyone knew each other's business, where a pie thief could be a critter from your own backyard, and where love, as quirky as it may come, was always just around the corner.

"Speaking of sitcoms, you should have seen your mom's face when she discovered one of Catherine's nest eggs in the back of the dresser in the room I put them in. She thought I was squirreling away funds behind your back."

Drew's eyes crinkled, a mixture of amusement and concern dancing across his features. "She said that to you?"

"Not in so many words, but the implication was there. I explained the vagaries of Catherine and took them on a tour of the addition. Your mom was all ready to start hunting for the crown jewels of some obscure monarchy. Her words, not mine."

He chuckled, though it was strained around the edges. "That sounds like Mom. She's always up for an adventure."

The humor ebbed away, and Drew's expression grew somber. "How are they holding up, really?" His voice dropped, a note of vulnerability threading through the words. "I know they're trying to be strong for me, but—"

"Your parents are some of the toughest people I've met, Drew." I meant every word, feeling their resilience as an echo of our own shared determination. "They're worried, sure, but they believe in you. And they're not alone in that."

"Thanks, hon." He reached out, fingers brushing

against mine between the bars, a fleeting touch that held the weight of the world.

We sat there in silence for a moment, the hum of the overhead lights and the distant murmur of activity outside the cell a stark reminder of where we were. Drew's hand retreated slowly, and I slid my keys out of my pocket.

"Guess it's time for me to head out," I said, the reluctance heavy in my voice. The shadows cast by the bars seemed to stretch longer now, as if unwilling to let go of the light.

"Thank you for helping me help Pete," Drew replied, his gaze never leaving mine. "And for everything else you're doing. For believing in me when it feels like the world doesn't."

"Always," I whispered, standing up and wrapping my arms around myself as if I could ward off the chill that had nothing to do with the temperature of the room.

"I love you."

"Same goes."

With one last look, I turned and walked away from the cell. As I left the station, the summer sun felt too bright, the bustle of town too cheerful for the turmoil churning inside me. But I carried on, fueled by the unshakeable belief that somehow, some way, we'd get through this catastrophe.

It was a few minutes shy of noon when I trudged up the steps to my house. The air was thick with the scent of summer blooms, a fragrant reminder of life's relentless march even when human affairs felt paused in uncertainty.

I pushed open the front door, expecting Molly to greet me, but instead, the murmur of familiar voices hit me like a welcome wave. There, in the heart of my home, were my parents and in-laws gathered around the kitchen table that was cluttered with the beginnings of an impromptu potluck lunch.

"There you are!" My mother's voice soared above the rest, and she enveloped me in a hug that smelled of rose-water and comfort. "We thought you could use some family time."

"Hey, kiddo," my dad added, his eyes crinkling at the edges as he gave me one of his patented hugs that somehow managed to squeeze the tension right out of me.

"We're having a getting-to-know-you lunch," my mother-in-law chimed, her smile warm and inviting.

"Indeed." My father-in-law nodded as he slid a foil-covered pan out of the oven where it had been keeping warm. "You were nearly late."

I allowed myself a small smile, aware of how much I needed this—their presence, their normalcy. The investigation into who had murdered Jerry Kaminski had hit a dead end, and my mind had become a carousel of worry and what-ifs. But here, at this moment, I was reminded that life still offered pockets of peace and joy.

"What have I missed so far?" I chuckled, slipping off my shoes and joining them at the table. My mom pushed a plate piled high with her famous meatloaf toward me while my dad poured me a glass of iced tea, beads of condensation forming to race down the side.

"Only your mom's hilarious retelling of the Great Garden Gnome Heist of '98," my mother-in-law teased, and we all laughed, the story as well-worn and comfortable as a favorite sweater.

Lunch passed in a blur of newly shared memories and gentle ribbing, the weight on my chest lightening with every chuckle and fond glance. It was these moments, I realized, that stitched the fabric of our lives together—simple threads of connection that held strong through the toughest times.

After my folks had gone, Drew's mother suggested watching a movie to keep our minds off the impending bail hearing. Quinn wanted action or sci-fi, while Cheryl preferred a comedy. We settled for Independence Day since it had elements of all three.

As evening settled in, painting the sky in shades of orange and purple, I found myself reluctant to let go of the cocoon of family warmth. But the day's worries finally caught up with me, and I needed a breather, so I faked a yawn.

"Time to turn in," Drew's dad observed with a knowing look.

"Big day tomorrow," Cheryl said softly. "We should all get some rest."

"Okay," I murmured, standing up and stretching. "I'm glad you're here."

With a chorus of goodnights and soft smiles, they climbed the stairs to their room while I let Molly out one last time and locked up. Jack had sent a steady stream of texts all day. First to tell me he'd struck out in Belfast and later to say Pete wasn't in Augusta, but somebody had seen him at the cemetery the day before, which was somewhat comforting news.

As I drifted off, I thought of Drew and the mess we were in. I hadn't felt like myself since I'd watched Ernie lead him from the atrium. This wasn't the same as when I'd left Paul. Walking away from him had set me adrift, but not like this. What I'd felt for him hadn't been love; if I hadn't realized that before, I did now. What I had with Drew was real. Deep and abiding.

Letting him go to prison for something he didn't do was not in my life plan. But, with no new leads, the only thing I could do was keep looking and put my trust in Patrea. She was a staunch friend and ally who would not let us down. And with that final thought, I surrendered to the embrace of dreams, ready to face whatever tomorrow might bring.

CHAPTER FOURTEEN

I'd just loaded the breakfast dishes into the dishwasher when my doorbell dinged two times, then paused and dinged three more. Martha Tipton's signature ring. With a sigh, I hit the button to start the cycle and opened the door to find Martha in her best Sunday clothes flanked by Bess Tate and Patricia Croft—the three women I least wanted to see right now because the unholy trio wouldn't be standing on my front porch unless they wanted something.

"Good morning, Everly," Martha greeted me, her voice carrying the same authority she wielded over town paperwork. Behind her, Bess frowned as if the petunias in my garden had personally offended her while Patricia offered me a smile that seemed to say, 'Brace yourself.'

Absolutely typical when it came to these three.

"Let me guess. We have another urgent matter at hand." I leaned against the door frame with feigned casualness. Maybe they'd take the hint and move on if I didn't invite them in.

"Is that coffee I smell?" Martha tilted her head to look past me, down the hallway toward the kitchen, then took a half step closer.

"Would you like to come in for a cup?" Resistance was futile, so I gave in.

"You have real cream?" Bess eyed me with a measuring gaze that suggested she was sure I didn't.

"Of course."

Since Ernie had finished with it, Drew's folks had taken his truck and gone to visit Jacy's parents for an hour or two. Probably to keep their minds off the impending hearing, which meant I couldn't even use them as an excuse, so I led Martha and her cohorts inside.

"Junior turned in his petition this morning, which led to the scheduling of an emergency town board meeting tonight," Martha announced as she stirred sugar into her coffee. "To discuss this pet cemetery thing."

"Pet cemetery? Whatever will people think of next?" Bess scoffed, crossing her arms. "We should be focusing on putting up new benches at the people cemetery, not some graveyard for critters."

"Animals are part of people's families, Bess," Martha shot back, her tone sharp enough to slice through the morning calm. "Besides, Junior's cat deserves a proper resting place, don't you think?"

Patricia stepped forward, the eternal peacemaker, her hands outstretched as if she could physically press the tension away. "Ladies, let's remember that people are all different, and what they find important might not be the same as your priorities."

"He only wants it because Ken Craven wouldn't sell him a headstone to stick in his backyard. Goes against regulations, and anyway, whoever heard of putting up a headstone for a cat? Next thing you know, we'll be holding dog funerals in the church. Ridiculous. He should just have the thing cremated and keep the ashes. Save everyone a lot of time and trouble."

While my opinion aligned more with Bess's on this one, I didn't see the harm in designating a piece of unused property for the burial of pets.

"I don't think it will come to that, Bess," I chimed in before Martha let fly whatever comment I saw she was winding up to deliver. "I'll admit the hullabaloo seems a bit silly, but I don't see the harm in something that many members of the community will appreciate."

Martha's gaze turned to me, her eyes narrowing slightly. "Hullabaloo? This is an important issue. We need you to work your magic. Get this thing some quick attention so people will turn up to support it."

"Martha, the last thing I want to do is spend this particular evening debating where to bury pets," I replied, but the set of her jaw told me she wasn't having any of it.

"Junior Pease is a respected member of our community," Martha pressed on. "He's been instrumental in keeping the VFW alive and working with the Legion. They do a lot to aid local veterans by teaching them about all the services available. Don't you think a pillar of our community has the right to give his cat a dignified send-off?"

"When you put it like that," I conceded, feeling a mix of exasperation and sympathy, "I don't see how I can refuse. I'll whip up some posts for the town's social media page and get my mother to pass the word along the phone tree. But Martha, I'm telling you, there's no way I'm attending that meeting."

"You're a damn fool for doing any of it," Bess said, shaking her head.

"Thank you, dear," she said, a small victory smile playing on her lips since she'd ultimately talked me into doing what she wanted me to do. "Every bit helps."

I couldn't help but feel a twinge of guilt mixed with amusement. Only in Mooselick River would a town emergency involve a pet burial dispute.

"Now that the stupidity is out of the way," Bess interjected, her voice cutting through the lingering tension like a well-sharpened knife, "I'd like a firsthand account of your mother tearing a strip off Ernie Polk's hide at the bowling alley. What did he say to set her off?" Sipping her coffee, she eyed me over the rim.

I leaned against the kitchen counter, accepting the familiar sensation of being put on the spot by these three. "I assume you've seen the video?"

"More than one. Kitty was in rare form," Bess said with the glee of someone who liked it when someone got stirred up. "Giving the police chief a piece of her mind, right there in front of God and everyone."

Going back to her earlier question, I said, "He didn't do anything to set her off. I think it was partly the tension over what's going on and a touch of guilt for doing something fun while our family is in the midst of a serious problem." Or maybe I was projecting my feelings onto my mother. But I'd been there to interrogate Don Giacomo, so it hadn't been all fun and games to me.

"Yep," Bess confirmed, reaching for her phone. "And it's all over the internet now. My grandson took a video and sent it to me. Want to see?"

"Absolutely not," I replied, but Martha was already crowding next to Bess, craning her neck to get a look at the screen.

"Play it, Bess," Martha commanded, and before I could protest, the tinny sound of Kitty's voice filled my cozy kitchen, amplified by the phone's speaker.

"You should be ashamed of yourself!" Kitty's voice rang out, passionate and incensed. "For wasting time trying to up your pitiful average while there's important work to be done."

"Turn it off," I muttered, rubbing my temples. But the next voice stopped me cold.

"I guess she told him," came Don Giacomo's casual drawl. "Not surprised Parker offed Jerry, though. Only a matter of time before someone did."

The four of us stood still as statues, the words hanging heavy in the air.

"Did he just say what I think he said?" Martha whispered, her usual composure slipping.

"Keep watching," Bess urged, pressing play again.

Don continued, the bitterness in his tone aligning with the gravity of his words. "I mean, I was tempted myself when he went after my sister. Guy was full-out stalking her before she moved out of town. I had a hot wife like Everly Dupree, you know I'd be doing something about it. Pretty stupid of him not to hide the body, though."

I didn't recognize the voice of the next speaker. "Could have been someone else. Jerry was in the chick-of-the-month club. Always out of his league and always already taken. Who was he chasing before he hit on Dupree?"

"Couldn't say," Donnie answered. "But Parker made damn sure she'd be the last."

"Uh oh," Martha breathed out, her face pale. "That's not good."

"Understatement of the year," I muttered.

"Doesn't look great for Drew, does it?" Bess commented softly, locking her phone and tucking it back into her purse.

"No, it doesn't," I admitted, feeling a growing unease. "If everyone thinks he did it, no one is likely to come forward with any evidence to the contrary. If the right man is locked up, why bother considering whether he's really guilty or not?"

"But we all know better," Martha said. "Surely there must be someone who saw something that would help."

"Not so far," I replied, though my thoughts were racing. Drew could be convicted by default if I didn't figure out a way to clear his name, and given what Donnie had said, I wasn't even close to finding all the suspects.

"Should we tell Ernie about the video?" Patricia asked hesitantly.

"Let's hold off on that," I decided quickly. "It might just add fuel to the fire."

"Right," Martha agreed, nodding slowly. "We don't want to make things worse for Drew."

"Or for Everly," Bess added, giving me a knowing look.

"Thanks," I said, forcing a smile. "Now, if you'll excuse me, I think I need to set up those posts and make a few phone calls."

"Of course, dear," Martha said, patting my arm as they prepared to leave. "I'll let you know what happens at the meeting."

"Thanks," I replied, my mind already racing with the implications of Don Giacomo's words. "One more thing before you go. Do any of you know who Jerry was chasing before he started coming after me?"

"Not a clue, dear," Martha said. "You might want to talk to Robin Thackery, though. She and Gina Giacomo were close. She might have kept an eye on things, you know, the way women do for each other. I assume they're still in contact."

As the door closed behind them, I let out a long breath, the weight of the situation settling heavier on my shoulders than ever. I dreaded what was to come, and now, I dreaded having to talk to Robin on purpose.

Still, going to the grocery store gave me something to do besides obsess about the outcome of the hearing, so I sorted through my fridge and cabinets and made a list.

"Be right back, Molls." She'd become Drew's dog as much as she was mine and had missed her morning runs with him. Quinn had tried to take up the slack, but it wasn't the same.

It wasn't luck that had me loading my groceries onto the conveyor without anyone else in line behind me. It was simple avoidance. The second register had a three-deep line, while Robin's was wide open.

"Got any coupons?" The voice hit my ears with an unwelcome ping, pulling me out of my spiraling thoughts. Robin Thackery leaned against the checkout counter at the grocery store and waited for my answer.

"Not today," I replied, watching her unwrap another stick of gum. "Someone told me you were friends with Gina Giacomo." I kept my tone light, knowing from experience that extracting reliable info from Robin was as unlikely as getting a straight answer from a politician. "And that Jerry Kaminski drove her out of town."

"Jerry?" Robin's brows knitted above heavily mascaraed eyelashes, and a frown tugged at her glossy lips. "Oh, him. That was over way before then. When she moved, she was hooked up with some guy from Dover."

"You're saying Jerry wasn't why Gina moved away?"

"Where did you come up with that?" Robin looked at me like I'd grown a second head while scanning the same loaf of bread three times.

"Her brother mentioned it, I guess." Not to me personally, but she didn't need to know that.

She slid a bag of oranges and two cucumbers right past the scanner. So far, I thought I was breaking even on the final bill.

"Don Giacomo is an idiot," she said. "Besides, it was the other way around. Gina was into Jerry, but he went from hot to cold once she dumped the guy she'd been seeing."

That supported Cindy's theory that Jerry was only in it for the chase. And it gave me an idea for how to handle him the next time he popped up.

I'd lost track of my mental tally and had no idea whether the store took a loss on my order by the time I ran my card through the reader. If Kirby didn't have the guts to fire Robin, I guessed the inventory and end-of-day receipts were his problem.

"Gina left for a job or something in Boston. Nothing to do with a man. I think the guy from Dover went with her. We lost touch. You know how it goes—out of sight, out of mind."

I suspected sight had very little to do with the things that went out of Robin's mind, but I kept that observation to myself.

"Do you know of anyone else Jerry bothered? Besides me, I mean?"

She arched her carefully shaped brow, gave me an up-and-down look that I should have found insulting, and said, "You don't seem like Jerry's type. He typically went for women with bigger boobs."

Crossing my arms over mine, I let that comment slide past.

"But there was someone." She squinted while she thought. "Oh! That's right. Linda...Laura...Something with an L. She worked at the bar. Now, she's working at the inn."

"Miranda Perkins?" Her name didn't even have an L in it, but she fit the description otherwise.

"No. I'm pretty sure her name was Lisa."

"Okay. Well, thanks." I picked up my bags, noting that she'd put the bread on the bottom and the oranges on top, and went back to my car to salvage what I could. Once I stashed the groceries and fired up the engine to get the AC going, I texted David. I knew he didn't have any employees named Lisa or whose name even started with L, but Miranda might know something.

— *Is Miranda working today?*

His response came back quickly.

—*I gave her time off to go to Connecticut with Toby. His mother slipped getting out of the tub and fractured her ankle. She had to have surgery, so they went to help her out for a few days.*

—*When did they leave?*

—*Last Monday, why? She'll be back tomorrow.*

—*Nothing major. I'll talk to her later.*

So much for a new suspect. Everyone who had a motive for Jerry's death also had an alibi except for Drew, unless Pete turned up with something useful, if he turned up at all. Which reminded me to text Jack for an update.

As I finished composing the text and hit send, someone tapped on my window.

"You got a minute?" The voice, hoarse and tinged with desperation, could only belong to one person in town: Junior Pease.

I put down my window to see the poor fellow looking even more wilted than he had the last time I'd seen him, his lips quivering with agitation. "Junior," I said in greeting, my voice heavy with both wariness and an inkling of concern. "You look upset. Is there anything I can do to help?"

"It's Mrs. Spiffles," he blurted out, eyes rimmed red and watery. "I can't stop thinking about her. Doc Hinkel will only keep her in the freezer at his place for so long, and then I'll have to have her cremated. It ain't right, you know. It just ain't right. Burning bodies. It's not how it should be. I can't bear for her to be all cold and alone like that."

Remind me never to open the freezer at Doc Hinkel's. Way too creepy.

"I'm sorry, Junior. That's rough." I meant it. Even though I saw spirits on a frequent basis, I couldn't imagine the sting of storing a loved one the same way I stored frozen peas and chicken breasts.

"Promise me you'll come tonight?" His plea was as raw as an open wound. "To the board meeting. They need to hear our voices and understand why our pets need a designated place to rest. With proper headstones and everything. I need this. She meant the world to me."

"Junior," My hesitation wavered under the weight of his gaze; those blue eyes bore into me, pleading for an ally. He'd stood up for Drew in front of Ernie, so maybe I owed him some loyalty, too. Besides, he was an older man who was missing his cat. A man who, despite everything, didn't deserve to have his last memories of Mrs. Spiffles be of her marooned in a vet's freezer.

"Okay," I conceded, squaring my shoulders. "I'll be there."

As I watched him shuffle away, part relief, part lingering anguish, I realized the depth of the community ties that bound us together into a tapestry of shared grief and joy, interwoven with threads of loss and hope. And like it or not, I was a part of it – the living, the dead, and those caught somewhere in between.

That's when it hit me: Mrs. Spiffles was probably the ghost cat that Dolly had taken in. Getting out of a freezer surely counted as unfinished business.

"Okay, Mrs. Spiffles," I whispered to no one in particular, my tone laced with humor to mask the unease settling in my stomach as the minutes passed. "Looks like your final resting place is about to become a town affair. Let's hope it works out so you can cross over."

With a sigh, I headed home. The bail hearing loomed over me like a thundercloud on the horizon, but for now, I had promises to keep and mysteries to unravel.

At home, I put the groceries away, took Molly out for some playtime, and then let myself sink into the momentary silence.

In my bedroom, I unfolded my murder board and scanned through the witness statements I'd read so many times that I almost knew them by heart.

"There's got to be something I missed. Something these aren't telling me," I said to Molly, who'd snuggled in her bed near mine. Robin's claim about a woman fleeing Jerry's creepy clutches niggled at me, an itch in the back of my brain. It obviously hadn't been Miranda since she still lived and worked in Mooselick River, and her name didn't begin with an L. But there could have been someone else. Someone Robin mistook for Miranda.

I pored over each statement, looking for names I could type into the search bar and check for female relatives with L names. Nearly an hour passed, the words blurring into a mosaic of unwoven statements that made my head spin. No matter how often I circled back, cross-referenced, or tried to read between the lines, I came up empty.

"Zip. Zilch. Nada." My voice bounced off the walls, met by the silent agreement of the house. "Either Robin's spinning tales or Ernie missed a connection." Or both, my brain supplied. As usual, Molly had nothing to say on the matter.

I heard the front door open, then the welcome call of Jacy's voice.

"Everly! Where are you at?"

"Right here." Rising, I left the useless search and met her in the hallway. She wasn't alone. "Hey, Neena. What are you guys doing here?"

"You didn't think we would let you go to the hearing alone, did you?"

"I was planning to go with Drew's parents," I said.

Jacy shook her head. "Change of plans. Quinn and Cheryl will ride over with your parents. You're going with us. Now, you need to pull one of those prim and proper business suits out of the back of your closet. If Ernie tries to make the case that Jerry was led on by some femme fatale and then murdered by a jealous fiancé, you need to look like anything but that. You get me?"

Too caught up in trying to figure out who killed Drew, I hadn't thought far enough ahead to consider today's strategy.

"You're right."

"I'll do your hair," Neena offered. "I think a nice, professional twist in the back should do it, and go easy on the makeup."

"Did Patrea send you over here?" This sounded like it had her fingerprints all over it.

"She might have," Jacy admitted, "but we all thought it was a good plan."

"No, it is. I agree. I'm glad someone has their head on straight because mine's all turned around. Martha and the Tiptonites showed up this morning and gave me some information I thought might pan out into a lead, but I struck out again. Jack hasn't been able to track down Pete, and I somehow got roped into going to a board meeting tonight to decide if we need a pet cemetery. Because that's what I need right now."

I knew I was rambling but could not stop the spew of words.

"It will all be okay. Trust Patrea. She's been working her butt off to poke enough holes in Ernie's case to get him to drop it entirely."

"She hasn't been keeping me in the loop," I said, realizing only now that this was true and beginning to feel somewhat annoyed. "Doesn't she trust me?"

"Don't go there," Jacy warned since she knew me well enough to see the stubborn set of my mouth. "This isn't a matter of trust. It's about managing expectations and giving you the mental space to pursue things independently. It's about coming at the problem from different directions. And we didn't know what her arguments would be until this morning, either. You need to trust her. She's doing everything in her power to fix this."

"I know." My annoyance deflated. "I trust her. You know, I do. I'm just tied up in knots."

"Of course you are. Anyone would be," Neena soothed. "Now, let's get you dressed and put your game face on. This thing isn't over yet."

"My mother and her minions have been tracking the grapevine down to its last tiny tendril, hoping to find someone who saw something. This isn't over. Not by a long shot."

CHAPTER FIFTEEN

The wooden benches in the county courthouse were never designed for comfort, something my backside could testify to as I shifted for the umpteenth time. Beside me, Drew's mother wrung her hands so tightly I thought she might squeeze lemonade from them. The rest of us—friends and family alike—were a collection of jittery leg bounces and bitten nails, all waiting for Drew's bail hearing to start. Except for Drew, who sat beside Patrea, facing forward and unmoving as a statue.

"Relax your jaw," Jacy murmured, her voice a blend of concern and that wry humor I needed right about now. "Before you crack a tooth."

"Sorry," I replied, rolling my shoulders and trying to let go of the tension. "Just trying not to think about what's coming." Mostly, I wished I could scoot forward and rub Drew's shoulders until the knots loosened. But Patrea had warned me against emotional outbursts of any kind, and if I touched him, one of those might erupt, so I stayed where I was and waited.

The tension in the room thickened like fog rolling in over the river when the bailiff announced the judge's entrance. "All rise."

The entire room stood in unison while a wave of anxious energy rose to meet Her Honor as she took her seat with the kind of deliberate grace that made it clear who ran the show. She adjusted her glasses, peering out over the courtroom like she could see right through every last one of us, our secrets laid bare beneath her gaze.

"Be seated," she intoned, and we obeyed, a collective sigh barely audible above the rustle of clothing and legal papers.

Sitting there, I tried to focus on anything but the fear gnawing at my insides. The way the sunlight filtered through the high windows, casting long shadows across the polished floor. The occasional creaks and groans of the old building, as if it too was nervous about the proceedings. Even the faint scent of my mother's lavender body lotion, usually so calming, did little to steady my racing heart.

"Today," the judge began, her voice drawing my attention back to the present moment, "we will hear the case for arraignment and bail regarding Andrew Parker."

Here we go, I thought, trying to keep from making a sound because if I did, I just might scream—or worse, sob uncontrollably. Drew needed me strong. And I'd be darned if I let him down.

The arraignment portion of the proceedings went quite quickly. The judge asked Drew to repeat his full name for the record and accepted his plea of not guilty.

Ernie Polk also stood, his posture rigid, like a fence-post that refused to sway in the harshest wind. He cleared his throat—a sound akin to gravel being tumbled in an old tin can—and fixed his eyes on the judge with a determination that raised the tiny hairs on my neck.

"Your Honor." When asked to recite the evidence in the case, Ernie enunciated with precision, as would any man who had been in this situation many times before, "The evidence against Mr. Parker is compelling." He paused, letting the weight of his words hang in the air before continuing. "We have the tire iron—the weapon used to bludgeon Jerry Kaminski to death—covered in the defendant's fingerprints."

Not one sound rose from the courtroom. We all knew the evidence weighed against him. Ernie's face remained as unreadable as one of those ancient hieroglyphs you'd need a Rosetta Stone to decipher.

"Furthermore," Ernie continued, now pacing like a caged animal eyeing its prey, "Mr. Parker had both motive and opportunity. The victim was romantically fixated on his fiancée, Ms. Everly Dupree—"

"Was" being the operative word, at least in Ernie's mind. He had no way of knowing Jerry's interest had continued after death.

"—and Mr. Parker's understandable jealousy presents a clear motive for murder."

And just like that, the room felt ten degrees warmer, the tension thick enough to spread on toast. While I worked up a satisfying mental image of Ernie Polk roasting over an open fire, Patrea rose, her height lending her a commanding presence that didn't require volume to convey authority.

"Your Honor," she said, her voice as smooth as the river outside but with an undertow strong enough to pull you under, "the prosecution paints a picture based on conjecture, not on concrete evidence." She turned slightly, sweeping the courtroom with a gaze that dared anyone to challenge her. "Chief Polk used the term understandable jealousy, which certainly begs the question of provability. Where are the incident reports that back up the claim? None of the witness statements mention Mr. Parker showing signs of jealousy on that night or any of the others when the deceased attempted to provoke an altercation. On the contrary, witness statements show just the opposite, and it was the deceased who had to be escorted from the tavern."

I nodded along, feeling a burst of admiration. That's my Patrea—calm, cool, collected. Unfortunately, the judge did not look convinced.

Patrea continued. "Furthermore, the timeline supports my client's innocence. Mr. Parker stepped outside to take a phone call in the relative quiet of the parking lot some thirty minutes after the deceased had left the premises. Phone records tell us the call lasted exactly nineteen minutes and fifteen seconds, after which Mr. Parker returned to his group of friends."

"The victim was found roughly three and a half miles from the tavern," the judge looked down at the paperwork before her to verify the fact. "Even staying within the speed limit, that distance easily could be driven within the time frame of the phone call."

"It could," Patrea shocked me by agreeing, then redeemed herself. "But only if Mr. Parker had meticulously planned for the phone call that gave him a reason to leave the premises. Only if Mr. Parker had engineered the confrontation that caused Mr. Kaminski to be ousted from the tavern. And only if Mr. Parker had known the deceased man's exact whereabouts some half an hour after he had been asked to leave the tavern."

In my time as a fundraising coordinator for a major foundation, I'd learned how to read people, and I'd thought I was pretty good at it until the moment when I looked at the judge's face and realized I had no idea what she was thinking.

"Most importantly," Patrea stressed, holding up a finger as if physically pinning her point in midair, "whoever committed this heinous act would undoubtedly be covered in the victim's blood. When Mr. Parker re-entered the tavern, multiple witnesses stated he immediately rejoined his party. Where and when would he have had time to remove all traces of the crime from his person? The police thoroughly searched my client's vehicle, his business, and his residence. Not a single drop of the victim's blood was found."

Patrea let the implication linger, as potent as the ghostly chill I so often felt. But the judge—stoic as the stone statue outside the courthouse—didn't seem swayed by logic or lack thereof.

"Mrs. Evergreen," the judge interjected with a skepticism that could curdle milk, "while your argument has certain points that seem difficult to overcome, the fingerprint evidence is particularly damning. I'm afraid I still find it possible that the crime could have been committed within the allotted time if we consider it a crime of convenience."

"Possible, yes," Patrea conceded with a half-shrug that belied the gravity of her argument, "but highly unlikely."

"Unlikely" was putting it mildly. Drew did nearly everything with a deliberation that most would envy. That included changing his clothes. Between us, he might be the morning person, but I could still bounce out of bed and be ready to leave the house in about the same time it took him to put on and tie his running shoes. Telling the judge that wouldn't help Drew's case.

"Thank you, Mrs. Evergreen," the judge said, her tone final, like the click of a lock snapping shut. "I'd like to take a moment to reread some of the witness statements."

I squeezed my eyes shut, willing away the image of Drew behind bars, his face a mask of stoic bravery. But courage couldn't scrub fingerprints from a tire iron or conjure alibis out of thin air. My heart hammered, each beat a morse code of fear—what if they never believed us? What if...

The vibration of my phone broke through the fog of my trepidation.

"Order," the judge had demanded earlier, her voice echoing like a decree from on high. Now, that very order was my enemy as I tried subtly tapping out my lock code. Any sudden movement could pop the bubble, turning all eyes on me and away from where they needed to be—on Drew.

"Come on…" I muttered under my breath, the tiny screen finally revealing Jack's message. My thumb hovered, trembling over the words that might just tip the scales. He'd found Pete, and his willingness to talk might be our lifeline, but how could I get this information to Patrea without setting off alarm bells?

"Patrea," I whispered.

Her shoulders twitched, but she didn't turn.

"I have a text about Pete."

Careful to hide the motion, she slid one hand behind her and wiggled her fingers impatiently.

My hands shook as I fumbled behind the wooden rails separating my seat from Patrea's, desperate to slide my phone through the narrow opening without drawing the watchful eyes of the bailiff or, heaven forbid, the judge. The courtroom was suspended in a silence punctuated only by the shuffling of papers and the occasional cough.

It wasn't the smoothest move I'd ever made, but I got the job done.

"Your Honor." After a quick scan of my phone screen, Patrea's voice was the sound of a velvet hammer, smooth but unyielding. She rose, and even though I was already sinking back in my seat, I could feel the shift in the room. "New information has come to light. May I approach the bench?"

As Ernie followed her up there and Patrea began to talk to the judge in a tone too low for the rest of us to hear, I allowed myself the smallest exhale of relief. My heart still raced like a startled rabbit, but I felt a shimmer of hope for the first time since this nightmare had begun—a ghostly whisper promising that the truth wasn't buried yet.

Returning to her seat, Patrea winked at me, and my heart soared.

The rustle of legal papers and the creak of leather announced the judge's intent to respond. The courtroom hushed as if the room's stale air itself were holding its breath. The judge cast a long, appraising look at Patrea, her eyes sharp as flint behind rimless glasses.

"Ms. Evergreen," she began, her voice steady, betraying no hint of sway in either direction. "The court acknowledges receipt of this...new development."

I bit my lip, my fingers curling around my purse strap so tightly my nails dug into my palm. The judge was a stalwart figure in her black robes, and right now, our entire future seemed balanced on her next words.

"Given the timing and nature of this testimony," she continued, tapping a pen against the bench—a metronome counting seconds of fate. "I have decided to postpone this bail hearing until tomorrow afternoon to give me time to review this new witness statement."

A collective breath escaped the room, and I felt mine hitch halfway. Postponement meant Drew had more time, but it also meant prolonged agony—another night of not knowing, of possibly being haunted by the annoying ghost of Drew's alleged crime.

"Please be advised," the judge addressed Patrea with an authoritative tilt of her head, "Mr. Casey's statement will need to be exceptionally compelling to tip the scales in favor of granting bail. I consider Mr. Parker to be a flight risk."

"Understood, Your Honor," Patrea replied, her confidence unshaken. She sat back down with the grace of a cat landing on its feet, while I, on the other hand, felt like said cat after a tumble in the dryer—static-charged and disoriented.

"Compelling," I muttered, rubbing at a temple where a stress headache threatened to bloom. "No pressure, Pete. Just the weight of Drew's world on your shoulders."

My gaze wandered over to where Ernie stood. As if feeling my gaze landing on him, he looked over and gave me the barest hint of a nod. I wanted to hate him for the part he was forced to play in this nightmare, but I knew he was doing everything in his power—even enlisting my help—to see that an innocent man wasn't sent to jail.

"What was all that?" Drew's mother reached over to squeeze my hand so hard I nearly yelped. "What new information?"

"Pete's been found, and he's willing to make a statement. It's not a slam dunk, but his testimony should help Drew's case."

Hope and uncertainty churned within me, an unwelcome concoction that tasted of sour apprehension. I needed Pete's statement to be more than just compelling; it had to be ironclad with enough detail to prove Drew couldn't have killed Jerry. Or at least to get Drew out on bail and buy us more time to find the real killer. I knew which scenario I preferred, but even the worst case was better than we'd had before.

As the judge rose, signaling the end of today's emotional rollercoaster, I gathered my wits about me. One thing was clear: tonight, there would be no rest for the weary or the wicked and certainly none for friends of the accused.

The judge's gavel struck with a finality that echoed through the courtroom, and I swear I could feel Drew's heart clenching along with mine. The sharp rap cut through the heavy air, a punctuation mark on a sentence we were all too anxious to finish.

"This court is adjourned," Judge Chase announced. As we rose to see her out, her eyes swept over the small knot of us who sat behind Drew—a sea of hopeful and harried faces—before she disappeared into her chambers with a swish of her robe.

Once she'd gone, I held Drew's hands in mine for about half a second before Ernie escorted him out through a side door and back to jail. The mood among our friends and family was an odd mix as we shuffled out of the courtroom.

"First order of business," Patrea murmured as she caught up to me. "Find out what Pete has to say. You pulled that one out at the last minute."

"It wasn't me. Thank Jack for going the extra mile to find Pete's hidey hole."

Outside, Jacy and Neena were anxious to know what Jack had said since they hadn't been sitting close enough to read the text before I passed my phone off to Patrea.

"All he said was that Pete had been found and wanted to make a statement. I don't think this is the time or place to call him for more information. Why don't we all go back to my house?"

We had to repeat the whole story for Brian, Chris, and David, who met us there, and then, with a whisper of hope, I reached for my phone and dialed Jack's number.

"Jack, it's me," I said when he picked up. "What happened with Pete? How's he holding up?"

"Well enough," Jack's voice rumbled through the line, steady as always. "I found him on the beach. Right where Drew said he'd be. It took him some time to come back to himself, and he's still a bit frazzled, but he's ready to talk tomorrow."

As much as I hated to, I said the words Drew would expect me to say. "He doesn't have to do this if it will be too much for him. I think Ernie would accept a written statement if it were signed in the presence of authority."

"I know, and so does he. But he's clear-headed now, and I think the chance to do something positive will do him a world of good. I'm not sure how much he remembers or if any of it will help, but I will get him cleaned up and ready."

"All we need is for him to tell the truth," I replied as

the knot in my stomach barely loosened. "I have to believe that will be enough."

"Understood. I've already spoken to your chief—a guy named Polk."

"Yes, that's right."

"We'll go straight to the station. First thing in the morning. Will you be there?"

"Wild horses couldn't keep me away. I'll see you tomorrow. Bright and early." I hung up with a weary smile. Jack had come through for us up to now. If anyone could ensure Pete showed up on time, it was him.

CHAPTER SIXTEEN

he scent of sugar and vanilla wafted through the air, mingling with a hint of cinnamon as I changed from the skirt and jacket I'd worn to the hearing. My friends had been gone only a few minutes, and Cheryl was already in her element with a dusting of flour on her nose as she stirred bananas into a bowl of batter.

"Smells like heaven, Cheryl," I said, trying to sound upbeat, but the lump in my throat didn't quite agree with my tone.

"Nothing like a bit of baking to calm the nerves, dear," she replied without looking up, her focus unbreakable as if her son's fate rested on the perfection of the loaf. "Nuts or no nuts? Drew loves them, but do you have a preference?"

I smiled because this was one more thing Drew and I had in common: "The more, the better, and I can only trust that things will fall into place and he'll be here to eat his fair share very soon." I planned to do everything in my power to make that the case.

"Okay, then." Her shoulders lost a bit of their tension. "Quinn took the dog out. I hope that's okay. When I'm upset, I bake. Quinn tends to walk off the tension."

I glanced out the window to see Quinn's towering silhouette disappearing down the street, Molly trotting beside him with more energy than I felt. They looked like they were going on a quest to walk every street in town.

"That's perfectly fine. Drew's the same way."

"Your friend's summation was quite impressive," Cheryl said as she folded in a cup of chopped walnuts. "Quinn has decided to stick with her rather than call in someone with more experience if the case goes to court."

I hadn't known another attorney was something they'd been considering. "Patrea's very good at her job. No one you could hire would be more determined to see this through."

Cheryl shrugged. "As I said, we were impressed. I just don't understand how the judge refused to look past the fingerprint evidence."

"I know."

With the house now wrapped in a silence punctuated only by the rhythmic clinking of kitchenware, a sense of restlessness took hold of me. I needed space, a breath of fresh air to clear the tension clinging to my brain.

"Cheryl, do you mind if I step out for a bit? Take a drive to clear my head?"

"Of course not, honey. Just remember this will be done in about an hour if you're like me and prefer the first slice while it's hot."

"Wouldn't miss it," I promised, though my mind was already miles away.

As I closed the door behind me, the late afternoon sun

cast long shadows over the town, lending it an eerie sense of stillness. I found myself driving almost automatically, the wheels turning toward the place where Jerry's life had been snuffed out—a spot so far out of the way it puzzled me every time I thought about it.

The gravel crunched under my car tires as I pulled up to the scene. A shiver ran down my spine, not from any ghostly chill but from the sheer isolation of the area. Trees loomed overhead, their leaves whispering secrets to one another, indifferent to the human drama that unfolded beneath them.

Why here, Jerry? What drew you to this lonely stretch of road? Had you come to meet someone? Or to sleep off a few too many?

Stepping out of the car, I wrapped my arms around myself, the breeze carrying the earthy scent of pine and the tang of the nearby river. It was a beautiful spot if you ignored the yellow police tape flapping lazily in the wind, cordoning off the site of a life violently ended.

My hair danced in the welcome breeze, little tendrils of rebellion refusing to stay put. I brushed it back from my face, wishing I could as easily sweep aside the unease creeping over me. There was something about being here, in the quiet where only nature and a murderer bore witness to Jerry's last moments—it unsettled me more than I cared to admit.

The way I was acting, you'd think this was my first murder or something. But it wasn't. It was, however, the first one that had been pinned on my husband, and I needed to get a grip. Even as I tried to muster the humor that usually buoyed my spirit, it slid away on the slick of worry that had taken up residence in my heart and head.

Taking a deep breath, I stepped closer to the police tape, my gaze fixed on the disturbed earth that marked where Jerry had fallen. There was no sign of him now, just an outline in what looked like spray paint on the ground and the weight of unanswered questions hanging in the air.

"Who else did you tick off, Jerry?" I said to the wind, expecting no response.

"Nobody." He popped up behind me with a quick chill, which was the only warning. "I was a hell of a guy. Maybe if you'd dumped Muscle Boy and taken up with a real man, we'd be cozied up in bed right now. But I guess I'll have to settle for the fact that you're out here beating the bushes for my killer."

The constant refrain was wearing that song about as thin as my last nerve. As if I'd spend my days tracking down his killer just for fun. It was bad enough that I had another death on my hands, but did it have to be a skirt-chasing Casanova?

That thought triggered a memory and then a plan.

"Fine, you've figured me out," I paused for dramatic effect. "I'm only out here trying to find out what happened to you because I've decided I can't live without you. The thought of spending another day on this cruel, Jerry-less earth is unbearable. So, I've decided—I'm going to find just enough evidence to get Drew out of jail and then tell him we had a torrid affair."

Jerry's eyes bugged out, but I cut him off before he could speak.

"Surprised? Well, hold your haunted horses. I'm not done yet." I leaned in closer, putting my grade school acting experience to use. "Then, because I'd need to be murdered to stay on the wrong side of the veil, I'll goad him until he tosses me off the nearest cliff so I can join you in ghostly matrimony. You know what's better than 'til death do us part,' don't you? When we can be together for eternity, which we can as long as neither murder is solved."

His face went from cocky to pale, which was quite a feat for a ghost. "You...what?" He held out both hands as if to ward me off. "Look, babe. You've got the wrong idea here. I just thought we could have had a little fun together. I wasn't looking for all that eternity stuff."

"Come on." In addition to having a case of the regular heebie-jeebies, getting all up in Jerry's face gave me the creeper-induced creeps, but I did it anyway. "You know you want me. You've been saying so to everyone and their dog for weeks now. Let's be together forever."

"That's not...I'm not...it's too much," he whizzed backward to get away from me. "You're moving way too fast. I can't keep up."

"Really?" I let the charade go and allowed scorn to show on my face. "Because apparently, according to town gossip, you only liked the chase, not the catch. So, how did it feel to have the tables turned on you?"

I watched as Jerry's ethereal form squirmed. "You mean you're not into me?"

"Relax, Jerry. I would rather kiss a rabid skunk right on the lips than follow you into the afterlife." I crossed my arms, enjoying the look of relief washing over him. "I never wanted you. This was just a ruse to get you to see how ridiculous you've been."

"Right, of course," he stammered, looking sheepish— or as sheepish as a dead man could look.

"Good. Now we've got that straight," I continued, "let's focus. I'm a happily married woman who would love nothing more than to take my husband on our honeymoon, and I'll do anything to solve this murder for his sake. Now tell me, why were you out here that night?"

"Uh, I don't know," Jerry admitted, shifting uncomfortably from foot to foot. "I was heading home and must have taken a wrong turn."

"Perfect," I muttered, more to myself than to him. "Unhelpful as ever. Maybe I'll tell the judge I can talk to ghosts and even Jerry didn't know where he was going that night, so Drew couldn't possibly have followed him. That ought to get him out of jail. Or put me in a padded room somewhere."

Despite the lingering tension, I couldn't help but inject a bit of humor into the grim situation. After all, if I didn't laugh, I might just cry, and tears wouldn't bring me any closer to the truth.

Clouds moved over the sun, threatening to bring a sudden summer rain as I stared at the one new addition to the area: a makeshift shrine that marked where Jerry Kaminski's life had been brutally snatched away. A wooden cross, crooked and hastily hammered together, jutted out from the earth, adorned with a bouquet of wildflowers someone must have picked from the nearby meadow. The petals were already wilting, their vibrant colors succumbing to the inevitability of decay.

Who had put it here? Maybe one of Jerry's drinking buddies. Just one more mystery to solve. Still, seeing that someone thought enough of him to make the effort made me feel a little ashamed of my attitude toward him. Presumably, the shrine-maker probably hadn't been someone like me—the object of Jerry's unwanted attention, but no one deserved to have their life brutally ended on the side of the road.

The weight of the situation settled in my bones, heavy and unyielding. Sometimes, it was easy to forget that behind every ghostly encounter and spectral whisper was a genuine loss. Someone had lost a child, sibling, or friend, and someone else had to carry the burden of being responsible for that void. Assuming the killer felt remorse, anyway.

"At least someone cared enough to set up a memorial," I said to Jerry. He was still hovering around, but there was no response—just the rustle of leaves and the distant chatter of river water trickling across stones.

Hearing myself say the word memorial snapped me

back to reality. "Oh, shoot!" I checked my phone. The time blinked accusingly at me, reminding me I was playing hooky from adult responsibilities. I should have been there two minutes ago for the emergency board meeting, but now I was late.

"Dammit, Jerry. I have to go. If anything else comes back to you—" I didn't finish the sentence as I turned on my heel and hurried back to my car. At least he didn't follow. My reputation for being on time for everything had just gone out the window.

An errant wind picked up just as I pushed open the town office door slamming it against the wall. Even from the entrance, I heard the meeting room fall into an abrupt hush, the kind that clings to the air when something unexpected happens. Walking through the doorway, I could feel every eye on me, curiosity piqued beneath furrowed brows and the occasional cocked head.

"Sorry, sorry," I murmured, trying to make myself as small as possible and failing miserably. My attempt at stealth fell flat. Chairs scraped against the linoleum floor as I sidled past knees and purses, aiming for the empty seat that seemed to be beckoning me like a beacon of hope.

"Where have you been?" Martha mouthed when I settled beside her, my face nearly as red as the giant purse sitting on her ample lap.

"I got held up. Sorry," I said, plastering on a smile that felt more like a grimace.

The newest board member—who just happened to be

my dad—cleared his throat, pulling focus back to the front. "If we can continue," he said, though his glance lingered on me just a second too long.

Red Belanger finished the explanation that my arrival had interrupted as to why Bog Road hadn't been graded since the first of the summer.

"We're digging ditches over on County Line Road this week. We'll get to Bog Road once that's done."

When the explanation failed to appease a woman I didn't recognize from the back, she called Red several names that turned the tips of my father's ears pink. It was then that I realized the discussion about the pet cemetery hadn't begun, and half the attendees were there for a different reason entirely.

"Hush up, Jenny," Martha stood and ordered. "You'd argue the sky was green just to stir up trouble."

"That road is riddled with potholes. I pay my taxes just like everyone else, and they get higher every year. Seems like I oughta get some benefit out of all the money it costs to fund one expensive event after another."

The room's tension was a living thing, crackling in the air like static before a storm.

"Every event we've put on has added to the town coffers, not taken money away. You'd know that if you ever hauled your haughty backside into town and offered to pull your weight." Martha ignored the looks she was getting from each of the board members and spoke her mind.

The sharp rap of a gavel put a stop to the argument.

"I'll get out there the first of the week," Red said, his face showing no emotion at all. "Best I can do." With that, he sat back down and waved a hand to indicate the meeting should continue. Jenny wasn't placated, but when the gavel rapped again, she took her seat and settled for taking turns staring daggers at Martha and Red.

Finally, Junior rose to make an impassioned speech covering the life and death of his beloved feline in far too much detail. He then cited the town ordinance preventing him from erecting a headstone on his property to mark the resting place he thought his cat deserved.

"I've done a lot for this town over the years, and I'm proud to call Mooselick River my home. But we're missing something vital in our community."

He'd made enough noise about it over the past few days that no one had to ask what he meant.

"I figured I wasn't the only one who thinks of their pets like they were members of the family, and I was right." Pulling out the petition I'd already signed, Junior stepped forward to place it on the table in front of the board members. "Over three hundred people signed, which I believe satisfies the minimum number of signatures needed to put this matter before the board."

First Chair, Miles Higgins, nodded and picked up the stapled sheets. Junior stood silent while Miles read the petition aloud and then flipped through the pages of signatures. Once finished, he handed the sheets to Second

Chair Ginger Martin, who barely bothered to look at them before handing them over to my father.

"Go ahead, Junior," Miles said.

"As I said, we got over three hundred signatures, and in a town this size, that's what I'd call a majority. All we're asking is for the board to sign the approval and let our furry friends have the resting place they deserve."

My father spoke up. "The way I see it, the costs would be minimal. The sextant already charges a fee for overseeing burials, and since I see her name on the list of signatures, I assume she has no objection to that or to the extra hour a week for mowing."

Muttering broke out across the room.

"May I speak?" Martha Tipton's voice cut through the murmur like a foghorn through the air, and all eyes swiveled toward her. With her years of handling town business, she had an air about her that could command attention without demanding it.

"Of course, Martha," Miles replied, gesturing for her to continue.

Martha stood, smoothing the fabric of her skirt with a practiced hand. "I think it would be remiss of us to overlook the importance of Junior Pease's proposal for a pet cemetery. It's not just about giving our furry friends a final resting place. It's about community." She glanced around the room, locking eyes with several attendees. "We all know how hard Junior took the loss of his cat. But he's channeling that grief into something positive that can bring our community together. If money is the only reason to say no, I'm sure we can set up an event to raise funds. It wouldn't be the first event we have done that benefitted pet owners, and I hope it wouldn't be the last."

I couldn't help but admire Martha's angle. The woman knew how to spin a tale that could warm hearts and open wallets. No doubt there'd be a plan designed to draw in more tourism if she was at the heart of it.

Bess Tate, on the other hand, was having none of it. She stood up abruptly, her chair scraping against the floor. "I'm sorry, Martha, but we have to be practical," she said, her voice steady but edged with frustration. "We spend enough time raising funds for this, that, and the other thing as it is. Maintaining a pet cemetery is an unnecessary expense."

"Unnecessary?" Martha countered, her eyebrows arching. "I'd say it's far from that. Have you no compassion? This is about healing and paying homage to the unconditional love we get from our pets."

Bess's lips pressed into a thin line, her stance unyielding. "Homage doesn't pay the bills, Martha. And it certainly doesn't mow the lawns. Besides, something like this has got to be done all legal, and we all know there ain't no lawyer who's gonna work for free. Not even that new one who married Christopher Evergreen."

The room buzzed with whispered opinions, divided between head and heart. I sat back, trying to keep my own thoughts from spiraling. Pet cemeteries were far from my top priority in the grand scheme of things. Yet here I was, caught up in the passion that always accompanies progress.

Still, these little squabbles were what made me glad I'd come back home. Our town might be a little bit quirky, but it was brimming with people who cared enough to show up and speak out, no matter the cause.

"May I have the floor?" Junior's voice was surprisingly strong, echoing off the high ceilings, and everyone hushed as it broke through the tense silence left by Bess and Martha's comments.

"Of course, Junior," said my dad, nodding at him with a respect that seemed woven into the fabric of our community.

Junior cleared his throat, his whiskers twitching like the tail of an agitated cat. "I've listened to the concerns about expenses," he began, glancing briefly at Bess, "and I reckon it's a fair point." He paused for dramatic effect or maybe just to catch his breath. "So, here's a different proposal. I'll make a donation to cover the maintenance of the pet cemetery for the next ten years and cover any legal costs involved in designating the property for it. That should ease any financial burden on the town."

There was a collective intake of breath. The notion of Junior Pease parting with his money was akin to witnessing a solar eclipse—rare, unexpected, and a tad eerie.

"Are you quite certain about this, Junior?" Ginger

asked, peering over her spectacles like she was trying to spot the fine print.

"It's my money. I think I know what I want to do with it," Junior affirmed, his gaze never wavering.

"Then I believe we should put it to a vote," declared my dad. The other chair members nodded and, with a solemnity reserved for moments of great importance, raised their hands and voted.

"Aye."

"Motion carried," Miles announced. "Mr. Pease will fund the pet cemetery for the next ten years. Motion approved."

The room erupted into applause, some out of relief, others genuinely moved by Junior's gesture. It was a testament to how tightly knit our little town was; even when we disagreed, we were always just a surprising act of generosity away from coming together.

"Thank you, everyone, for your participation," Ginger said, standing up as she signaled the conclusion of the meeting. "This meeting is adjourned."

Chairs screeched against the floor as people began to trickle out of what had been the third-grade classroom when I attended school here, their chatter mingling with the hum of fluorescent lights. Some patted Junior on the back as they passed, while others simply nodded in acknowledgment of the day's events.

I lingered a moment longer, my gaze drifting toward Junior, who let his shoulders slump once the rest of the crowd had left. If I hadn't been looking at his face and seen something else there, I'd have assumed he'd given in to relief.

"You don't seem as excited as you should," I mentioned as I stepped closer. "Everything okay with you, Junior?"

CHAPTER SEVENTEEN

I don't know why, but something about Junior always reminded me of an affable wizard gearing up for a spell.

"Me? Oh, I'm fine, Everly," he said, his voice calm and reassuring, but his smile didn't reach his eyes. "Actually, quite happy about the cemetery. But you seem upset. How'd the bail hearing go?"

"Postponed," I replied, tucking my purse tighter under my arm. "Until tomorrow to give the judge time to review a new witness statement. We're hoping to prove he never left Cappy's parking lot that night."

"Sounds promising," he nodded slowly, his face going grave. "I can say with certainty Drew didn't kill anyone." Junior leaned closer, lowering his voice as if sharing a secret, though we were nearly the only ones left in the building. "He's too good a man. Too helpful and kind for the Jerrys of this world to get under his skin. He saved my bacon the other day like the Good Samaritan that he is. I can't tell you how grateful I was to see him pull over after three or four other vehicles passed by."

"Thanks, Junior," I said, offering a smile, hoping my

gratitude would mask the unease twisting in my gut. It felt strange discussing my husband's predicament with Junior, who tended to overshare his feelings on the subject. But we weren't exactly in public at the moment, so he wouldn't be causing a scene if he did.

Before I could delve deeper into that conversation, Martha Tipton marched up to us, her gaze fixed on me with an urgency that couldn't be ignored. Or it could have been, but I was thankful for the distraction for once.

"Everly, dear, I need a moment of your time." Martha sounded annoyed.

"Sure thing, Martha," I said, curiosity piqued. I turned to Junior, giving him a nod. "We'll catch up later?"

"Of course," he replied and pushed through the door leading to the parking lot.

Martha led me to a quieter corner of the room, her heels clicking against the tiles. The scent of stale coffee wafted from the meeting room, mingling with the lingering aroma of chalk dust that no amount of cleaning could remove.

Junior's shadow had barely cleared the doorway when Martha leaned in, her voice dropping to a conspiratorial whisper that seemed to fill the space he'd left. "Bess is tap dancing on my last nerve," she confided, her eyes darting around as if Bess might pop out from behind one of the musty filing cabinets.

"Martha, come on," I said, tilting my head and giving her a half-smile. "Bess is just...Bess." I knew their friendship was like an old bridge—sturdy but needing constant maintenance to avoid a collapse.

"She thinks we should add a clown parade to the Harvest Festival! A clown parade." Her hands fluttered to her chest. "I can't begin to imagine what goes on in that head of hers."

I couldn't help but chuckle at the thought of a phalanx of clowns marching down Main Street, honking noses in harmony with the high school band. "It's her way of getting you riled up about one thing when she really wants something else. You just need to be calm and wait for her backup idea because that will be the one she wants to do."

Martha pursed her lips, clearly unconvinced, but I could see the affectionate glint in her eye, so I offered several examples to bolster my opinion. "Well, isn't that perceptive of you? Now that you mention it, she does have a pattern. I can't believe I've missed that all these years."

"Trust me," I said, my tone reassuring. "Bess does have good ideas sometimes. She just likes to keep you off track until she's ready to reveal them. And she's a champion pot stirrer who constantly needs to defend her title." I winked, hoping to soften the edges of Martha's exasperation.

"Let's hope so," Martha sighed, her shoulders relaxing slightly. "For the sake of this town—and my sanity."

Stepping out of the Town Office, I looked at the deepening sky and thought of how time must be moving so slowly for Drew since there were no windows in the jail cells to help mark its passage. That's when I saw an old Chevy Suburban, its two-tone gray and black paint job looking flat in the slanting light.

"Would you look at that," I murmured, hands on my hips. The hulking vehicle lumbered out of the parking lot with all the grace of a bear waking up from hibernation. A shiver ran down my spine—not from the chill in the air, but from a memory nudging insistently at the edges of my consciousness.

"It was an old gray truck," Gomp had said as he breathed a cloud of beer breath in my direction. "Nearly turned me into roadkill the night Jerry met his maker."

"Coincidence?" I mused, my gaze trailing the Chevy as it turned onto the main road. "Or clue?" The possibility of the latter made my detective senses tingle with anticipation.

I headed for my car as I watched the Suburban disappear around the corner. The two-tone paint made it look like a pickup truck with a cap on the back, just like Gomp described. Maybe I hadn't given Ernie enough information when I asked him to run a search.

"This could be the key to this whole mess," I whispered under my breath, the thought both thrilling and terrifying.

With a sense of urgency nipping at my heels, I yanked open the door and slid into my car. The Chevy's taillights receded in the distance, like the last crumbs of a trail leading to a gingerbread house, but this one had less sugar and spice and more sinister secrets.

"Come on. Move it!" I muttered as I tried to peel out of the parking lot at the exact moment a blue minivan dawdled its way down the street at a maddeningly leisurely pace.

"Today, please!" I hissed, banging my hand on the steering wheel and resisting the urge to lay on the horn. By the time it had trundled past, the Chevy Suburban had vanished like a ghost—and not the kind I could chat up for directions.

Just what I needed—a game of vehicular hide and seek.

I took a right at the end of the street, squinting in the rearview mirror, half-expecting the Suburban to materialize behind me. Which would have been creepy, but at least I'd have found it.

The stretch of road ahead seemed to unspool like a ribbon from some forgotten gift, winding its way into the countryside. The town's familiar sights fell away behind me, replaced by open fields and clusters of trees. My car hummed along, eating a couple of miles in no time, but there were no taillights in sight—only the occasional porch light from a farmhouse or the distant twinkle of stars beginning to appear in the twilight sky.

"Should've seen it by now," I grumbled, kicking the AC down a notch. It was like the truck had disappeared into thin air, much like the spirits I so often encountered. But unlike my unwanted visitors from the other side, I couldn't summon this vehicle back with a few choice words.

Sighing, I hung a U-turn, tires crunching on the gravel at the edge of the paved road, and headed back the other way, my headlight beams sweeping across the fields like searching spotlights. Maybe I'd chosen wrong. Perhaps the truck had gone left instead of right. There was only one way to find out, and I could only hope my hunch that this was the vehicle that had nearly taken Gomp out was worth its salt—or at least worth the gas I was burning.

I retraced my route until I reached the first turn I'd taken and veered the other way this time, my heart thumping with hope and frustration. Just outside of town, I gunned it and finally saw something—a vehicle up ahead. Could it be?

"Come on, come on," I urged, jamming my foot down on the pedal. The gap between us closed, and for a moment, my pulse raced with the thrill of the chase. But as I drew nearer, the sinking feeling of disappointment squashed the excitement flat. It wasn't the Suburban I'd been hunting at all. Just a Jeep that looked like it had been rolled through a mud pie a few times.

Waste of time.

I kept driving for a while longer, but I knew I was already too late and that continuing would be nothing more than a series of wrong turns and bad decisions. Too many choices, not enough clues. I had a better chance of getting hit by lightning than catching up to the Suburban.

So much for my detective skills. I probably wouldn't be any better at stakeouts, either. Not that I had any plans to get a PI license.

Annoyed with minivan drivers everywhere—except for Jacy, of course—I admitted defeat. Whatever secret the Suburban held, it wouldn't reveal itself tonight. With a resigned exhale, I pointed my car back toward town and another evening with my in-laws, followed by another sleepless night.

CHAPTER EIGHTEEN

The heavy door to the police station swung open with a thud that seemed to echo through my bones. Jack and Pete ambled in ahead of me, a contrast in emotions. Jack's jaw was set, his eyes darting from Pete to the drab walls with silent concern. Pete, on the other hand, wearing clothes that hung on his gaunt frame, paid little attention to his surroundings. While Jack spoke to Carole Ann at the front desk, Pete turned back to me.

"How's he holding up?" Above light brown eyes, his bushy brows furrowed in concern.

I took a deep breath of air that had gone stagnant with the scent of stale coffee and a hint of anxiety. "As well as can be expected, I guess."

"Good luck," Carole Ann murmured, almost under her breath as we passed by. Even though she liked Drew, I'd bet my house she'd be listening, and whatever Pete had to say would hit the grapevine as fast as he got the words out.

We reached Ernie's office, and the door creaked ominously as Pete stepped inside. The small space felt even more cramped with the addition of serious-faced Ernie Polk and his desk cluttered with paperwork.

"Sit down, Pete," Ernie said, gesturing to one of the chairs that looked like they'd been stolen from a 1950s schoolroom. His voice was gruff but not unkind, the tone of a man who'd been doing this job long enough that he just wanted to get on with it. "We won't be needing an audience." That last was directed at Jack and me, but Ernie didn't seem to mind that I left the door open.

Jack and I moved toward the holding cell where Drew was waiting, our steps slow, the tension clinging to the air around us. As I glanced through the open door behind me, I could see Ernie leaning forward, elbows on his desk, giving Pete his full attention. There was no humor in his eyes now, just the laser focus of an officer ready to dig for the truth.

"Thanks for coming in, Mr. Casey," Ernie started, his all-business tone still audible though he tried to keep his voice down. "Now, tell me everything you remember about the phone call between yourself and Drew Parker last Tuesday night."

Stepping closer, Drew offered Jack a grateful look but didn't speak. None of us did. Jack leaned against the wall, arms crossed, while Drew wrapped his hand around mine. The drone of their voices carried through the thin walls, steady and relentless, as Ernie asked Pete to confirm his name and contact information.

"Let's hope Pete remembers something useful," I whispered, squeezing Drew's hand. He nodded and swallowed hard.

"You need to remember he was in rough shape that

night. If what he says isn't helpful, I need to know you won't hold it against him," Drew said, his voice steady, but I could see the tiny lines of tension around his eyes.

"I would never, but I'm sure he'll do the best he can," I replied, mustering as much cheer as possible. But deep down, I knew we were all walking a tightrope, and below us, the webbed net of the investigation was either waiting to catch us or split to let us crash to the ground.

Pete's hands were shaking when he and Jack arrived. I'd noticed it when he gripped the door frame as if trying to steady himself against a storm only he could feel. They were shaking still. From our vantage point, we could see into Ernie's office through the mirror attached to the wall that let Ernie keep an eye on the holding cell.

"I get anxious sometimes," Pete began, his voice a notch higher than usual. "Something happens that takes me back to...well...it takes me back, and I spiral. Sometimes I get through it on my own. Sometimes I need help. This was one of those times, so I called Drew."

"And you talked for," Ernie consulted his notes, "around twenty minutes."

"Sounds about right, but I can't say for sure. It's hard to keep track when you're in the hole. Harder yet when the hole is in you," Pete spoke honestly about his mental status. "You can check my phone, though. It keeps a log of calls."

We heard the sound of a phone sliding across the desk.

"Did you hear anything unusual during the call?"

Ernie asked, his brows knitting together like he was trying to piece together a jigsaw puzzle with half the pieces missing.

"Unusual?" Pete echoed, leaning back in his seat. "There was music playing when he answered and voices. It sounded like he was at a bar, which made sense because he was getting married the next day."

"Could you hear the talking and music during the entire call?" Ernie leaned in, his eyes boring into Pete.

I held my breath, feeling Drew tense beside me. This detail mattered; it could establish a timeline and corroborate Drew's alibi.

"I—I'm not sure," Pete stammered, raking a hand through his hair. "It was louder when we started talking, but then...I don't know. I think maybe it got quieter, like if he went outside. I was more focused on my own stuff, you know?"

Ernie nodded, and I felt a sharp twang of disappointment, like a guitar string snapping under too much strain. That wasn't the concrete confirmation we needed. It was as if the ground beneath us had turned to quicksand, and with each word from Pete's mouth, we sank deeper into uncertainty.

"Why don't you tell me what you do remember," Ernie said, his pen poised to take down Pete's statement in his own words, only interrupting to clarify several minor points. Nothing was said that was particularly damning, but neither was anything especially helpful in establishing Drew's alibi.

"Did Parker speak to anyone else while he was on the phone with you?"

"Not to the best of my recollection."

"Do you remember hearing any ambient noise? Such as the slamming of a car door or the rev of an engine?"

"Not that I can think of."

Most of what Pete remembered had to do with his state of mind at the time and how Drew helped ease him away from dire thoughts.

"Okay," I muttered under my breath, exchanging a look with Drew. His eyes were a mirror of my frustration, reflecting the grim realization that we were no more than a few tiny steps ahead of where we'd been before as Ernie escorted Pete from his office.

"Ten minutes, Dupree." Ernie nodded toward the door but also grabbed a chair for Pete to sit in while he spoke to Drew. He looked too fragile to stand for any length of time. "Then I want you all out of here." When he returned to his office, Ernie left the door open to make it clear he'd be listening to whatever we said.

"I wish I could be more help," Pete mumbled, unaware of the sinking feeling that had taken up residence in my stomach. "But all I can say is that I don't see how Drew could have been killing anyone while he was so focused on talking me down off the ledge."

"Don't beat yourself up, Pete. It's a huge deal that you were able to pull it together to come and make a statement," Drew told him. "If you could do this for me, I know you could do the same and more for yourself."

"You're trying to get me into a program," Pete said.

"Only because I think it will help, and if I can't be there for you every step of the way, I know I can depend on Jack to lend his support." Tilting his head, Drew looked to Jack for his response.

"You know I will, brother." Stepping forward, Jack clapped a hand on Pete's shoulder.

Whatever else happened here, seeing Pete nod his head was enough to make Drew smile. "Good," he said. "I'm glad to hear it."

"So am I." my voice didn't carry the conviction I hoped for, sounding hollow instead. Drew gave my hand a reassuring squeeze, and I forced a smile for his sake. But inside, my mind was racing.

Pete's face crumpled like a paper bag caught in the rain, his eyes brimming with a helplessness that echoed through the sterile walls of the police station. He leaned forward in the hard plastic chair, elbows on knees, as if trying to push the words out physically.

"I just...I wish I knew something that would have helped more, you know?" His voice was a whisper, laced with the kind of frustration that comes from deep within. "You've always been there for me. Every time life knocked me down, you picked me up and dusted me off. I feel like you're my own personal Good Samaritan."

Something about the way Pete said 'Good Samaritan' tickled the back of my mind, a memory teasing at the edge of consciousness. I watched Pete's earnest expression, his admiration for Drew shining through despite the grimness of our situation. It was heartwarming and gut-wrenching all at once, knowing how much Drew meant to him.

"Hey," I said, reaching out to gently squeeze Pete's hand. "You came, and you told the truth. That's all we asked for, and everything you didn't hear might be enough to get the judge to grant bail. All we need is more time to figure out what happened to Jerry, and this will all be over. Since we *all* know Drew didn't kill him." I raised my voice on that last sentence to drive the point home with Eavesdropping Ernie.

Pete managed a weak smile, but it didn't quite reach his eyes. And that's when it hit me—the phrase. 'Good Samaritan.' Junior had used those exact words just the night before, standing in the town office after the board meeting. He'd been talking about Drew, too, saying how helpful he was.

"Junior," I muttered, my pulse picking up speed. "He said the same thing."

"Who?" Pete looked up, confusion knitting his brows together.

"Junior Pease. Called Drew a Good Samaritan, like you just did." My thoughts were racing now, each one tripping over the next. It couldn't be a coincidence.

"Everly?" Drew's voice broke through my reverie, concern etched in every syllable.

"Sorry, just thinking out loud." I shook my head, trying to dispel the fog of speculation. "It's probably nothing."

But it wasn't nothing. Not really. The connection was tenuous, sure, but even coincidences sometimes meant something. This was one of those times, and I intended to find out what.

"Or maybe it's something."

To find out, I needed more information. Ignoring Pete for a moment, I fixed my gaze on Drew's. There was a look in his eyes I couldn't quite place—a mixture of concern and hope as he studied my face, trying to read the thoughts racing behind my eyes.

"Drew," I started, my voice low and steady. "Have you been doing a lot of favors for folks around town lately?"

His brows furrowed, and he gave a small, uncertain nod. "Uh, yeah, I guess. Nothing out of the ordinary, though. You know how it is here—neighbors helping neighbors with small acts of kindness. I like to pay it forward. Why do you ask?"

I tapped my fingers against his, feeling the weight of every second that ticked by. It was like I could sense the puzzle pieces floating around us, ethereal and just out of reach. If only I could snatch them from the air and fit them into place.

"You know that's part of why I love you, don't you?" I couldn't help saying. Between the two of us, he really was the best. "But I need to know more about your most recent acts of kindness." I pressed on, scrutinizing his face for any flicker of realization or resistance. "It might be important."

"Important? I don't see how." Drew's voice held a note

of frustration now. His brow furrowed as he tried to understand the direction of my questioning. "You're not making much sense."

"Trust me," I said, hoping my smile didn't look as forced as it felt. "I have a hunch, and it's convoluted, but I need to know who you've been helping lately." My heart was pounding, a relentless drumbeat echoing in my ears.

Drew scrubbed a hand over his face, clearly thrown by my line of inquiry. "I'm not sure why this matters, but okay. I mean, I've done the usual stuff—helped Tim unload one of the delivery trucks last week when the driver wasn't feeling well. I fixed a broken hinge on the back door of the diner for Mabel."

He trailed off, looking more puzzled than ever. Good deeds meant less to him if they came with recognition. His willing cooperation made it all the more challenging to press him for information if he couldn't see its relevance. But my gut told me there was something we were both missing here.

"Anything else?" I prodded, achingly aware that every detail mattered, no matter how small or mundane it seemed.

"Everly," Drew said slowly, his steady gaze holding mine, "I don't see—"

"Just humor me, okay?" I interrupted more sharply than I intended. A part of me hated putting him through this, but I couldn't shake the feeling that these small actions were a breadcrumb trail leading us somewhere significant.

"Sure," he conceded with a sigh, though his expression remained a portrait of bewilderment. "I bagged and carried out Mrs. Allen's groceries and paid for Bess Tate's muffin and coffee at the bakery the other day."

"Boy Scout," Jack coughed as if to hide a minor insult. Not that Drew would take it that way.

"I gave Leandra a hand with a box of books she was loading in her car. Are you sure this is all important?"

Bless the man for looking embarrassed about detailing the ways he made himself helpful to his adopted community. Reason #579 why I loved him.

"I am," I murmured, offering a weak smile. "I'm pretty sure none of those had anything to do with Jerry. Anything else?"

He shook his head making it clear he couldn't keep up with my mental gymnastics, but his trust in me kept his doubts at bay—for now. "I can't think of anything."

"Are you sure?"

"Well, there was Junior's tire." Drew rubbed the back of his neck, looking almost embarrassed by his own generosity. "He was stranded on the side of the road and couldn't get the lug nuts loose."

"Junior," I said more to myself than to Drew as alarm bells clanged in my head.

"Everly?" Drew's voice cut through my thoughts, laced with concern. "You're looking a bit pale."

"Sorry," I said, forcing a smile. "Just thinking about what a big heart you have. It's one of the many reasons I love you." It was the truth.

"Love you, too." He reached across the table, squeezing my hand. "But you've got that look in your eye. The one that means you think you've stumbled onto something big."

"Maybe," I admitted, the weight of my suspicions anchoring me in place. Pieces of the truth behind the murder might be fitting themselves together, and not in the way I'd hoped or even in a way I understood fully.

At that moment, our small-town charm felt like a double-edged sword—a weapon that could protect or betray with equal ease. And I was beginning to fear that Drew's kindness had cut deep into the heart of a mystery far more tangled than any of us had anticipated.

"Cherries lead to cherry pits," I murmured almost inaudibly, my voice a whisper that barely disturbed the air between us.

"Are you sure it's not the other way around?" he asked, looking at me like he expected my marbles to roll across the floor at any moment.

"No. It's fine. It's nothing," I said quickly, brushing off his concern with a shake of my head. But it wasn't nothing. My mind was hurtling back to the night before, to the peculiar sight that had greeted me as I returned to my car—a constellation of cherry pits scattered across the asphalt like a breadcrumb trail left by an absentminded snacker, or...something more sinister.

I had thought little of them then, dismissing them as the careless leavings of a passerby. But now, with every detail of Drew's helpful nature laid bare, those discarded pits took on new meaning. From what Jerry had told me, they were not merely litter—they were clues, tiny sentinels silently pointing to truths hidden in plain sight.

"I don't like it." Drew's voice was tinged with concern, his eyes searching mine, looking for answers I wasn't sure I wanted to give. "You're planning something dangerous."

"I'm not," I said, trying to sound nonchalant. "My brain's just doing that thing where it makes mountains out of molehills—or, in this case, murder plots out of cherry pits. The more I think about it, the more I think it's probably nothing. Just one more minor mystery."

"Are there such things?" Drew wanted to know.

"Speaking of mysteries," I began, trying to sound casual as I navigated the treacherous waters of my next question, "What kind of vehicle does Junior drive?"

CHAPTER NINETEEN

The revelation hit me like a slap from a cold, wet fish as Drew casually mentioned Junior's ride —a gray and black Suburban, the exact beast of a vehicle I had been tailing down all the wrong roads last night. My heart did a jitterbug in my chest. "You're kidding," I said, trying to keep my voice level, "I think I saw it last night. He drives that tank?"

Drew nodded, his brow furrowed with concern. "He does. Bought it used from the old Sawyers lot down near Bangor. Why? You look like you've seen a ghost."

"Not this time," I muttered under my breath, considering the possibility that the friendly, white-haired gentleman could be connected to Jerry's untimely departure from the living.

"Everly?" Drew's voice softened, his protective instincts kicking in. "What's going on?"

"Nothing for you to worry about," I assured him with a pat on the hand, mentally adding 'yet' as an invisible postscript. I had to handle this delicately. No need to worry him until I absolutely had to.

"We need to head out," Jack said, glancing toward Pete with concern. He'd agreed to start a program through one of the veterans organizations, and none of us wanted to delay getting him there. He was a proven flight risk.

It had begun to rain as I left the station, and since it was still early enough, I made my way to Mabel's diner, where Junior was known to be a breakfast-time regular. The bell above the door jingled a greeting as I stepped inside, the scent of sizzling bacon and fresh coffee wrapping around me like a warm blanket. The place was a hive of activity, clinking cutlery providing a soundtrack to local gossip.

There he was, Junior Pease, parked in his usual spot at the counter, hunched over but still managed to seem tall. His fluff of hair and beard gave him an air of benevolence, which would have been quite endearing if I didn't suspect him of murder.

"Morning, Everly!" Mabel called out from the kitchen window, her hands expertly flipping pancakes. "Your usual spot just cleared up."

"Thanks, Mabel," I replied, flashing her a smile before making a beeline for the stools at the counter instead. "Mind if I join you, Junior?"

On the way in, I'd taken a moment to check the tires of what I now knew was his vehicle and was not surprised to find they matched the photo of the tread marks we'd seen near the crime scene. I was at least ninety percent certain I was about to have breakfast with a killer.

He looked up, his expression unreadable. "Of course not," he said, gesturing to the empty stool beside him. "I was just thinking of you and Drew's predicament."

"Thanks." I perched quickly, the vinyl squeaking beneath me. My gut churned with a mix of nerves and the heavy burden of suspicion. "It *has* been hard on him to be accused of a crime he didn't commit. I suppose Jerry's killer is happy, though, thinking he got off scot-free."

If I hadn't been certain before, the change in Junior's demeanor pushed away all doubt. He shrank in his seat.

"I wouldn't be so sure about that," he said. "It could be that the guilt is weighing on him."

"Not enough to confess, though. Right?" It wasn't easy to keep my tone light and even. "Unless something changes soon, Drew's headed to Thomaston this afternoon. He doesn't deserve that."

Strong emotions flickered through Junior's eyes, and I wondered if I could play on his sense of community and whatever moral fortitude he might have left and get him to make a full confession. It would be the best for everyone.

"Not when he has a full life ahead of him. Not when he's the type of guy who helps anyone who needs it. I worry that his helpful nature is somehow to blame for him being arrested."

Junior flinched. Maybe I was getting through to him. I lowered my voice. "We were planning to start a family." Leaning my elbow on the table, I cupped my cheek with my hand and heaved a sigh that might have been a tad theatrical. "It's just so unfair."

"Life so often is."

He hadn't jumped up to go to the station and get Drew off the hook. Maybe I needed to poke him harder.

"I have a theory that whoever murdered Jerry did it in a fit of rage. Probably for something Jerry had done."

"Is that so?" Junior's voice was low, almost a growl that rumbled from deep within.

"Yep," I said, popping the 'p' for emphasis. "And I think you might know something about it."

The diner's chatter faded into the background, leaving only the sound of our breathing and the distant clatter of Mabel working her griddle magic. I'd laid my cards on the table; now it was time to see how Junior would play his hand.

"Mind if we talk somewhere more private?" Junior glanced nervously toward the rain-smeared windows, the air bristling with the tension that now hung between us.

"Sure," I said, though my instincts screamed at me to keep things public. But curiosity, that darn cat killer, nudged me forward. "Lead the way, Junior."

He shuffled out the door, and I followed, wincing as the deluge outside welcomed us with a soggy embrace. The cold, wet slap of a Maine summer downpour quickly replaced the diner's warmth. He pointed to his Suburban parked at the curb, its gray and black paint job looking like a storm cloud on wheels.

"Let's sit in the truck," he suggested, hunching against the rain.

"Right behind you."

I took a deep breath, watching Junior round the front

of the vehicle. When he was out of sight, I whipped out my phone, muted all sounds, pulled up the voice recorder app, and slid it back into my bag. My heart hammered as if I'd just run the town's annual charity 5K.

Slipping into the passenger seat of the Suburban, a shiver chased up my spine, not entirely from the cold. My feet slipped on a handful of cherry pits scattered across the rubber floor mat like tiny confessions. Jerry had said he smelled cherries. The pits might not hold up in court, but I knew what they meant.

"Junior," I began, my voice steady despite the rising tide of anxiety, "I know it was you."

His hands gripped the steering wheel as if it were a lifeline, knuckles whiter than his hair, but he didn't answer; instead, Junior's weathered hand started the engine and shifted the gear into drive. Now we were moving, the rain outside blurring everything into smudges of gray and mist.

Under the cover of the top of my handbag, I keyed in the number to the station, praying Ernie was still chained to his desk, and tapped the speaker button so that whoever answered would hear whatever was being said in the Suburban without Junior knowing I'd made the call.

"Jerry..." Junior's voice cracked, the sound nearly lost beneath the patter of rain on the roof. "That man had no respect for life—not even a sweet little cat's."

"What exactly are you saying?" I pressed, my heart pounding against my ribcage like it wanted out.

"He'd been at the bar, of course. Drinking and driving as usual, I—" He choked on his words, sucked in a deep breath that did nothing to steady him. "I saw him go past, and then I found her lying in the road. My poor baby. And Jerry just sped off. Didn't even stop."

"Junior, I'm so sorry." My voice was barely above a whisper, a stark contrast to the thunderous drumming of water against the window.

"I knew she was hurt too badly. She couldn't be saved, so I gave her the mercy he hadn't bothered with," he continued, eyes fixed on the road ahead, windshield wipers slashing through the downpour. "It broke my heart."

"I can understand that. I have a dog named Molly, and I would be gutted if anything happened to her."

Junior nodded as he took the turn at the end of Main Street, which would lead us out of town. A frisson of concern washed over me, but at the same time, he was about to confess to murder, and I needed to keep him talking. Not that I had to push much. Once the floodgates had opened, he was ready to share the entire sordid tale.

"Then, I was heading back from the VFW meeting last Tuesday, and I saw him. Stopped on the side of the road, pissing into the bushes, swaying from drinking too much. I just...I snapped. What if it wasn't just a poor cat the next time he got behind the wheel like that? What if he hit a child? I had to do something. I had to stop him."

Once past the town line, Junior put his foot down on the gas. The big truck leaped forward.

"Junior, please," I urged, though my mind screamed it might be a good idea to open the door and jump out to escape this rolling deathtrap of a confession booth. "Slow down. You're scaring me."

But at this point, I'd pretty much ceased to exist for him. Instead, he was talking to his cat. His cat, who, coincidentally appeared on the seat between us. Her bottle brush tail flicked across my arm to chill my already damp sleeve.

"I thought I could live without you, but even now that I've dealt with your murderer, I can't. We'll be together again. On the other side."

Not if whatever was keeping her from crossing the rainbow bridge didn't get cleared up, he wouldn't. Should I tell him she was with us? Could I get the cat to show herself to him, and would that help? Too many questions chased through my head.

"Junior, you know I'm still here, right?" I said loudly. "You don't have to do this. Whatever 'this' is."

"I can't live with what I've done, and I can't live without Mrs. Spiffles. There's the bridge near Dead Man's Curve. I think that will do the trick. It's fitting, isn't it?" His laugh was hollow, more haunting than any spirit I'd ever encountered.

I had no idea if Ernie was hearing any of this. If not, Junior would die. I would die, and Drew would still go to jail. I couldn't let that happen. Dead Man's Curve was a good ten minutes away, even at this rate of speed. I needed to talk fast.

"Junior, what you're planning is not the answer. We can find another way, a better way," I said, my voice laced with forced optimism as my hand clung to the door handle, ready to enact my great escape if needed. "Mrs. Spiffles wouldn't want this. She wouldn't want you to take an innocent life. I haven't done anything to deserve what's happening."

"I can't live with what I did," he muttered, his resolve hardening like the concrete of the bridge we were rapidly approaching. "This is the only way to atone."

"Please, Junior. Think about Drew, your friends, everyone who cares about you." I implored, trying to pierce the stormy veil of his despair.

"Jerry's the one who should've thought before he got into his car," he whispered, almost to himself. As minutes ticked away, I wondered how badly it would hurt to jump out of a car doing better than fifty miles an hour. Somehow, I didn't like my chances.

The rain pelted the windshield in a furious torrent, as if Mother Nature was trying to wash away Junior's sins and my last shred of hope. The wipers could barely keep up, smearing the water into ghostly trails that blurred my vision—though not as much as the dread fogged my mind.

"Junior," I began, swallowing the panic that threatened to choke my words. "You've always been the heart of this town. Killing an innocent woman isn't the legacy you want to leave behind."

"Legacy?" He scoffed, his knuckles white as they

gripped the steering wheel. "What kind of legacy is there for a man who took another's life over a cat? This way, no one else will ever find out."

Unless my call to the station had gone through, but would telling him that make things worse or better? I wasn't sure.

"Maybe it wasn't your finest moment," My voice was steady, but inside, my heart raced like a hummingbird's wings.

He didn't respond, gaze fixed on the road, but I sensed a flicker of hesitation. It was frail, nearly smothered by his anguish and the storm's relentless assault on the truck, but it was there. And I clung to it like a lifeline.

"What's going on?" Jerry's voice cut through my head just as the chill of his presence washed over my body, and I shivered. "Why's there a cat in here?"

Mrs. Spiffles had curled up next to Junior and laid her head on his leg.

"You don't want to do this, Junior. You already have Jerry's death on your conscience. You don't want to die with another black mark on your soul. Taking me over the bridge at Dead Man's Curve with you won't erase what you've done." It was the only way to speak to Jerry without Junior knowing he was there.

Out of the corner of my eye, I saw Jerry's mouth drop open as he looked from me to Junior. A ghost can't tell me of their death or name their murderer, but when the truth is staring them in the face, there's a sense of recognition that comes over them. I saw it in Jerry now.

"He killed me? Why?"

"Mrs. Spiffles wouldn't want you to seek vengeance. Besides, what are the chances that you'll join your beautiful cat if you willfully kill an innocent? You know there are consequences in death just as there are in life."

"He killed me over a cat?" Jerry's voice shredded my last nerve.

"Jerry might have been too drunk to know he'd taken a life, but you're not. Please let me out, Junior. I don't want to die."

The first curve of the stretch of road leading to what we all called Dead Man's Curve had come into view. There would be thirteen curves to navigate before the Suburban careened off the bridge at the end of the final one. I had four or five minutes to get through to Junor, but not much more.

"Pull over," I said, pleading with every fiber of my being. "Let me out."

The bridge loomed closer, a final threshold. Would it be a path to redemption or a plunge into darkness?

"Junior, please..."

"Hell with that," Jerry's voice sounded loud in my ear. "He's not listening. I'll distract him. You do whatever it takes to get control of the wheel."

Before I could tell him to be careful, Jerry winked out of the truck.

CHAPTER TWENTY

We came out of the other side of the storm just as Jerry reappeared at the beginning of the only section of straight road between us and the bridge. Seeing him, Junior yelped and swerved. Sure, I thought. Avoid hitting the ghost, but don't give a second thought to the living woman in the car with you.

When the truck passed right through Jerry, Junior yelped again.

I could almost hear his pulse racing over the engine's growl. He clenched the wheel with a vice-like grip. Seeing Jerry, the very man he'd killed, seemed to strike a chord so deep within him that his well-meaning façade crumbled like my worst attempt at pie crust.

"Jerry?" His voice was a strangled whisper, nearly drowned out by the hum of the tires.

Dead and gone but not quite departed, Jerry popped right back up in front of us, his face set in a hideous grimace meant to scare Junior into stopping. Even though I knew what he was doing, it gave me the creeps.

That's when Junior went from startled to full-blown panic. His face turned as pale as his hair, his breathing becoming short and frantic. When his entire body went rigid, his foot jamming down hard on the gas pedal, I didn't need my psychic senses to tell me something was terribly wrong.

"Junior!" I shouted again, my voice laced with fear. Jerry's actions had taken this situation from bad to worse.

But before I could blink, Junior's body jerked violently, and he took his hands off the wheel to clutch his chest. The truck veered sharply as if it had a mind of its own, careening towards the side of the road. My heart skipped a beat as I grabbed the wheel.

"Hey, hey, stay with me! I think you're having a heart attack. If anyone can hear me, I need help!"

Junior's eyes were wide, staring at something only he could see, maybe his life flashing before him as the weight of his guilt manifested in physical distress. Probably a heart attack from the looks of things.

My purse slipped out of my lap as I shed the seat belt and tried to shove Junior's foot off the gas while keeping the truck from veering too far onto the tree-lined side of the road. Maybe the gravel verge would slow us down some, or maybe dropping off the pavement would send us even more out of control. Either way, I had little time to develop a better idea.

When Jerry reappeared, and the truck drove right through him again, he realized something was wrong.

We barreled forward over steam-drying pavement, the truck of death like a spooked horse, unhinged and wild.

"What's going on?" Jerry popped into the back seat and took in the situation.

"Junior's out cold. I think he had a heart attack. I can't get his foot off the gas, and we're going too fast to make Dead Man's Curve."

"County Line Road's coming up. Can you make the turn?"

Getting off this road would give me a better chance of survival, and the turn on County Line wasn't nearly as sharp as Dead Man's Curve. Still, I wasn't sure if we could make it unless I got the truck to slow down.

I grabbed the shifter, thinking I could drop it down into second gear and let the transmission act as a braking system, but it wouldn't budge.

Making himself visible to Junior had taken a lot out of Jerry. He had already begun to shimmer around the edges when he phased through the seat and fully materialized on the floor, his body wedged against my legs. I barely noticed the heebie jeebifying sensation as he tried to shove Junior's foot off the gas.

"Dammit," he said and tried again. "I can't get him to budge. He's gone rigid."

I heard the faint sound of Ernie's siren just before I saw the flashing lights coming down County Line Road. He must have taken Bog Road to cut us off. At least now I knew he'd heard Junior's confession, but there was no way I could make the turn now. Not without hitting Ernie head-on.

I had no choice but to stay on course and hope for a

miracle. I wrestled the steering wheel, mustering my strength to make the gentle turn that marked the end of the straightaway. The tires spun a bit on a still-damp patch of road, costing the truck just enough speed that I managed to haul us around the curve and straighten out again. That's when I caught sight of Ernie's cruiser in the rearview mirror, barreling up behind us with determined speed.

"Come on," I muttered under my breath, giving Jerry's semi-solid body a nudge with my leg just as Ernie came up alongside. I saw Drew's face in the passenger side window but didn't have time to wonder why when Ernie passed, whipped his car in front of us, then hit his brakes.

The Suburban crashed into the back of the cruiser with a sickening thud. The impact shifted Junior's body enough that his foot slid slightly sideways while Ernie braked, slowing both vehicles as much as he could. Tires screamed and smoked, but the ploy was working.

"I'm a moron," Jerry said, letting go of Junior's foot and pressing down on the brake instead. The truck shuddered violently but slowed even more. It looked like I might have a chance after all.

"Oh, hell. I'm sorry, Everly," Jerry said, "I can't hang —" His body shivering like a leaf in a hurricane, he poofed.

The truck sped up slightly, pushing the limits of Ernie's braking capability since the truck was so much heavier than his car. But Jerry had slowed things down enough that we hit Dead Man's Curve at an unsafe but manageable speed.

The two vehicles mated, we slid around the corner, and flew across the bridge without ending up in the river. Score one for the team.

Now that we were on a longer straightaway and running at a speed that allowed it, I took both hands off the wheel, reached down, and finally shifted Junior's leaden foot off the accelerator.

The world slowed down. The only sounds were the screeching of tires and my labored breathing. As Ernie eased both vehicles to a stop, I finally shoved the shifter into Park. We were safe. Or I was safe, anyway. Junior wasn't.

"Everly?" Drew's voice snapped me back to reality as he dragged the passenger door open. "Talk to me."

"I'm okay. I'm alive." I let out a laugh that sounded more hysterical than humorous. "And probably in need of new underwear, but that's neither here nor there."

"Backup's on the way," Ernie instructed, but I barely heard him over the sound of my ragged sighs.

"I think Junior had a heart attack." By now, Drew had pulled me from the wreckage—minor wreckage, all things considered, but still. The smell of burning rubber clawed at my nostrils. I blinked, trying to steady my world that had been lurching violently only moments before. My heart still raced like a jackrabbit on a caffeine binge. "I'm okay. You need to help him."

His first priority being the safety of everyone involved,

Ernie had pulled Junior out of the driver's seat, then reached in to turn the key and kill the engine. Drew left me long enough to assess Junior's condition.

"He not breathing," Drew's voice cut through the adrenaline haze.

I watched, half in awe, half in shock, as Drew tilted Junior's head back and started CPR.

"Come on, Junior," Drew grunted between compressions, sweat beading on his forehead. "Don't you quit on me now!"

Ernie, meanwhile, was on his radio, barking orders like a drill sergeant with a sore throat. "I need an ambulance at the north end of River Bridge. Possible heart attack. And someone get a wrecker out here to clear this mess off the road!"

He glanced over at me, his usual gruff exterior softened by something that looked suspiciously like concern. "You good?"

"Five-by-five, Ernie," I said, though my legs felt like they'd been replaced with overstretched rubber bands. "Just glad I won't be adding 'truck surfing' to my resume today."

"Save the jokes, Dupree." But even as he said it, the corner of his mouth twitched upward. "Good thing you called me to come and save the day."

"Well, thanks," I mused, watching Drew continue his life-saving efforts. I couldn't help but feel a swell of pride for my husband, doing his best under the worst circumstances.

It didn't take long for the wail of sirens to shatter the relative calm, the ambulance arriving in a blur of lights and urgency. The paramedics took over from Drew, who stepped back, wiping his brow and watching them intently as they worked on Junior.

"Hey, Drew," Ernie called out once the medics had Junior loaded up and were ready to speed away. "You did good. Real good."

"Thanks." Drew's voice was hoarse, his eyes never leaving the ambulance as it pulled away. "I'm off the hook now, right?"

"Damn straight." Ernie clapped him on the shoulder. "Just to make it official—"

The words hung between them, and I could feel the weight of worry lift as Ernie delivered the news I'd been waiting to hear.

"All charges against you are dropped. You're free to go, Parker."

Drew didn't move for a moment, as if the words needed time to find their way through the thick fog of adrenaline-fueled aftermath. Then, slowly, a smile spread across his face, reaching his eyes and lighting them up like fireworks on the Fourth of July.

"Free to go," he repeated as if tasting the freedom in each syllable. "I like the sound of that."

"Go on," Ernie said, with a dismissive wave of his hand that didn't quite match the warmth in his eyes. "Get outta here. Everly looks like she could use a good cup of coffee and maybe a dozen donuts."

"Make it two dozen," I called out, finding my voice again. "But, um, it's a long walk back to town."

"Your ride's coming," Ernie handed me my purse and nodded toward the vehicle just pulling up behind the flatbed Bennie had loaded with Junior's truck. "I had Carole Ann call to let them know."

Drew's folk's faces peered out through the windshield of my car, both pale as they viewed the wreckage, but neither could hide smiles as they saw their son standing before them without a single handcuff in sight.

"Thanks, Ernie."

"Yeah, thanks," Drew agreed, coming over to wrap an arm around my shoulders. "Let's go home, Everly."

"Home," I echoed, leaning into him. "Tell your dad to drive slow, okay? I've had enough speed for one day."

"Sounds perfect," he said, and together, we walked away from the chaos toward the promise of peace, powdered sugar, and a future free from the specter of suspicion.

The sun was beginning to dip below the horizon, casting an orange glow over the town that seemed to fit my current mood. Drew's hand found mine, his grip steady and grounding. We stood in our backyard for a moment, taking in deep breaths of summer air that smelled like someone's nearby barbecue and freedom while Molly cavorted across the grass. She'd missed Drew almost as much as I had and couldn't contain her joy at spending time with him again.

We'd spent the afternoon telling friends and family

the story of my near-death experience and Drew's subsequent release. Ernie had called to let us know that Junior survived his heart attack thanks to Drew's actions. We had one more night with Drew's parents before they went back home, and we planned to make it a good one.

"Everly," he began, his voice thick with emotion. "I can't believe how close I came to losing you. Junior wasn't the only one who nearly died of heart failure."

I nodded, feeling a smile tug at my lips. "It's over now," I said. "Justice is served, and your name is cleared."

He let out a long sigh, the kind that seemed to carry the weight of the world with it as it left his body. "You want to tell me the rest of it now?"

"It was all Jerry's fault, but he did help save me in the end."

"He saved you?" Drew echoed, confusion knitting his brows together. "I thought it was Ernie's quick thinking that did that."

"When Jerry realized Junior planned to commit suicide with me as a ridealong, he materialized and tried to help." I chewed on my lower lip, wondering if I'd ever get over that one. "He thought showing himself to Junior would be a good idea."

"Seriously?" Drew's eyes widened, but not with disbelief. After everything we'd been through, ghosts were just another part of our new normal.

"Dead serious," I joked, then winced at my own pun and told him the rest of the story. "I haven't seen him since. I'm hoping he went into the light already, but I wouldn't be surprised if he turned up to annoy me one final time. Still, he did his part to save my life in the end, so I guess I owe him that much."

"Sounds like I owe him one, too," Drew said thoughtfully, staring off into space while settling the events of the day in his head.

"Oh, I think after what his death put us through, you're even," I suggested. "In fact, let's not speak of trucks, ghosts, or near-death experiences for a while. Deal?"

"Deal," Drew agreed, squeezing my hand. "So, what now?"

"Now, we spend a nice evening with your folks, eat those two dozen donuts, and enjoy the quiet life for a change." I glanced up at the first stars peeking through the twilight. "Let's just enjoy being married."

"Sounds perfect," Drew said, pulling me close. "Do you feel any different now that we've made it official?"

"To be honest," I chuckled, shaking my head. "I haven't had a minute to think about it. What about you?"

"Oh, I had plenty of time to think while I was sitting in that jail cell. Everly," he turned me in his arms and rested his forehead against mine. "I want to start a family."

"Not today," he said when my body jerked in surprise. "But soon."

Not giving me time to form an answer, he went on. "We said 'for better or for worse,' and it wasn't even a minute before it got worse. But we came through like we always will, you know?" His voice was light, but I sensed the depth of emotion behind it.

"Definitely heavy on the 'worse' for a few days there," I mused, "but I wouldn't trade 'better' with anyone else. We're a team, Drew. Wherever life leads us, and whatever little surprises that come along. Even the planned ones."

"Team Dupree-Parker." He grinned, and I couldn't help but return the smile, feeling the rightness of it all.

"Sounds like a detective agency from a noir film," I joked, but there was pride in my voice.

"Or a series of cozy mystery novels." He winked, and I laughed again, the sound mingling with the night as if it belonged here among the whispers of the wind.

"Starring Everly, the red-haired ghost tamer and her dashing sidekick, Drew." I played along, loving the way his eyes lit up with amusement.

"Sidekick?" He feigned outrage, and I nudged him gently with my elbow.

"Okay, okay, co-conspirator," I conceded, and we fell into a comfortable silence.

The world around us felt expansive yet intimate, as if the entire universe had narrowed down to just the two of us and Molly. We sat on the back steps for a while, neither of us needing to fill the quiet with words. Our shared experience bound us in ways that went beyond language, beyond even the touch of our entwined hands.

In that moment, I realized that no matter what specters might come our way, the true strength lay in the living—in the love and loyalty that tethered one soul to another. There would be more mysteries to solve and more dangers to face, but as long as Drew and I stood side by side, we were invincible.

"I'm ready, too." I eventually said. "For that family you were talking about."

"Let's get started, then," he answered with a grin.

"Maybe not with your parents hovering around." I nudged him with an elbow. "But after the honeymoon, for sure."

CHAPTER TWENTY-ONE

The morning sun spilled a gentle warmth across the room as I stretched out from the tangled comfort of my sheets, lingering in that perfect moment of peace before Molly leaned in to slather my face with kisses. With Drew's parents leaving late the day before, the house was ours again—quiet, serene, and blessedly free of unsolicited advice on how to properly deadhead roses or sort the recycling.

"Ah," I sighed, wrapping my arms around my new husband, "the sweet sound of absolutely nothing."

Nuzzling close, he whispered in my ear, "I'm not opposed to making a little noise."

When Molly snuffled and thumped her tail on the floor, I knew one of us would have to let her out before long anyway. It might be worth installing one of those electronic doggie doors so we could both sleep in once in a while. Or not sleep in. Whatever we wanted to do.

"Dog and coffee now, noise later." I kissed him, and the way he kissed me back would have changed my mind if Molly hadn't whined.

"Okay, girl," Drew sighed, rolled out of bed, and echoed my earlier thoughts. "But we're getting you a doggie door. You stay there, I'll let her out, and coffee can wait."

I couldn't argue with that.

Later, a familiar chill crept through the air as I poured a dollop of cream into my cup. A shiver danced down my spine despite the summer heat that promised another sweltering day ahead. Jerry stood in the doorway, his usual leer replaced by something that resembled...was it remorse?

"Morning, Everly," he said, his voice tinged with emotion so heavy it seemed to weigh on the very atmosphere.

"Jerry," I greeted him, pulling my bathrobe tighter around me—partly for modesty's sake and partly because Jerry still hadn't learned about personal space bubbles. "What can I do for you?" As if I hadn't already done enough.

He shuffled his feet, a gesture that would have been endearing if it weren't for the fact that he was, you know, dead and had once been a tad too interested in yours truly. "I came to say goodbye. I've caused you enough trouble, and, well..." He looked down at his insubstantial shoes. "I'm sorry, Everly. Truly. I never meant to bring danger to your doorstep."

There it was—the apology I didn't know I needed until it floated in front of me with sad, puppy-dog eyes. It was hard to stay mad at someone earnestly seeking redemption, even if they were doing so post-mortem.

"I know you meant well, even if your actions took a

detour through 'What the heck were you thinking?'ville." I offered him a small smile, hoping it conveyed forgiveness. "Thank you for helping me out there in the end. You saved my life."

"Guess I did, huh?" A hint of his old cheekiness peeked through. "Everly Dupree, saved by Jerry Kaminski. Who would've thought?"

"Don't let it go to your head—or wherever your thoughts hang out these days." I chuckled, shaking my head. "Do you see the light?"

Looking to his left, he nodded. "It's there."

"Go find your peace, Jerry. You've earned it. Or if you haven't, I certainly have."

Nodding, he turned and took two steps to his left. The temperature in the room returned to normal as Jerry's presence faded away.

"Have a good afterlife," I muttered to the empty space where he'd just been. Then, with a deep breath, I sipped my coffee, ready to face a day without unforeseen ghostly interventions.

I had just finished my second cup of coffee, the liquid warmth doing little to stave off the chill that had nothing to do with ghosts and everything to do with the notification blinking at the top of my phone screen.

"Reservation canceled?" I muttered aloud, the words tasting bitter on my tongue. "No, no, no." My finger jabbed at the screen, bringing up the details in the travel app that shattered the morning's tranquility. We should have left on Monday for our honeymoon in Greece. I'd been looking forward to white walls, azure sea, peace, and no phantoms needing favors. Instead, the stark words 'cancellation' and 'refund' stood out like unwanted omens.

"What the hell," I grumbled, feeling the frustration bubble up when I remembered Drew's mom telling me she'd spoken to someone at the hotel and assured me they would let us check in late but still keep our reservations. We'd planned to fly out tomorrow, sacrificing a couple of days there and making them up by spending time in Boston on the way home.

"What's up?" Drew came in with Molly, her tongue lolling from a good run.

"Our reservations got canceled. I need to talk to your mom." I picked up the phone. "Or better yet, I need to call the travel agency."

Dismay settling over me, I dialed the travel agent's number. The hold music, a tinny rendition of Vivaldi's Four Seasons, did nothing for my sour mood.

"Wanderer's Travel Agency, Darian speaking. How may I help you today?" The chipper voice eventually came through the speaker.

"Hi, Darian, it's Everly Dupree. I just received a notification that my reservation was canceled. There must be some mistake."

"Really? I'm not seeing anything on my end. Can you hold for just a second?"

The Vivaldi came back before I had a chance to answer, and Darian's second turned into several minutes before his voice came back on the line sounding far less chipper than it had before. "According to the reservation agent at the hotel, the booking was canceled by you on account of Drew developing cancer."

"Excuse me?" I couldn't even begin to understand what might have happened.

"They offered their best wishes for his health and assured me that they'd given you a full refund rather than the percentage they'd have normally allowed for a last-minute cancellation."

"I don't even...I don't understand any of this. Do they have another room available? It doesn't have to be the honeymoon suite. Anything will do."

I could almost hear Darian shaking his head over the phone. "I'm sorry, but you know this is one of the smaller hotels. We had to schedule nearly a month in advance as it was. Milos has a reputation for being less crowded than some of the other islands, but it's still a popular destination during honeymoon season."

"What about somewhere else on the island?" Surely, Drew's parents would understand if we didn't go to the same hotel they'd stayed in thirty-two years before. We could still visit the beach they remembered so fondly. They'd talked about their magical trip so many times Drew and I had both become enthralled with the idea of going there.

The pause between my question and Darian's answer drew out so long a sinking feeling told me I wouldn't like the answer.

"I'm sorry, Everly. I'm scanning through every resource available, but there isn't a room to be had on the entire island until the middle of September when wedding season starts to taper off."

"That's over a month away." We could probably rearrange our schedules, but it seemed like a long time to wait for a honeymoon. "Are you sure?"

"Positive. I've checked every resource I have. You know how these things go sometimes. There's nothing I can do."

"Well, thanks for trying. Go ahead and book us for two weeks in September." I hung up the phone gently despite the storm brewing within me.

"It looks like our honeymoon will have to be postponed for a few weeks," I told Drew. "I'm not sure what your mom said when she called, but somehow, the booking agent at the hotel got the idea you'd been diagnosed with cancer."

The way his eyes widened, I assumed there wasn't something dire he'd been hiding from me.

"I'll call her right now. This is just plain weird."

"But I know that I said incarcerated," Cheryl insisted a few minutes later when Drew put her on speaker. "Incarcerated, not cancer."

Maybe the two words sounded the same to someone for whom English was a second language.

"Don't worry about it, Mom. We'll just postpone." Drew grinned at me, his good nature and sense of the absurd lightening the mood. "It will be fine."

"At least take a few days and go somewhere now, though," his mother ordered. "You could use a vacation after what you've been through."

"We'll think about it," Drew said, ringing off. "What do you think?"

"I guess it's time for plan B." Whatever that was.

"As long as we're together," Drew said, not seeming upset, "I'm fine with Plan B."

"Okay," I sighed, slumping onto the couch. "If only I had one."

Just then, the ringtone I'd set for Amethyst, one of the friends I'd made since the whole ghost-seeing thing started, cut through the stillness—a whimsical chime that usually brought a smile to my face. Today, my face wouldn't cooperate.

"Hey, Amethyst," I answered, the weight of disappointment heavy in my voice. "How are things in Oakville?"

"Better than they seem to be in Mooselick River." Her voice was deep and warm, a comforting blanket woven with concern and a hint of amusement. "I can see the disruption in your aura from here."

Since a run-in with her guardian angel, Amethyst's aura reading capabilities had been boosted to the point where she could dial in on her friends even from a distance. I was lucky enough to be counted in that group.

"Ah, you know, just the universe conspiring to keep me away from fancy cocktails and breathtaking Aegean views," I replied, trying to muster some of my usual humor. "It's probably good you didn't tune in on your way home from the reception."

She and my other Oakville friends had come for the wedding but left before Ernie showed up and ruined the end of my reception, so I gave her the Cliff Notes version of events ending with the rotten cherry on the spoiled sundae. "And now, our honeymoon is on hold."

"Say no more. I've got something that might cheer you up. How does a week in a private vacation rental sound? On the lake in Oakville?" There was an expectant lilt to her voice, the kind that suggested she was hiding a grin.

"Oakville?" I repeated, my interest piqued despite myself. "It's no Greece…"

"Think secluded, think serene. The water won't be as blue or the sand as white, but the place has its own beach and a sweet little boat tied up at the dock. It's a friend's place, and I know she hasn't rented it for the next couple of weeks." She named a price that was on the lower side of reasonable. "The place is outfitted with everything except food. You can even bring the dog with you. Honestly, I can't think of anyone who deserves a bit of peace more than you two lovebirds. What do you say?"

Since I'd put her on speaker and Drew was wearing a similar expression to Molly when someone said 'treat,' I guessed my answer was yes.

"Amethyst, you're a gem." I couldn't help but chuckle. "A lake house retreat might be just the ticket."

"Consider it yours. I'll make the arrangements. All you need to do is pack and show up. I'll text you some photos and the address and pop the key under the mat. And Everly? No ghosts, I promise."

"Perfect," I said with a relieved smile. "A ghost-free week on the water sounds like heaven right about now."

"Great!" Amethyst chimed brightly. "And hey, nothing says you can't have fancy cocktails by the lake. I'm sure you can whip up something with an umbrella in it."

"Umbrella drinks on the lake it is, then," I replied, my cloud of disappointment beginning to lift. "Thanks, Amethyst. You're a lifesaver."

"Anytime, hon. You just focus on enjoying yourself. Clean up that dark aura cloud that's bringing me down."

With a click, the call ended, leaving me in a silence that suddenly didn't feel so oppressive. A serene lake house. Just Drew and me, and a week of doing absolutely nothing but boating and swimming...maybe Plan B wasn't such a bad idea after all.

The decision made, we grabbed coolers from our camping supplies, packed up the contents of the fridge, added a few staples from the cupboards, and let our family and friends know where we were headed.

The car was packed, and the quiet hum of the engine was our soundtrack as we pulled out onto the street. Drew reached over and squeezed my hand, his touch grounding me to the moment.

"Ready for our adventure, Mrs. Everly Parker-Dupree?" he asked, eyes crinkling at the corners with that boyish charm.

"More than ready, Mr. Drew Dupree-Parker," I replied,

feeling that familiar warmth of his presence. We hadn't decided on last names yet. That was a detail in the landscape of our new life. It was the comfort of knowing that together, we could weather any storm—even those of the supernatural variety. "Amethyst promised a ghost-free week."

I chuckled, tipping my head against the headrest and watching the landscape change from the familiar to the new as we drove further from home. The anticipation built with each passing mile, a bubbling mix of excitement and relief. It wasn't Greece, but it was an escape, a slice of serenity we both craved after the chaos of the last few days.

"Did she?" he quirked a brow. "You know she probably jinxed it."

"I sincerely hope you're wrong." But for now, it was just Drew and me—no ghosts allowed.

I should have known the universe would have other plans.

❧

Thanks for reading!

We know you love Everly, but if you want to hear Drew's side of things, you can read a bonus scene from his perspective HERE.

And if you're wondering what's next for Everly, keep

reading for a preview of Mourning After, where her cozy routine is about to be upended again—this time by a missing woman, an unexpected return, and a visit from some friends you're sure to recognize 😜.

~Also Available in Audiobook & Paperback Versions~

Quick Author's Note

You probably know by now that we're a mother-daughter writing team. What you might not know is that ReGina started writing first—and she didn't have to twist Erin's arm too hard to join her. Writing was always Erin's dream, so when the opportunity came along to dive into the world of cozy mysteries and ghostly mayhem, it was a no-brainer.

But before Everly Dupree started wrangling ghosts and solving murders, ReGina wrote the Psychic Seasons series —a story about four very different but equally amazing women who are drawn together by mystery and adventure, and ultimately form a lifelong friendship. And now? Those same ladies are about to shake things up in Everly's world.

In Mourning After, Everly's dream honeymoon takes a sharp left turn when a woman connected to the local food truck scene goes missing. And as usual, her knack for attracting restless spirits puts her right in the middle of it.

But here's where things get really interesting...
Our favorite ladies from Psychic Seasons are making an appearance, and let's just say—when it comes to meddling in Everly's life, these women are bringing more than just psychic intuition.

We're not saying Everly's honeymoon is completely ruined... but when you mix missing persons, ghostly opinions, and a few psychic surprises? Let's just say dessert is about to take a backseat to danger.

Stick around—because Everly's next adventure is going to be one for the books.

Anyway, if you've come this far with us and not decided we're complete and total whackadoodles...and especially if you have, we're offering a chance to sign up for our newsletters— the best place to get new release updates, sales notifications, and other fun content.

You can sign up for ReGina's newsletter and/or Erin's newsletter and as a thank-you gift for hanging out with us, you'll also get a FREE novella that isn't available anywhere else. And of course, we promise not to SPAM your inbox!

Love, hugs, and happy reading,
ReGina & Erin

~

P. S. If you enjoyed this book, it would be great if you could leave a review or recommendation on Amazon, GoodReads, or BookBub.

Your reviews help indie authors sell more books!

BOOK 14 OF THE HAUNTED
EVERLY AFTER MYSTERIES

*A*T HAYWARD HOUSE

"A little to the left," Julie Kingsley directed her best friend Gustavia, who was standing on a step ladder nearby. "No. Your other left."

"Sorry." Gustavia tilted the reflector the other way so the soft morning light streaming through the window bounced off its silver lining to highlight the pretty teapot glazed in turquoise and white. "How's that? Better?"

"Perfect. Kat, could you tilt your hand just a little more toward me?" Julie peered through her camera's viewfinder to line up the shot. "Right there. That's good."

"What about me?" Amethyst held the position she'd been in for the past five minutes but felt a case of the shakes coming on. "Are you about done yet?"

"You're fine. Don't move." Julie clicked the shutter twice. "Almost done, now. Move into the second position. And hold." The shutter clicked twice more. "And done."

"Phew," Kat said, shaking her wrist to get the feeling back in her hand. "You wouldn't think a teacup was so heavy until you've held one in the same position for half an hour. I hope we got the shots you needed."

Her grin wide, Julie flipped her laptop around to show off a series of gorgeous photos featuring the teapot and matching cups cradled in her friend's hands. "They're perfect. Amaya's gonna sell a lot of teapots thanks to your pretty hands and Gustavia's head for heights."

"I'll take the flattery," Amethyst rose and stretched to ease the kinks from sitting still for so long. "And the standard model fee since we decided to go with the premium windows Finn's been harping on about. I'll be glad when the building phase is complete."

Having climbed down the stepladder, Gustavia spun and clapped her hands. Yards of paisley in a sunny yellow swirled around bracelet-adorned ankles. "I stopped by on my way here to check on the progress. The addition is coming right along. I can't wait until you start buying fixtures. The best part of any remodel is putting in those personal touches."

Helping Julie gather the cups to take to the kitchen so they could be washed and repacked for shipping, Kat teased, "Three guesses what the color scheme will be."

Since purple had been Amethyst's signature color for a few years, it wasn't much of a leap to assume its varied shades would figure highly into her decorating.

"You might be surprised to learn I've decided to go with neutrals for the walls." Amethyst's chin tilted up in mock defense. "It was Reid's idea, but I've been considering a change anyway."

Three sets of eyes widened at the declaration.

"No kidding?" Julie tilted her head and let her eyes go slightly unfocused while imagining Amethyst in various shades. "I could see you as a Ruby or maybe Sapphire. With your skin tone, you should stay away from yellows. I can't see you becoming a Citrine or Sandstone. Jewel tones look better on you."

"Citrine would be better than plain Jane." Even though plain had never been a word to describe her, Amethyst's dislike of her given name had driven her to change it legally. "But I think I'll keep the name and just try some different colors on for size."

"Twenty bucks says you're back in purple by the end of the summer," Kat fished inside her pocket and pulled out the folded twenty she kept on hand for just this reason. She and Amethyst would put their money on the table for almost any reason.

"You're on." A second twenty joined the first. "Sucker bet." Still, they shook on it.

Since many hands make light work, twenty minutes saw the teacups washed and packed and a fresh pot of tea brewed to share.

"Did Everly and Drew get checked in okay?" Gustavia asked Amethyst while she added a dollop of cream to her tea, followed it up with a spoonful of honey, and selected an oatmeal raisin cookie from the plate Julie placed in the center of the table.

"As far as I know. She messaged me when they arrived

but not since, so I figure they're settling in and doing the honeymoon thing. Didn't want to disturb."

Waiting for her tea to cool, Kat began to shuffle the Tarot deck she'd pulled from her purse, "I could read for her. Or just pull a card for one of you." She scanned her friend's faces.

"I'm good," Julie said, as usual.

"Same." Gustavia chose a second cookie, broke off a chunk, and popped it into her mouth. "Ammie?"

"Read for Everly. I've got no burning life questions at the moment—unless the cards can help me decide between Steely Gray and Morning Fog for my bedroom walls." Rising, she retrieved her purse and pulled out two paint sample chips.

"Morning Fog," Kat glanced at the samples and cut the deck. "It's softer. More bedroomy."

"Is that the technical term?" Julie teased.

"It is," Kat said, nodding her head with enthusiasm as she shuffled again and chose a five-card spread. She laid the cards face down on the table, all in a row, pausing theatrically before turning over the first. Her brows shot up with the revelation. "The High Priestess. Now that's interesting."

"I've had that one before," Amethyst said, leaning forward to get a better look. She reached across and tapped the card. "She stands for intuition and secrets, right? Do you think something's up with Drew? Maybe he's hiding something from her. Not the best way to start a marriage."

"Could be Everly with the secrets," Kat mused, tapping her lip with the tip of her finger. "She's been known to keep a thing or two to herself."

Julie cradled her teacup and blew gently on the surface to cool it. "Probably wise in her case since few people would believe her if she told the truth."

Shrugging, Kat turned over the rest of the cards, showing the Page of Swords, the Tower, the Five of Cups, and Judgment. She frowned at the combination. "Hmm. Definitely interesting and more than a little concerning." She glanced up at her friends, gauging their reactions before diving deeper into the interpretation.

"Why?" Julie asked, curious and without the others' depth of insight into what the cards meant.

Kat pointed to the Page of Swords. "Well, this little guy suggests curiosity and a search for the truth, maybe even some cleverness or manipulation involved. It could mean someone's hiding something, and Everly's on the hunt to figure out what it is. Then there's the Tower, which represents unexpected events or an upheaval that leads to a breaking down of existing forms. Probably means she'll get more than she bargained for. Shocking secrets, maybe?" Her eyes sparkled a bit at the dramatic turn of events the cards predicted but softened as she considered Everly's penchant for landing in hot water.

Julie's brows drew together in concern. "Like, something's going to happen to shake things up?"

"Exactly. Most likely when she's not expecting it. And it doesn't look like it will be a small thing. Very disruptive." Kat sighed and tapped the Five of Cups, her finger lingering on the dark card.

Gustavia frowned down at it.

"This doesn't bode well." Kat turned to Amethyst. "See all these spilled cups? Maybe Drew has something in his past. Something Everly won't be happy to find out about. This card is all about disappointment and emotional loss."

"I'm not buying it," Amethyst declared. "There's nothing in Drew's aura to suggest a sordid past. Couple of dark spots, but nothing different than I've seen with other veterans."

"The cards don't lie," Kat said, her tone mild. "But they could be open to other interpretations depending on the circumstances. It's hard to tell, but this is not the reading I'd want to get on my honeymoon, and three major cards out of five lend more weight."

"And just when will that be, anyway?" Gustavia quirked a brow at Kat. "You and Zack have been married for almost a year. Seems like the honeymoon phase is over, and you missed it."

Grinning, Kat scooped up the cards and returned them to the deck. "We haven't figured out a destination, and Zack couldn't get time off right away. And you know he has to think every decision to death."

"Pfft." Gustavia waved that away. "I love my brother, but he's an idiot."

"He's not." Kat defended her man. "And I'm not in any rush. I like the scenery here."

"What about Everly?" Julie offered a gentle reminder. "Should we drop by and see how things are going? I don't want to be a honeymoon crasher, but if something's up…"

"Something's definitely up," Kat agreed, nodding.

"Then we should go." Gustavia began to rise.

"I think we have time to finish our tea first," Amethyst said, picking up a cookie. "Then we'll go."

"Should we call first?" Julie wondered.

"Not if we want to get a solid impression of things. Better to show up without warning, I think."

"You're probably right."

Mourning After is available now, or if you want to save money you can pick up the box set of books 13-15 at a discount. Keep reading for a preview of the free novella you'll get for joining our newsletters.

Enjoyed meeting Everly? Not ready for her story to end?

Sign up for either or both of our newsletters and you'll receive *A Snowball's Chance in Spell*, a prequel novella featuring characters from the *Mag & Clara Balefire Mysteries*, the *Haunted Everly After Mysteries*, and the *Psychic Seasons* series.

Christmas is canceled! Lexi Balefire's faerie godmothers didn't mean to knock Santa Claus and his sleigh out of the sky, but now his reindeer are missing, and it's up to Lexi to find them all before time runs out and Christmas is ruined!

Excerpt from A Snowball's Chance in Spell

*L*ightning flirted in shadows of the dark clouds hovering over my house when I came home from work the afternoon before my twenty-second Christmas Eve. Nothing unusual there. With three elemental faeries living in the house, weird weather happened all the time. Or rather, every time my temperamental godmothers mounted some sort of snit.

The godmothers idled at snit.

Going back to work wasn't an option. I'd cleared the last match of the year—a lovely couple with a shared affection for online gaming—and I was no coward. When it came to diffusing faerie fights, I consider myself an expert, and this one didn't look like it rated more than a two on the volcano scale.

Yes, you heard right. I measure faerie fights on the scale of whether or not a volcano might erupt in my backyard. Living with faeries is never boring. Occasionally dangerous—especially because I have yet to come into the magic that is my birthright, but never boring.

A quick check proved they'd contained the madness to the inside and/or the backyard. The two feet of snow on the front lawn was still there and still white—you try explaining black snow to your neighbors sometime. I didn't see any winged denizens—fae or otherwise—dotting the roof ridge, or hear any ominous sounds. If not for the fact that lightning is rare in Maine during the winter, and rarer still when confined to a single area, I'd have thought it was a quiet day in the household.

In my head, I downgraded the threat to a level one, and went inside.

For the most part, my place looks like an ordinary, New England style home. Built by my great grandparents, it's the oldest house in a neighborhood that grew up around it when the suburbs expanded into what was once a rural area. Because, I think, the faeries wanted to give me a normal upbringing, they left the house in mostly the same condition it was in when they came to take care of me and only added on a wing for their own use.

I stepped into the front hall expecting...well, just about anything. Did I mention the faeries love holidays? Maybe they don't have them in the faelands, or maybe they do and go overboard there, too. I can't say since I've never been, but I could tell at a glance there were more decorations than there had been when I left.

"Terra!" I yelled, but got no answer. Terra, faerie of earth, held sway over all the flora and fauna found on dry land. She would be the one responsible for the pine boughs twining over anything that held still long enough. Fire faerie, Soleil, contributed by setting sparks of faerie light to twinkle inside the delicate ice bubbles crafted by her sister, Evian, mistress of water. The effect was lovely, but not as lovely as the three women could be when their faces weren't twisted, as they were now, with rage.

I came upon them in their favorite fighting grounds: the kitchen. It looked like I'd caught this one early since there was relatively little damage done so far. Steam rose from a puddle of water at Soleil's feet which I assumed had come from Evian. Vines snaked from between the kitchen tiles to twine around Evian's ankles, and there were a few smoking embers dotting Terra's hair. Nothing more than a minor spat.

Keeping it casual, I asked, "What's going on?" There's no rhyme or reason to what will settle a fight or send one into the red zone.

Terra turned one granite pink eye in my direction. "This doesn't concern you." The fingers of her left hand twitched and the vines slithered from Evian's ankles to her knees.

Retaliating, Evian conjured a gush of water from thin air, and doused the smoking embers. The scent of pine boughs couldn't compete with the stench of burnt hair, or the pungent funk erupting from the flowers that burst into bloom near her feet.

"Now look," I pointed out to Terra before she conjured something worse. "Evian is trying to help."

"Was not." Evian snapped her fingers and turned Terra's wet hair white with frost, except because the vines were now questing higher, she overshot the mark and doused a few of Soleil's decorative sparkles.

That was the moment I lost control.

Oh, who am I kidding? I never had control.

Soleil let out a screech and lobbed a fireball at Evian, who encased it in a ball of water and batted it toward Terra. I felt scoured clean when Terra called all the dirt and dust in the house to form a layer over the bobbing ball of doom which now resembled a small planet whizzing back toward Soleil.

It might have ended better if I'd have kept my mouth shut, but I didn't.

"You're going to put an eye out with that thing."

The ire of three faeries is a potent thing, but not as potent as a flaming mudball. I ducked, rolled, and hit the latch on the patio door in what I'd like to think was a graceful move. Probably looked like a seal rolling off a rock.

The flaming fireball arced over my head, its warm breeze tossing my hair, and rocketed off into the sky.

Crisis averted. Except, it wasn't. I should have known.

A Snowball's Chance in Spell is only available by signing up for one of our newsletters here:
https://reginawelling.com
https://erinlynnwrites.com

If you'd like to meet more people who live rent-free in our heads, here's a list of other series we've written. Our books are all set in fictional towns in Maine, and some characters like to flit back and forth between series. The cast of Psychic Seasons hangs out with Everly and also with Lexi Balefire from the Fate Weaver series. Mag and Clara Balefire are Lexi's grand-mother and aunt!

Psychic Seasons
Four women, four love stories, and a whole lot of supernatural surprises. In the quaint town of Oakville, Maine, psychic visions, ghostly whispers, and fate itself conspire to change lives—and hearts—forever

Haunted Everly After
Everly Dupree came home for a fresh start—not a full-time gig solving ghostly murders. But when the dearly departed start demanding justice, what's a reluctant medium to do?

Ponderosa Pines Mysteries

Nothing bad ever happens in the weird little town of Ponderosa Pines...until someone dies. Now it's up to best friends Chloe and EV to solve the mystery—before the town's secrets bury them too.

Fate Weaver
Lexi Balefire—matchmaker, witch, and accidental fate-weaver—must balance love, magic, and a family legacy of chaos before destiny decides for her!

Mag and Clara Balefire Mysteries
Sister witches Mag and Clara Balefire move to a sleepy Maine town for a fresh start—only to find themselves conjuring up trouble, solving murders, and keeping their magic under wraps in this charmingly witchy cozy mystery series

Laurel Haven Witches
Four witches, destined by blood and magic, must embrace their power, battle a dark legacy, and surrender to the love that could break the curse—or bind them to it forever.

Nell Page: Accidental Investigator
Nell Page owns a bookstore, drinks too much coffee, and has a habit of noticing things she probably shouldn't. With warmth, wit, and an accidental talent for investigating, Nell tackles mysteries that don't always involve murder—but always matter.